The ⬛⬛⬛ Roses

Rich Goldhaber

Copyright © 2014 Rich Goldhaber

ISBN -13: 978-1500514648

ISBN – 10: 1500514640

ACKNOWLEDGEMENTS

The author would once again like to thank a wonderful group of friends who have helped to make this novel better in many ways. The following individuals are deserving of special recognition.

Kathlene and Lu Wolf have helped with editing and a critical review of this work. Their feedback is excellent and is always appreciated.

Miriam And Luis Blanco's thoughtful comments added to the accuracy of this novel.

Don Tendick's inputs have added greatly to the accuracy of this story's plot.

My wife Jeanne continues to live up to her reputation as my Editor in Chief.

ALSO BY RICH GOLDHABER

The Lawson Novels

The 26th 0f June

Succession Plan

Vector

Stolen Treasure

Risky Behavior

Other Novels

The Cure

The Four Roses

Prologue

Sam Johnson stood looking into the bathroom mirror, staring beyond the dark almost black eyes and into a soul demanding of affection but devoid of real love; a soul unable to feel guilt, compassion, or remorse; a soul incapable of distinguishing between right and wrong, or good and evil. The voice, this time demanding in its tone, once again ordered Sam to act. Sam's head began to throb with almost unbearable pain. It was the same every time the voice spoke, always the same, and the agony wouldn't cease until Sam obeyed. Sam was certain the voice was nothing more than the subconscious mind reminding once again of the need to execute the plan, because hearing outside voices would denote psychotic behavior, and Sam was certainly not crazy; committed yes, cunning yes, vengeful yes, but certainly not crazy.

This inner voice had guided Sam and helped plan revenge for years. The mission was simple; terminate the lives of four people not worthy of living. The world would certainly be a better place without The Four Roses.

A translucent haze descended like a curtain over the mirror, and four faces appeared in the mist. The Four Roses seemed to float inside the mirror, and they were once again laughing. They were mocking Sam, repeating the words *first time, first time, first time....*

Sam screamed into the mirror, "You'll all pay for this; don't worry, you'll all pay."

A white porcelain vase next to the bathroom sink held four freshly cut long-stem roses. Four roses, each a different color, each representing one of the four women destined for death. Sam had filled the vase with fresh flowers each week, a tradition Sam had adhered to with unfailing dedication.

In Sam's mind, killing did not create an ethical problem. Sam wasn't even remotely concerned with issues of right and wrong. This was a matter of revenge, pure and simple, and Sam was prepared to be the instrument of the Almighty to exact retribution and end their miserable lives. Wronged by these women in the past, Sam would demonstrate to each one who was really in control of their destiny.

Four roses for four young women, each of whom would soon be meeting an unexpected but well deserved fate. Sam had planned revenge since that horrible day ten years ago when The Four Roses had altered an innocent person's life forever.

The four women had been tracked and studied meticulously over the years. Each of their daily habits was known in great detail, and each Rose was definitely vulnerable. There was only one problem. Sam didn't know which one of the four had been the ringleader, the one who had hatched their vile plot, the one who had changed Sam's life in the cruelest way possible, and Sam wanted to ensure the ringleader was the last to die; and that bitch would be in store for a special death, one befitting the role she had played in bringing such havoc into Sam's young life.

Sam reached for the vase, held it reverently in front of the mirror, and kissed it four times, once for each Rose. "One of you will be dead within the week. Which one will it be?"

The voice responded, "It must be Carol, and she will know who the ringleader is. She's a follower, not a leader."

Sam agreed; it would certainly have to be Carol. Sam held up the yellow rose and inhaled its intense aroma. "It will be you Carol. You will have the honor of being first."

The voice, whispering in a somber tone, said, "It must be soon Sam; it must be very soon. On Thursday, Carol will come home late after her usual night at the bar with her friends. You must do it on Thursday."

"Yes," Sam said to the voice, "it will start on Thursday. The beginning of the end is here at last."

Chapter 1

Detective Dan Lawson looked with foggy eyes at the clock on the nightstand as the phone woke him from a deep sleep. He looked again, and the time finally registered in his mind. It was 4:17 a.m., much too early for civilized people to be pulled from their sleep. His wife Sally answered the phone. As a doctor, she was used to middle of the night disturbances.

She passed the phone to him and collapsed back onto her pillow. "It's Joey. He says it's important."

Dan sat up and tried to clear the cobwebs. "Joey, what's up?"

"I just got a call from the precinct. There's been a bad one over in Bucktown. Billy says the beat cops are saying it's the worst they've ever seen. I've alerted Forensics and the Medical Examiner's office. They're on the way. I hate to say it, but this one is going to be high exposure; I can feel it in my bones, so I'm giving this one to you. I'll farm out your other cases as soon as I get to the office. The address is over on West Cortez Street, just east of Hoyne."

"What do you know?"

"Not much; a young woman in her twenties, her body was mutilated. Talk to Art Fuller, he was first on the scene and has the scoop. Keep me posted. And by the way, Art says Channel 9 news is already on the scene."

Sally looked up from her pillow. "What's up?"

"Homicide over on West Cortez. Joey says it's bad. I've got to get over there."

Dan leaned over and gave Sally a kiss. Then he headed for his bedroom closet. No time for a shave and shower, just enough time to get dressed and grab a bagel from the freezer.

Ten minutes later he was thawing his breakfast in the microwave. He had it down to a science, thirty-nine seconds for a cinnamon raisin bagel. What did people in a hurry do before bagels? That's why bagels were putting the cereal makers out of business; you can't have a bowl of cereal while driving in the car, coffee yes, a donut yes, a bagel yes, but cereal no.

The microwave signaled the bagel was ready. Dan pulled it from the oven and tossed it from hand to hand while it cooled off. He looked at his watch as he left the backdoor leading to the garage, 4:33 a.m. Not bad, just sixteen minutes from Joey's call to out the door.

It was the time of day when streets are empty. The party-goers and drunks are already home in bed, and the garbage truck drivers and street cleaners are just waking up. Dan turned on the car's flashing blue lights but decided he didn't need the siren. Why disturb the good citizens of Chicago.

It was late May, and the cool nights created an eerie effect as steam rose from the sewers beneath the street and quickly condensed into a foggy mist as the vapor hit the cold air. From Oak Park, where Dan and Sally lived, it was only a short ride to the scene of the crime.

Dan didn't need an exact address because as he turned onto Cortez Street, he could see a grouping of official City of Chicago cars double-parked out in front of a three-story brownstone. The lights were on in all six apartments. Dan parked behind the Forensics van and turned off his flashing lights.

Art Fuller walked up to Dan as he stepped out of his car. Dan had met Art a few times, a regular guy who liked to work nights. There were always a few crazies like Art who enjoyed working the vampire shift. They shook hands, and then Art confessed. "Dan, I'm sorry but as soon as I saw the body, I barfed on the floor. I've never done anything like that before, but wait till you see her. I can't believe anyone would do that. It's the worst I've ever seen."

Dan ignored Art's apology. "What have you got?"

Art took out his notebook and read from his notes. "The woman, her name's Carol McCowen, was found by her boyfriend at about three o'clock. The station got a call at 3:07 a.m. I got here at 3:11 a.m., and the boyfriend immediately showed me the body. The boyfriend says they were both with friends at Bar Louie until just after midnight. When he got to his place he remembered he had given her his wallet and called to remind her to bring it to work the next day.

"She never answered the call. He tried again several times over the next two hours and then, thinking something was wrong, drove over to make sure she was alright. She didn't answer the door. He has a key, and after entering the apartment, he found the body. He made it to the bathroom before he threw up, and then he called the police."

"Do the neighbors know anything?"

"I've checked with them all but none of them heard anything until the boyfriend found the body. When you see the body, I think you'll understand why."

"Where's the body?"

"Second floor on the right."

"Listen Art, I want your people to go up and down the street and alley looking for security cameras. If you find any, wake the people up and see if there're any recordings worth keeping. If there are, take them as evidence."

"Will do."

Dan left Art and walked up the six concrete steps to the apartment's entrance. The building looked old but was in pretty good condition. Dan guessed it was a product of the pre-depression building boom. There were no security cameras, and no lock on the front door. Inside, a small vestibule held six mailboxes and an umbrella stand.

Walking up the stairs to the second floor, Dan was greeted by a motley collection of residents in various stages of dress who were observing events unfolding in real-time. Fires and homicides had a way of attracting gawkers.

Dan carefully opened the door to the apartment. He first reacted to the smell, which was overpowering. It seemed Art had decided to upchuck right by the front door. Dan inspected the pile of vomit as he avoided stepping in the mess. It looked like Art had polished off a pepperoni pizza just before arriving on the scene, probably a deep-dish.

As Dan moved into the living room, he was greeted by the sound of a familiar voice coming from the bedroom. Amber Carlson, the Medical Examiner stuck her head out and greeted Dan. "So they got you up too. My boss got me out of bed. He said I wouldn't want to miss this one."

"Well hello to you. It seems like we always find the strangest places to meet. What you got?"

Amber, who was wearing a white disposable jumpsuit and gloves, said, "Get ready for the worst homicide you've ever seen. I would have barfed just like Art except I had nothing in my stomach."

Even with Amber's warning, Dan was not prepared for the terrible smell of feces filling the air as he followed Amber into the bedroom. The body of the naked victim was bound spread-eagle to the four corners of the bed with grey duct tape and a six inch section of tape had been placed over the victim's mouth. The scene was horrific. The woman's belly had been slit open from her vagina up to her sternum. The contents of the woman's body were strewn over the once white linen bedspread; a combination of blood, fecal material, and intestines. Sometime during or just prior to death, the woman had urinated and defecated onto the bed. And to top things off, the number fourteen had been cut into the victim's forehead with a razor or other sharp instrument. A trail of blood led from the bed across the room and ended near the door leading to the bathroom.

Dan had to step away from the bed and regroup outside the bedroom. Amber followed him into the living room. "One hell of a crime scene, don't you think?"

"I've never seen anything like it. What can you tell me?"

"Not much yet. With her liver just exposed like that, it's going to be hard to give you an accurate time of death. I'm not sure when she died, but I can tell you she was alive when her belly was slit open. You can see the lacerations around the duct tape as she struggled to free herself. And the blood and innards splattered all over the bed and floor shows that it took some time before she died. It must have been a horrible death."

"What do you make of the number fourteen?"

"It was cut with a razor blade or X-acto knife or maybe even a scalpel; definitely something very sharp. It's the cut that opened up her belly that's most interesting. I'm pretty sure it was made with one slice. It looks like the killer started in the woman's vagina and ran the blade all the way up to the sternum in one single cut. It must have been one special knife to be able to do that. I might be able to tell you more when I get the body back to the morgue. Oh, and by the way, she was hit over the head a few minutes prior to death. There's a pretty large contusion on the back of her head."

"Who did they send from Forensics?"

"Julie, she's in the library dusting for prints. The boyfriend who found her is in the kitchen."

Dan composed himself and walked into the kitchen. A young man in his late twenties sat at the kitchen table staring at a picture taped to the refrigerator. The photograph was of the young man and the victim in front of Buckingham Fountain. Obviously in shock, his body shook uncontrollably. "I'm Detective Dan Lawson with the Chicago Police Department. I know I've caught you at the worst possible time, but if you can, I'd appreciate your answering a few questions."

The man stood up and introduced himself as Bryce Collier. They both sat down at the kitchen table and Dan said, "Mr. Collier, if you could, I'd like you to tell me about what happened tonight."

Dan took out his notebook and got ready to take notes. "Carol and I spent the night at Bar Louie. We meet our friends there every Thursday night for dinner, and we watch whatever sports are on their TVs. We all left a little after midnight. I tried calling Carol when I got home."

"Why did you call her Bryce?"

"She had my wallet. I forgot I gave it to her to keep in her purse because it kept falling out of my pocket. When I got home I remembered she had it, and I wanted to remind her to bring it to work in the morning. I can't believe she's dead. Who could have done such a thing? I mean the way she was killed!"

Bryce held his face in his hands and began to sob quietly. Dan found some Kleenex in the powder room and handed him the box. The young man finally composed himself and continued. "I'm sorry detective. I just can't believe someone would do this."

"Can you continue Bryce or would you like to do this tomorrow?"

"No, let's go on," he said. "I tried calling her several times, but she never answered the phone. I got really worried. She would always answer the phone, so after trying for over two hours, I decided to drive over. I was sure something was wrong."

"How did you get in?"

"We both have keys to each other's apartments. We're engaged; we were going to get married in June; she always wanted a June wedding. Then I saw her on the bed, and I knew right away she was dead. My God, how could someone have done such a horrible thing?"

That's when Bryce lost it. He just broke down in tears, an uncontrollable emotional breakdown. Dan decided to leave and let Bryce deal with his loss in total privacy. Julie Westerman, the head of Forensics was dusting for prints in the library. "Julie, Hi; it looks like they've sent all the pros to deal with this one."

"Yea, I was sound asleep when my boss called and ordered me to get my ass down here ASAP."

"What have you got for me?"

"Not much. I've taken a full set of pictures; I found the boyfriend's prints on the doorknob, but it was wiped clean by someone before the boyfriend came in the door. Check out the security chain on the front door; it looks like it was forced open."

Dan walked over to the front door and studied the brass security chain hanging from the door. The chain had been torn right out of the doorframe, and the wood screws were lying on the floor just in front of the door. Why do people think these chains offer any security?

Dan returned to the kitchen to find Bryce back in control of his emotions. His eyes were red and swollen, and his nose was dripping. "I'm sorry detective; I just lost it. I still can't believe she's dead."

"Don't worry about it Bryce; you've been through a lot and witnessed a terrible thing. You're doing better than I could do if I were in your situation. Any ideas on who could have done this?"

Bryce shook his head in a negative response. "That's what I've been thinking about, and I don't have a clue. Carol didn't have any enemies, absolutely none."

"Okay Bryce, you need to go home and get out of here. Write down your address and telephone number, and I'll call you later today. Do you feel up to driving?"

"Sure, I can drive myself."

"Where are you parked?"

"Down the block."

"Go out the backdoor and don't talk to any reporters."

"I need to talk to Carol's parents."

"I'll do that. Do you have their number?"

Bryce pulled out his cellphone and found their telephone number. "Can I tell people what happened?"

"Sure, but please leave out anything about the crime scene."

Just after Bryce left, some more people from the morgue arrived. They placed the body in a black body bag, zipped it up, and wheeled it out on a gurney. The body was gone, but the smell still lingered. Julie had bagged up the bedspread, and one of her assistants had cleaned up the messes Art and Bryce had left on the floor.

Art walked into the apartment shaking his head. There aren't any cameras in alleys, backyards, or front yards for two blocks in both directions"

Dan looked at his watch. It was close to six o'clock. Boy, how time flies when you're having fun. It was time for some interviews with the neighbors. He walked out into the hallway and talked to the seven residents milling around. "I'm going to need to talk to each of you." Dan pointed to the apartment across the hall. "Who lives there?"

An elderly couple dressed in robes stepped forward. Dan pointed to their apartment and the three of them walked inside. "Where's a good place to talk?" Dan asked.

The lady who introduced herself as Emma Phillips led the way into the kitchen. She asked if Dan wanted a cup of coffee. "Mrs. Phillips, I'd love a cup of coffee."

While Emma brewed a fresh pot, her husband Ralph and Dan sat down at the kitchen table. Ralph asked, "It was bad wasn't it?"

"Yes, Mr. Phillips, it was very bad. Did either of you hear anything tonight?"

Emma Phillips answered, "Ralph can't hear at all without his hearing aids. We were both sleeping when I heard Carol's boyfriend screaming for help. When I opened the front door, Carol's door was open, and I could see him talking to someone. I guess it was 911."

"Where was he standing when you saw him?"

"Just in front of the coffee table."

"What happened then?"

"Well, after he hung up he started screaming that someone had killed her. I walked over to the bedroom and looked in. I've never seen anything so terrible in all my days. I took one look and then sat down next to Bryce; he's her boyfriend; they were going to get married in June. I tried to comfort him, but he just couldn't control himself."

Ralph Phillips handed his wife a box of Kleenex as tears streamed down her cheeks. "How could anyone do this? God, it was awful, and they were such a nice couple and so much in love."

"How long have you known Miss McCowen?"

"She moved in about two, no wait, three years ago. I guess we treated her like the child we never had. We had her over for dinner a couple times a month, and she and Bryce were always talking to us about their upcoming wedding."

"Do either of you know of anyone who would want to kill her?"

Emma Phillips blew her nose while Ralph shook his head. "Detective Lawson," Ralph said, "Carol was a wonderful person. I can't think of anyone who would have wanted to kill her."

Dan sipped at his coffee preparing to ask the most difficult question. "Did Carol and Bryce ever get into any arguments?"

Emma Phillips' face turned angry, "I think I know where you're going with that question, and I can tell you I never saw them get into an argument; and Bryce loved her and would never have hurt her. He is a tender, loving, young man."

Dan knew it was time to end the discussion. He handed the couple his business card and asked them to call if they could think of anything.

Ralph Phillips walked him to the door and Dan entered an empty hallway. Evidently the gawkers had decided to get ready for a new day without their young neighbor. Dan walked up to the third floor to begin interviewing the other residents in the building.

The middle-aged couple above McCowen's apartment heard nothing until the police came. They had just moved in the month before and didn't know Carol McCowen.

The other apartment on the third floor was another matter. A guy about thirty, dressed in a suit and tie, answered the knock. His name was Jeffrey Smothers. He had heard the sirens but chose not to get involved. He had stayed in his apartment while all the other residents had gathered in the hallway. He seemed nervous and explained he was going to have to leave in a few minutes or he'd be late for work.

"Just a couple of questions Mr. Smothers. Did you know the victim?'

"We were just casual acquaintances detective. We saw each other at the mail box from time to time."

"Any idea who may have killed her?"

"I didn't know she was dead detective. I don't like getting involved in things not affecting me. And as for who might have killed her, I have no idea. Now if you'll excuse me, I have to get to work."

"Thanks for your time Mr. Smothers. If you can think of anything important regarding the case, please give me a call."

Dan handed Jeffrey Smothers his business card and made a note to talk to him again. His behavior was just strange. What kind of person wouldn't have at least checked with the neighbors to find out what was going on?

The three residents on the first floor knew nothing, heard nothing, and saw nothing; just your typical excellent eyewitnesses. Dan decided to check with Emma Phillips again, the only resident who seemed to have her act together. She answered the door and invited him inside.

"Just a few more questions Mrs. Phillips. Did Jeffrey Smothers come downstairs to see what happened in Carol McCowen's apartment?"

"No Detective Lawson. I don't recall seeing him."

"Don't you think that's a little odd?"

"Not for Jeffery; he's one weird bird."

"What do you mean?"

"He's a loner; he never says hello when I see him at the mailbox. He plays a lot of loud classical music in his apartment at night, but other than that, you wouldn't know he exists."

Dan thanked Mrs. Phillips for her time and left her apartment.

Chapter 2

So other than Ralph and Emma Phillips, none of the other tenants in the building knew anything. They were all awakened from their sleep by the arrival of the police cars with their sirens blaring. Typical, typical.

Dan walked back into the crime scene and watched the Forensics people doing their thing. He finally had some time to ponder the evidence. What had really happened here? What did he know, and what information was missing?

He examined the broken security chain again. The conclusion was rather obvious; someone forced the door open after the victim had answered a late night knock. Dan looked through the small round security peephole in the door. He had a clear view of the hallway, and if Carol McCowen had used it prior to opening the front door, she would have gotten a good look at the person on the other side.

Dan thought about the implications. If he was a young city girl, he would have been sensitive to any intruders, certainly someone knocking on her door after midnight. She might have known the person knocking but still wasn't sure, so she had kept the security chain fastened.

The intruder forces the door open, breaking the security chain, and somehow stops Carol from screaming. This wasn't like the movies where the young girl facing the guy in the hockey mask can't find the ability to scream. But Emma Phillips heard nothing until she heard Bryce screaming. Her hearing was good enough to hear screams, and therefore perhaps Carol McCowen never screamed. If that was the case, then why the broken chain? That was a question searching for an answer.

Dan walked across the living room carpet toward the bedroom and noticed two shallow depressions in the carpet leading to the bedroom. He hadn't seen them before. He called out to Julie, who emerged from the library. "What do you make of this?"

Julie walked around the tracks in the carpet. "We didn't do this. It must have been here before we arrived."

"Amber said the victim was hit over the head before she died. Maybe she was hit over the head by the front door, then dragged into the bedroom, and then tied to the bed while she was still unconscious. That might explain why there weren't any screams and no struggle."

Julie said, "If those are her heel marks, she may have had some skin cells scraped off. I'll vacuum the area and see if we can find anything with a microscope."

Dan, with Julie following, walked into the bedroom. Carol's body had been removed, and Julie's team had removed the blood stained bedding. A mixture of blood and shit was splattered around the bed on the light beige carpeting. Bloody smudges, perhaps footprints, led from the side of the bed to near the bathroom doorway. Dan could picture the victim struggling violently as she bled out, splattering bodily fluids throughout the room. Some stains had even reached the walls. There was definitely a lot of blood, but strangely the carpeting was free of blood stains in a square area near the bathroom. Why?

"The killer changed clothes here."

"What do you mean?" Julie said.

"Look, the place is a bloody mess. Blood and shit everywhere, but nothing in the living room and nothing in this area. I think the killer placed a tarp over here where there aren't any stains. Then, after the killing, the killer put his bloody clothes on the tarp and changed into clean clothes. He wraps all the bloody stuff in the tarp and leaves."

"I see your point; it would explain a lot. That implies a lot of preplanning."

"Right you are Julie; this was no impulsive killing; this was premeditated, and the killer planned everything out in great detail."

Julie went back to the kitchen, and Dan began a search of the apartment after gloving up. He found a cellphone in Carol McCowen's purse and looked in the call history file. She had seven missed calls from Bryce beginning at 12:45 a.m. At least Bryce's story seemed to check out, but he certainly could have made the calls from anywhere, including the crime scene. Unfortunately crimes of passion were usually committed by someone close to the victim. Dan found Bryce's wallet in the victim's purse. Bryce's story made sense, but he was definitely not out of the woods, at least not yet.

Dan returned the phone to McCowen's purse and placed the purse in an evidence bag. He'd inspect it again back at the precinct.

Dan walked over to the front door and looked at the doorknob. Julie said it had been wiped clean of fingerprints, except for Bryce's prints. Bryce probably wouldn't have bothered to wipe his prints off the doorknob just to put fresh prints back on. Probably the killer had wiped the place clean of prints before leaving the crime scene. Of course Bryce Collier could have wiped the doorknob clean just to misdirect the police. Dan guessed Julie wouldn't be finding any prints left behind by the killer.

He suddenly had a thought. Did the victim answer the door in the nude or had she been wearing a robe or something else. If so, where were the clothes? Had the killer hung them up in the closet?

In the bedroom walk-in closet, he found a terrycloth robe on a hanger, but there was also a large pink porcelain hook on the back of the closet door. The same place Dan's wife always hung her robe.

The smell still lingered in the apartment, and would probably remain there for many days to come. Dan was running out of gas. He looked at his watch. It was a little past ten o'clock, and he needed to get back to the office and let Joey know what was happening. He'd come back later in the day and do a more detailed search

As he left the apartment, he was surrounded by a half-dozen reporters from the local TV stations. Art had set up a crime scene barrier with the usual yellow tape, but the tape didn't stop the reporters from blocking access to his car. A reporter he recognized shouted above the throng, "What can you tell us detective?"

"Nothing Miss, nothing. No comment at this time."

Chapter 3

Joey saw Dan enter the precinct's office area and waved him into his office. "What you got?"

Dan gave him the update. Joey, a good detective back in the day, sat back in his chair and thoughtfully considered Dan's account. "I don't think it's the boyfriend. The killing's too gruesome."

"I agree," Dan said, "but we can't rule him out yet. So far his story checks out, but I'll see what the victim's friends have to say."

Joey pointed his finger at Dan. "Just remember, it sounds like she probably knew the person she let in, so one of those so called friends may have done it."

"I hear you boss, I hear you."

Dan sat down at his desk and readied himself for the unsavory task of calling Carol McCowen's parents and telling them their daughter had been murdered. The area code Bryce had given him indicated a northern suburb of Chicago. Police protocol stated a face to face visit was the preferred method of delivering this type of news, but Dan didn't want to waste a half day on a trip up north. He wanted to find the killer.

Dan punched in the number and waited. He hoped he didn't get an answering machine because leaving a message from the police department was never the way anyone wanted to hear bad news. The phone was answered on the fourth ring by a woman.

"Is this Mrs. McCowen?"

"Yes, who's calling please?"

"My name is Detective Dan Lawson. I'm with the Chicago Police Department. I'm sorry to have to convey some tragic news. Early this morning your daughter was the victim of a homicide."

"Oh goodness, is she alright?"

"I'm afraid not mam; she was found dead in her apartment."

"Who's making this call? How could you play such a cruel joke on a mother?"

"Mam, I'm a detective with the Homicide Division, and your daughter was found dead in her apartment early this morning by her fiancé Bryce Collier."

Dan heard the phone drop to the floor, and Mrs. McCowen shrieked at the top of her voice. In the background Dan could hear a man approach the woman, and she screamed, "Carol's dead; our Carol's dead; someone killed my little baby."

A shaky voice suddenly spoke on the phone. "Who is this?"

"Mr. McCowen, this is Detective Dan Lawson with the Chicago Police Department. Early this morning your daughter was the victim of a homicide. Bryce Collier found her dead in her apartment."

The silence on the other end of the phone seemed to drag on forever. He couldn't imagine what these two parents were going through. Getting this type of news was like getting hit over the head with a sledge hammer. How could a person process this death notice and still remain rational? Dan knew it was impossible, and he would just have to give them time to come to terms with the sudden and unexpected loss of their daughter.

Finally Mr. McCowen spoke again. Dan couldn't see the man's face, but he could feel the anguish written across his face. "Detective, what happened?"

"Mr. McCowen, please accept my deepest sympathy for the loss of your daughter. I want to explain in detail what we know, but I'd like to do it in person. I know Bryce wants to talk to you, but I asked him to let me talk to you first. I'd like to see both you and your wife tomorrow morning. I think you'll both be better prepared for a discussion at that time."

Mr. McCowen's voice suddenly turned angry. "Just name the time Detective Lawson. Please for the love of God, find the person who did this."

"I promise to do everything I can to find the person who killed her. Let's meet at nine o'clock at your house. Bryce gave me the address."

The called ended and Dan looked at Amy Green at the desk next to his. She said, "A tough one huh?"

"You have no idea."

Dan gave Amy the ten minute summary, and when he described the body, she gritted her teeth.

By the time he had finished the debriefing she was squeezing the blood from her arms. She just sat there stunned, not knowing what to say.

Finally she looked at Dan and said, "I want in. I'm going to see Joey and tell him either he lets me help you on the case or I quit, and if I catch the guy who did this, I'm going to cut off his balls. Murder is one thing, but this is beyond being human."

Amy, a detective after his own heart, got up from her chair and burst into Joey's office. She slammed the door behind her and after ten minutes emerged from the boss's office with a look of determination on her face. "You're the lead; just tell me what you want me to do."

"What did Joey say?"

"He wouldn't do it until I handed him my badge and gun. Then he finally said yes."

Dan knew he could count on Amy, and he was glad to have her help on the case. Dan looked at his watch. Let's go back to the crime scene and then let's talk to Bryce Collier at the end of the day. I want to give him some time to process the death of his fiancée. He was pretty shook up this morning."

Amy began clearing her desk, and after handing in some case folders to Joey, she returned to a clean desk fired up and ready to go.

Dan said, "Let's get some lunch. I don't know if I can keep any food down, but all I've had today is a bagel and a half cup of coffee."

Dan and Amy had lunch at a nearby Subway. After eating in silence for a few minutes, Amy asked, "How's Debbie doing?"

Dan smiled at the question about his one-year old daughter. "She's doing great. She's actually walking almost like a pro, and she loves our au pair. She looks just like Sally. You know when I was breaking the news of their daughter's death to the McCowens, I kept thinking how I would react if Debbie suddenly died, and you know what; I couldn't even begin to imagine. Just thinking about the possibility was beyond what my mind could deal with."

"That's why I wanted in Dan. I kept seeing my daughter with her belly cut open, and the thought was so offensive, I knew I had to help catch this guy."

They both finished their lunch deep in very personal thoughts.

Chapter 4

The crime scene looked the same in the afternoon sun. The lock on the apartment's front door had been replaced with a special lock by one of Julie's people along with the usual yellow crime scene tape, and a note plastered to the door warned unauthorized people not to enter. Dan took out a special key and unlocked the door.

As they entered the apartment the smell of death still permeated the small one bedroom unit. Dan opened a few windows to let in some fresh air and then explained what had happened. Amy asked a few questions, but for the most part just listened.

It would be a fresh start for Dan. With the body removed, and the chaos surrounding Forensics and the Medical Examiners' Office doing their thing over, a calm almost anticlimactic air filled the apartment. Dan looked around the place and tried to capture a feel for how the victim had lived.

It was remarkable in that it was totally unremarkable. If you had a picture in your mind of what a twenty something single woman might live like, this was it. The place was sparsely decorated, probably with some hand-me-downs from mom and dad. The living room walls, painted in depressing beige, were void of any works of art, just a few pictures of friends and places where Carol McCowen may have vacationed. The apartment certainly wasn't uncomfortable, just exactly what you might expect from a young single person with only a little extra money to spend on non-functional necessities.

The bedroom was furnished with one of those cheap five-piece bedroom sets you see advertised on TV; *and all for the incredibly low price of $999.95.* Several stuffed animals were displayed on a small round table in front of the bedroom window, probably of great sentimental value to the victim, and Dan guessed it would now become a cherished keepsake for her distraught parents.

Dan said, "Amy I'll take the desk; why don't you take the rest of the place. Both Amy and Dan knew the drill. It wasn't like either needed a checklist of things to look for, so they parted ways and left to complete their work.

Dan sat down at the victim's small black Ikea desk, assembled by the buyer with only a Phillips screwdriver. He began gathering evidence. His highest priority was to make a list of everyone who might have been an acquaintance of Carol McCowen. He started with her desktop computer. Luckily, it wasn't password protected. He opened her browser and a Google Home Page filled the screen. He clicked on g-mail and began looking at her recent correspondence with the outside world. Carol McCowen was heavy into getting advertisements and announcements from every retailer in the Chicago area.

It took Dan almost an hour to sift through the trivia and read all of the e-mails to her friends. For the most part, they were nothing more than the usual banter between close friends about clothes, young men, and other friends; nothing in the least bit unusual.

Dan printed out her list of contacts. At least the list was complete: names, e-mail addresses, telephone numbers, and even a few pictures. Then he checked her deleted items, and they were more of the same. A quick check of her Word and Excel files revealed nothing out of the ordinary. In short, the entire ninety minute exercise, except for the names, had been a total waste of time.

Amy shouted from the kitchen. "Where's her purse?"

"Bagged up as evidence. We can look at it back at the station."

After she left, Dan started on the paper files located inside the victim's desk. Some recent bank statements showed a minimal balance in her checking account, and her Visa statements indicated she was in debt to the tune of a little over nine-thousand dollars. Dan shook his head. Why couldn't young people live within their means? He just didn't get it.

He left the desk with a printout of all her contacts and nothing more. Absolutely nothing; usually he found something; but the truth was this young lady was living a rather uncomplicated life, apparently free of stress other than being overextended financially, and that was certainly not unusual for this age group.

Dan sat down on the living room couch and sank down almost to the floor. This was not an upscale piece of furniture. The beat up coffee table in front of the couch held a few knickknacks and a photo album, but little of great interest.

Dan began looking through the scrapbook of pictures. The photos were arranged in chronological order. There weren't any baby pictures. The first pages were of a young girl, perhaps ten-years old, and as Dan turned the pages the pictorial story of Carol McCowen's life unfolded before his eyes. Carol at her birthday parties, Carol at a summer camp, Carol graduating from grade school, then high school, and finally college. Pictures of Carol on vacations with her friends and family, and near the end some pictures of Bryce and some of her friends; just the usual photographs people keep to remember the good times. No pictures of funerals, bad days at the office, arguments between friends or work colleagues; none of the bad things making up a person's real life, the things people try to forget.

"Hey Amy, where are you putting the evidence pile?"

"There isn't one yet. You can start the pile anywhere you want."

Dan walked into the kitchen and placed his list of contacts and the photo album on the Formica kitchen counter and returned to the desk for one final bit of investigative necessity. He looked in a file labelled Spartan Industries and discovered where Carol McCowen made her living. She was Comptroller for a small specialty metal fabricator on the Near Northside. Dan found a letter to Carol offering the recent college graduate a position in the company working in Finance, and she had recently been promoted to Comptroller with a salary of $32,000 per year. It was above the poverty line but not the kind of yearly salary most college graduates would envy.

Amy walked into the room and threw a Ziploc bag containing what looked to be about an ounce of weed. "I found it hidden inside a box of tampons."

"Not the most original of hiding places," Dan suggested. "We'll have to talk to her fiancé about that."

Amy sat down in an old loveseat facing the desk. "Other than the weed, I couldn't find anything of interest."

"You're a woman; tell me about her; what was she like as a person?"

Amy thought for a moment. "Typical twenty something single woman. Her clothes labels suggest she shopped at The Gap. She was a neat and orderly person. Her closet was highly organized by colors. She was on the pill. She and her fiancé had an active sex life."

Dan interrupted, "How do you know that?"

"From the almost empty tube of KY jelly in her nightstand."

Dan laughed at the imagery.

Amy continued, "She liked to cook; her herbs and other ingredients were of the more expensive variety. She did her grocery shopping at Whole Foods, and all of her pots and pans have been used extensively. She wore contact lenses, and had a few nice pieces of old style jewelry, maybe hand-me-downs from a grandmother. In short, she was unremarkable, but trying to move upward in society."

"But she died," Dan said, "and it was a cruel death. Her life was cut short by some crazy asshole who, for some unknown reason, decided it was time for Carol McCowen to die. And now, we've got to figure out who did this and bring him to justice."

Amy answered back, "Profound Detective Lawson, but save that speech for the press conference. I'm figuring the boss will have a stick up his ass placed there by the Mayor. What happened in this bedroom is going to leak to the press, and they're going to have a field day with the headlines. It'll be front page for sure. Just mark my words; I'm guessing we have one more day before the shit hits the fan, and Joey tells you to talk to the press."

Dan sat silently, thinking about Amy's prediction. She was probably right. Somehow, someway, this story would leak. It was only a matter of time.

Dan looked at his watch. It was almost four o'clock. He took out his cellphone and called Bryce Collier. "Mr. Collier, this is Detective Lawson. I wonder if you're feeling up to answering a few questions?"

Bryce was at home, and he agreed to meet there for the discussion.

Chapter 5

Bryce Collier shared an apartment with another guy who Bryce said was still at work. Dan and Amy stepped into a typical single male's apartment; that is to say cluttered with sports equipment still smelling from several lengthy workouts, and messy beyond anything Dan had seen in years. There were probably thousands of cockroaches lurking under every dirty dish waiting for darkness to start another day of feasting on three day old takeout food.

The furnishings made Carol McCowen's apartment look like a palace fit for a queen. Bryce led them back into the kitchen where they sat down at a cheap Formica kitchen table. A half empty bottle of scotch sat on the kitchen counter, and Bryce looked like the bottle might have been unopened when he had started drinking. His eyes were red and swollen as he sat quietly at the table facing Dan.

After introducing Amy, Dan asked how Bryce was doing. "Just peachy," Bryce answered in slurred speech. "I still can't get over it. She was so happy when we left Bar Louie, and then, wamo, she's dead. Not just dead, but the way she died. Who would do such a thing, and why her? Everyone loved Carol."

Dan answered, "I wish we could answer those questions Bryce, but that's why Detective Green and

I are here. The more information you can give us, the quicker we'll be able to get answers."

"Whatever I can do to help detective, just ask and I'll do it.

Dan took out his notebook along with Amy. "Bryce, we think Carol might have known the person who did this. She answered the front door after midnight. Would she have looked through the peep hole before she opened the door?"

"I really don't know detective. There weren't too many times when I was at her place and someone came to the door."

"Bryce, this might sound like a strange question, but did Carol sleep in the nude?"

Bryce looked dumbfounded. "Why do you care about that?"

"Because we found Carol nude on her bed and no clothes in the bedroom."

"Yes, she usually slept in the nude."

"Well, if she was in bed when there was a knock on her door, would she have gone to answer it naked?"

"No, that's not like Carol; she would have put on her robe. It's a blue one, and she keeps it in the closet."

"On a hanger?"

"No on a hook in back of the closet door."

"Are you sure she never puts it on a hanger?"

"Maybe, all I can say is I've always seen her put it on that hook. Why is this important?"

"I'm sorry Bryce, but I can't tell you why right now. Tell me what the number fourteen means to Carol?"

Bryce was silent for a long time. He finally smiled and spoke. "One of her cousins just turned fourteen."

"Could there be anything else?"

Bryce grabbed some Kleenex and blew his nose. "I don't know! I don't know!"

"Bryce, did you get a close-up view of Carol's body?"

"When I first saw her, I thought she was asleep on the bed, but then I saw her arms and feet tied to the bed and then I saw her entire stomach slit open and that terrible smell. That's when I ran to the bathroom and threw up."

"Did you see her face?"

"Not up close, but close enough to see it was her."

"How did you and Carol meet?"

"We both work at Spartan. I'm in the Engineering Department. She started working there right out of college in Finance. We met at a party." He had a smile on his face as he remembered the night. "I had just gotten there, and she was just sitting by herself out on the patio sipping on a martini. I came up with this stupid line, *haven't I seen you at work,* and she just smiled at me with this wonderful smile. I'll always remember that smile."

"Bryce, we found about an ounce of weed in Carol's apartment. Now I want you to understand,

Detective Green and I aren't with drug enforcement, and we don't really care if you and Carol smoked a joint from time to time. I even smoked a few joints when I was in college. Detective Green and I only want to catch the person who did this, and maybe the person who Carol bought the weed from had something to do with her death. Do you know where she got the marijuana?"

Bryce wasn't sure if he wanted to answer the question. He had a hard time believing any cop wouldn't care if he smoked a joint, but Carol had died, and Bryce wanted the guy caught. "We were walking in Humboldt Park last week and this guy approached us. He sold us two ounces. We tried some in the park. It was at night and nobody was around. We never went back to see the guy, and I have no idea who he was."

The interview went on for another hour. Dan wrote down the names of the friends who were together at Bar Louie. When they were finished Dan was convinced Bryce Collier had absolutely nothing to do with Carol's murder. As Dan and Amy left, Bryce asked, "Did you talk to Mr. and Mrs. McCowen?"

Dan answered, "I did Bryce, and they took it pretty hard. I think they would really appreciate a call from you. Just remember; please don't mention anything about what you saw."

Back in their car, Amy said, "He's a good kid. He's got nothing to do with her murder."

"I agree, just a young guy who just lost his future wife."

Dan dropped Amy back at the precinct and headed home after a very long day.

Chapter 6

Dan arrived home to a hero's welcome from his year-old daughter Debbie. She waddled from the au pair into Dan's arms, and he lifted her high into the air much to her delight. She screaked until he put her down. With the greeting over, Debbie walked back to the au pair, and the creative art project taking place on the family room floor resumed.

Susana, the Columbian au pair, said, "Sally got home about ten minutes ago. She's taking a shower."

Dan found Sally drying off in the master bedroom. She took one look at her tired husband and knew it had been a rough day. "Was it bad?"

"You have no idea."

Dan reviewed his day, and as he described in detail how the body had been found, Sally grimaced in horror. Sally, the head of Emergency Medicine at Northwestern Hospital, saw the horrors of death every day, but nothing like Dan's description.

"Any suspects?" she asked.

"Not yet. I'm just hoping it's not the first of many killings."

There, he had finally said what he had been thinking about all day. It had been in the back of his mind, but now it was there, out in the open for him to contemplate. What if this was the work of a serial killer? Only one fact moved the possibility to the backburner. Carol McCowen probably knew the person at the door. That's why she opened it. Of course people being people, she might have just opened the door without knowing who was there. People do stupid things like that all of the time.

Dan took his turn in the shower. His clothes smelled of death and he wanted to wash away the day's misery. He could clean his body, but not his mind. He kept on thinking about the homicide, and one fact remained; the killing had been brutal, beyond anything Dan had ever experienced. What was the motive?

The number fourteen inscribed in Carol McCowen's head offered the only hint of motive. Somehow Dan knew understanding the significance of that number would provide an important clue.

Over dinner, three adults, with one toddler looking on, discussed the significance of what the number fourteen might mean. Susana wasn't told the details of where the number was found, but nonetheless had her own theory. "Could this be the fourteenth person this guy killed?"

"Not with this type of murder," Dan said. "We would have heard about it if it happened anywhere else in the country."

Sally was thinking out loud. "Obviously the number has significance to the person who did this.

Something between the victim and the killer; something in their past; maybe the killer knew the victim and it happened to them when one of them was fourteen years old."

Dan had a different thought. "Maybe this is a serial killer who plans on killing fourteen people, and this was the first."

With that pleasant thought, they finished their dinner in silence.

Chapter 7

The McCowen house was located in Wilmette, an affluent suburb just north of Chicago alongside Lake Michigan. Their house wasn't one of those mansions sitting along the lake, but a modest house in an older section of town near the Metra train stop. Amy and Dan parked on the street and walked up to the front door. Door chimes announced their arrival, and the sound of footsteps on creaking wood floors prepared them for the front door opening.

George McCowen, anticipating the visit, asked, "Detective Lawson?"

"Yes Mr. McCowen and this is Detective Green."

George McCowen led them into the living room where his wife Emily sat fidgeting on a plush dark-brown couch. She rose as George introduced the two detectives. Emily McCowen said, "I would have had coffee ready, but somehow it just didn't seem appropriate."

Dan said, "Thank you anyway Mrs. McCowen. You're probably right; it just doesn't seem like a coffee day.

George started the conversation. "We got a call last night from Bryce, but he told us you asked him not to talk about what happened. What can you tell us?"

Dan thought about how to answer. Minimal information might lead to minimal cooperation, but providing too much detail might cause such anguish as to create the same effect. He chose the middle ground. "A little after midnight last night, someone entered your daughter's apartment. We think she may have known the person. Although I don't have the medical examiner's report yet, we believe she was knocked unconscious, and then she died from a knife wound."

At the word *died*, Emily McCowen clutched her body with both arms and began weeping. Her husband, who was sitting next to her, tried to comfort her but without much success. Emily suddenly sat up and said, "I'm so sorry; I promised myself I was going to be strong, but it's a promise I can't keep. She was our only child. Now we have nothing, absolutely nothing."

"I know it's difficult for both of you, but Detective Green and I need to ask you several questions. The more information you can provide, the better our chances of finding the person who did this as soon as possible."

George McCowen, who was holding up better, answered, "We understand detective; we'll try our best to answer whatever questions you have."

"Detective Green and I appreciate that. As I said before, we think the person who did this knew your daughter."

George interrupted, "Why is that detective?"

"She evidently opened the door with the security chain attached. She probably could see the person who knocked through the peep hole, but she felt confident enough to open the door, but not so sure that she removed the security chain. After the door was opened, the person forced the security chain open and then knocked your daughter unconscious."

Emily asked, "Didn't she scream for help? Didn't someone hear her?"

"Evidently not Mrs. McCowen. The lady living across the hall from your daughter heard Bryce scream for help after he found the body, but she never heard your daughter scream."

"Was that Mrs. Phillips?" Emily asked.

"Yes it was. She and her husband seemed to really like Carol and Bryce."

"Yes, I know, and Carol liked them as well."

"What I really need your help with is the killer left the number fourteen written at the crime scene. Do either of you have any idea about what the number might mean?"

It was one of those moments when you're asked a question by someone about something very important, but you have absolutely no idea how to answer the question. Dan could see it in their eyes. They had no clue whatsoever. They looked at each other as they searched for an answer, but there was not even a flicker of an idea as to what the number might mean, and they both seemed ashamed at not being able to answer the question. They just shook their heads in ignorance.

Dan, after waiting an appropriate amount of time, asked, "Did your daughter have any enemies; people who she didn't like or problems at work; any of those types of things?"

George answered, "She loved her job and just got a promotion. The people there loved her."

Emily answered, "Carol never had enemies. Even at school, she seemed to get along with everyone."

Dan asked, "I wonder if we can take a look at Carol's room. The place she grew up in might offer some clues."

Mrs. McCowen led the way up a narrow staircase to a good-sized room on the second floor. Emily said, "We'll wait for you downstairs. Take your time."

Amy closed the door and the two detectives looked around a room apparently not used for several years. It was a nice room painted pink, the perfect color for a young girl growing up. A large window overlooked the backyard. A nice mahogany dresser held a variety of pictures including one picture of Carol McCowen with her fiancé Bryce Collier.

A half hour search of the room turned up nothing in the way of insight into the homicide. Dan held onto the picture of Carol and Bryce as they walked downstairs and met once again with the McCowens. "Do you mind if we borrow this picture of Carol? It will help us with our investigation."

George said, "Of course, whatever else we can do, just ask."

That was the sign for the meeting to end. Dan and Amy thanked the McCowens for their time and assured them they both would be working on the case fulltime until they caught whoever had killed their daughter. Dan and Amy handed them their business cards, and Dan asked them to please call if they could think of the meaning of the number fourteen.

Chapter 8

As they were leaving the McCowen's house, Dan's phone rang. It was Amber Carlson "I've got some preliminary information for you on the McCowen case. When do you want to meet?"

"As soon as possible. Amy Green and I are in Wilmette. We'll be at your place as soon as we can."

Dan hated the morgue. It wasn't the dead bodies all around. It had more to do with the architecture: tile floors, tile walls, extremely bright lights, tools of the trade lying all around; and of course there were the autopsy tables, ten of them to be exact. You would think ten would be more than enough to keep up with the workload, but you'd be wrong. Luckily from Amber's perspective, there was adequate refrigerator space to temporarily store the excess corpses.

Amber was sitting in her office just outside the autopsy room munching on a Kit Kat candy bar. She quickly stuffed the last piece into her mouth and stood up to greet them.

"What have you got?" Dan asked.

"You understand everything I'm going to tell you is preliminary?"

"We know the drill," Amy said.

"Well first, let's look at the time of death. With the victims innards all over the bed, liver temp, which is usually the best method, wasn't going to work. A rectal temperature indicated she probably died between 11:30 p.m. and 3:00 a.m."

Dan said, "It probably took thirty minutes to drive home from the bar, so we can say between 12:30 a. m. and 3:00 a.m."

"Works for me," Amber said. "Okay, now let's get to the interesting stuff. I believe the sequence of events were as follows. The victim got struck in the right rear quadrant of her skull with a blunt object and was rendered unconscious. While unconscious, she was placed on the bed and bound with duct tape. When she was slit open, she was certainly alive; the marks around her limbs under the duct tape indicate she was struggling to free herself, and also the spray pattern of blood and other bodily fluids scattered throughout the room also substantiate this conclusion."

"What about the number fourteen?"

"I believe the number was cut into her forehead after she died. First because the lines are very straight indicating a lack of a struggle and secondly, there was very little blood flowing from the wounds which also indicates death had already occurred."

"Anything about the weapon used?" Amy asked.

"Well now Amy, you've asked about the most interesting part of my findings. The weapon used was about eight inches long and very sharp, almost like a surgeon's scalpel. The weapon was inserted in the victim's vagina, and it appears the cut was made in a single stroke: through the Mons pubis, taking a nick out of the pubis symphysis, and then past the bladder and uterus. The blade then cut through the colon and small intestine, then the abdominal aorta, the left renal vein, the diaphragm, the lower lobe of the left lung, and finally nicked a bone fragment from the xiphoid process just below the sternum where it finally came to rest before it was with-drawn."

Dan said, "Cut the medical mumbo jumbo; what are you telling me?"

"I'm telling you the young lady was gutted like a fish!"

"Was the weapon a knife?"

"That seems to be the most likely weapon, but here's the thing, I've seen thousands of knife wounds, and I can tell you it's unlike any knife wound I've ever seen."

"How so?" Amy asked.

"I don't know yet; it's just different; that's why this is all preliminary. Preliminary as in I don't have a fucking clue yet as to the exact nature of the weapon."

"What about the blood workup?" Dan asked.

"Nothing unusual except for a trace of marijuana. I'm guessing she had a joint, maybe two, a couple of days ago. She definitely wasn't a chronic user. And that's about it. I'm sorry I don't have more. I wish I could tell you more about the weapon. Maybe I'll figure it out. If I do, I'll give you a call."

On that less than happy note, Amy and Dan thanked Amber and headed back to their car.

"Not a lot to go on," Amy said.

"You're right about that. Let's check in with Julie and see what she's got."

Chapter 9

Julie Westerman's lab was less foreboding than the morgue. It looked more like a college chemistry lab, and in many respects it was exactly that. Julie was looking through a microscope when the two detectives arrived unannounced. "I was going to call you after I finished checking out this fiber under the microscope. Look at this."

Julie backed away from the stereo zoom microscope and let Dan and Amy peer into the instrument. Dan looked first and adjusted the focus. A long twisted blue-colored fiber came into focus. "What is it?" he asked.

"We found it in the area in the carpet that was free of any blood. It's a spun polyolefin material; either polyethylene or polypropylene, I'm not sure which, but it's the kind of fiber typically used to make plastic tarps used by painters. Like we talked about at the crime scene, it looks like the guy who did this laid the tarp out on the carpet and then put all the bloody things on the tarp and cleaned up before he left the apartment."

As Dan let Amy look through the microscope, he said, "Amber gave us very little. We're hoping you've got something to help us."

The three walked back to Julie's off sat down around her desk. She pulled out a and organized the contents. "Here's what we've got so far. All the blood we found appears to be the victim's, at least based on blood type. We'll have DNA results back in two weeks to confirm. The duct tape appears to be your garden variety. You could buy it at any Home Depot or Ace Hardware anywhere in the country. We found epithelial cells along the depressions in the carpet, probably from the victim's feet as she was dragged into the bedroom. We'll have DNA confirmation again in two weeks.

"As I mentioned at the scene, the front doorknob was wiped clean recently, and the only prints we could find were of the boyfriend. I took sample prints from him at the scene."

Dan asked, "Was he cooperative?"

"Yes, once I explained why I needed them. There're a couple of unidentified prints, but none in the actual location of the crime. What I did find was traces of talcum powder, the type used in medical examination gloves on the bedspread. The victim had no talcum powder in the apartment, so I'm assuming the killer wore disposable examination gloves and therefore no prints were picked up."

"Do you know what types of disposable gloves use talcum powder?" Dan asked

"These days most are powder free because some people are allergic to talcum powder, but you can still buy them with talc in thousands of places."

"So you're telling me the gloves didn't come from a doctor's office or hospital."

"No, I'm not saying that, I'm just saying the guy could have purchased the gloves anywhere;

there're nothing out of the ordinary; some doctors may still use them."

"Anything else?" Dan asked.

"I found a white polyolefin fiber on the bedspread. It may be too big a leap, but it might have come from one of those cleanroom bunny outfits, you know, similar to what I wear at messy crime scenes to prevent contamination. They're also used in high-tech products being manufactured."

Amy said, "That might explain the gloves too. Those would also be consistent with cleanroom manufacturing operations."

Julie was skeptical. "Not with the talcum powder. They would never allow talcum powder in a cleanroom."

Dan thought out loud as he began to put the pieces of evidence together. "So the killer knocks on Carol McCowen's door. She knows the guy, but is still apprehensive and keeps the security chain locked. The killer forces the door open and breaks the security chain. Then he hits her over the head and she falls unconscious. The guy drags her with her feet scraping along the carpet into the bedroom, and after taking off her robe and putting it on a hanger, he binds her to the bed with the duct tape and places more duct tape over her mouth."

"We're with you," Amy said.

"He then goes back out into the hallway and brings in a bag or valise and puts the bunny suit over his clothes and gloves over his hands. He spreads a blue tarp on the carpet and waits for the victim to wake up and then kills her slowly and during the process the victim struggles and blo bodily fluids are spread throughout the room. Afterward, he cuts the number fourteen in her forehead, places the bloody bunny suit and the weapon on the tarp. Then he puts the folded tarp back in the bag or valise and walks out the door after wiping his fingerprints off the doorknob. After leaving the building, he removes the gloves and walks away."

Amy said, "Possible, maybe even likely, but it's still too early to buy into your theory, but it is definitely worth considering until we have more evidence."

Dan continued thinking out loud. "She opens the door but keeps the security chain locked. I'm thinking she knew the guy, but he wasn't a close friend. The weird guy living on the third floor fits the description perfectly. We'll have to talk to him again."

Dan and Amy left the crime lab and stopped at a fast-food dive a few blocks away. Dan knew it well, and was sure he personally was helping the owner turn a monthly profit.

While feasting on an Italian Beef sandwich and fries, Dan thought about the crime. "What do we know? First, this was a well-planned crime. The killer was probably waiting for the victim, maybe sitting in a car parked out in front. The guy waits a few minutes until the victim is in bed and then knocks on the door.

"Second, and here's the key, there's a high probability she knew the guy. It all depends on whether she looked through that peep hole. You're a woman Amy. What are the chances she would have opened the door without looking?"

"Zero. In today's world any single woman alone in an apartment late at night would definitely assume the worst. She would have to be totally drunk not to look through that peep hole."

"So when we interview her friends, let's make sure we find out how much she had to drink at the bar."

"You know this guy's sick and for some reason he hated her," Dan said. "The way he killed her is just too brutal. After lunch let's get back to the precinct and check out whatever evidence Julie checked in. And then we definitely need to talk to this guy Jeffery Smothers living on the third floor."

Chapter 10

Dan sat at his desk waiting for Amy to bring up the things checked into the Evidence Locker. Some time to think and some time to reflect on the case. Without a doubt, this was the most brutal homicide he had ever worked on. He had seen many killings that taxed his humanity, but this was the worst.

Over the years, he had stopped terrorists and even worked on many cases for the FBI. In fact, that's how he met Sally. They had worked on a homicide case that had morphed into terrorism. The head of the FBI, fearing an inside mole in his organization, had wanted Dan and Sally to continue working on the case. Dan's best friend Jimmy Davis, the head of Chicago's FBI office, had worked with the two of them, and it had been Sally, almost single-handedly, who had saved Washington from a nuclear disaster.

And through all those cases, this was absolutely the worst, and as of right now they had almost no leads. In the back of Dan's mind an uncomfortable feeling emerged again. Sometimes a horrible murder with no apparent motive was the mark of a serial killer. Was there a new Jack the Ripper loose? The thought turned his stomach. *Please God, not a serial killer.*

Amy arrived with the evidence: one bag of weed, a photo album, a list of contacts from Carol McCowen's computer, and the victim's purse. Amy scattered the contents of the purse onto her desk. She created two piles: cosmetics and other items with no connection to the case, and a second pile of critical evidence. There was only one problem. The second pile only contained Carol's and Bryce's wallets, a checkbook, and the victim's cellphone. Amy returned the first pile to the purse and placed the two wallets on Dan's desk. "Some haul huh?"

"It's depressing Amy. We've got nada, absolutely nada."

Amy looked through the photo album while Dan sorted through the list of contacts taken from the victim's cellphone and computer. Bryce had given Dan the names of the friends who were at Bar Louie the night of the murder. These would be their first interviews. Was Carol McCowen drunk? Was there an argument between Bryce and Carol? What time did she leave? Did the victim have any enemies?

These were all the obvious questions, but the important thing was to extract what these people thought, not just what they knew, because mere suspicion was sometimes the key to unlocking a crime with no apparent motive.

Dan turned on the victim's cellphone and found her calendar app. Luckily, she seemed to record all of her appointments. As Dan flipped back in time, he began to get a feel for Carol McCowen's life in reverse: meetings at work, the Thursday night Bar Louie evenings, dates with Bryce, dinners with her parents, meetings with friends, a doctor's appointment, and two trips to the dentist. Nothing out of the ordinary, just a young single girl doing what young single girls do.

Joey burst out of his office and headed for Dan's desk. "Oh shit!" Amy said.

"Guys, I just a got a call from a reporter at Channel 9 news. They know about the girl's gut slit open. They want a statement. I played dumb, but I can tell the heat's going to get turned up. We can expect a front-page headline in the Tribune tomorrow. If the story runs, prepare yourself for a news conference, and Dan, you're going to be the senior detective answering questions."

"That's great Joey. Thanks for the heads up, and I appreciate your dumping all the shit in my lap."

"Hey my friend, that's why I get paid the big bucks, so I can delegate the shit to poor detectives like you."

Joey was actually laughing at his own humor as he returned to his office and closed the door.

Even Amy laughed, "Man are you going to catch shit tomorrow. I can't wait for you to answer every question with *no comment.*"

Dan, ignoring her prediction of tomorrow's press conference said, "Amy, can you chase down the victim's phone records and her recent Visa bill charges. Better get a court order and make it as general as possible so we don't have to go back again."

Amy asked, "What are you going to do?"

"I'm going to interview the friends who were at Bar Louie last night, and then talk to Jeffrey Smothers."

As Amy left to get a court order to gain access to the victim's confidential information, Dan took out Carol McCowen's check book and studied all of the transactions during the last year. Bills paid, checks from work being deposited. One check made out to Jimmy Wrangles for $2000 was the only suspicious transaction. Dan made a note in his little black book.

Dan turned to his list of the friends who last saw the victim at Bar Louie. He started at the top of the list and punched in Gloria Steinberg's cellphone number. She answered on the second ring. "Ms. Steinberg, this is Detective Dan Lawson with the Chicago Police Department. I'm calling with regard to the death of Carol McCowen."

She answered quickly. "Bryce called me a couple hours ago. Did you catch the person yet?"

"No we haven't Ms. Steinberg. The reason I'm calling is that I'd like to schedule some time with you. I have several questions, and your inputs may be able to shed some light on what actually happened. When's a good time?"

"Well detective, I doubt whether I have any useful information, but anything I can do to help. I'm free in the afternoon. Can we meet then?"

They agreed to meet at Gloria Steinberg's apartment at three o'clock.

Dan proceeded down his list and thirty minutes later had scheduled meetings with all of Carol's friends who were at the bar that night.

Chapter 11

Gloria Steinberg buzzed Dan into her apartment a little after three o'clock. The young lady who answered the door was one of those women who you can't keep your eyes off of, and Dan knew that she knew it and enjoyed every minute playing the role. Dark black hair flowed down to her waist; a perfect light bronze tan covered a high cheek-boned face; a short tight bright-red skirt showed off every curve on her perfect butt. This young lady enjoyed being looked at.

She led Dan into her living room and sat down across from him on the couch. As she slowly crossed her legs, nothing was left to Dan's imagination. "I can't believe anyone would want to hurt Carol. Everyone loved her."

Dan asked, "When did you first meet Carol?"

"We both went to the University of Illinois and pledged the same sorority. We roomed together junior and senior year."

"So you were good friends and knew each other very well."

"Absolutely, she asked me to be her maid of honor at the wedding."

"Tell me about Bryce and Carol."

"What do you want to know?"

"Everything."

"Well they met at work at some company function and immediately began dating. Bryce asked to marry her three months ago. Carol knew he was the one after their first date."

"Did they ever get into any arguments?"

"Are you kidding, it was like true love. If they ever argued Carol would have told me."

"Did Carol have any boyfriends before Bryce?"

"She dated a lot of different guys at college, but nothing serious. She dated one guy before Bryce, but the guy dumped her. They're still good friends though, and now he lives in California."

"Tell me about what happened at Bar Louie that night."

"We meet there every Thursday. I was late because of a meeting at work, so by the time I got there at seven o'clock, everyone was already onto their dinners. We watched the Bulls game until eleven and then left the bar just after midnight."

"How much did Carol have to drink?"

"I don't know; we were sharing pitchers, but Carol wasn't a drinker. If she had a total of three beers that night, I'd be surprised."

"Gloria, you knew Carol for a longtime. If she was alone in her apartment after midnight and someone knocked at the door, would she have opened the door without looking through the peephole?"

"No way! One of our friends was raped on campus when we were there, and she just opened her door and let a stranger in. Carol and I were both on guard against strangers entering our apartment."

"Did Carol have any enemies?"

Gloria thought for a long time. "I know this is an important question, but I'll tell you, I can't think of anyone who hated her let alone disliked her. I've been thinking about that question since Bryce called, and I just can't think of anyone who would have wanted to kill her."

"She wrote a check for $2000 to a person by the name of Jimmy Wrangles. Do you know anything about that?"

"Sure, that was a deposit for the band at their wedding."

Dan asked her about the number fourteen, but she could offer no help with the meaning of the number.

The meeting went on for another hour. Dan noted for someone who was best friends with the victim, Gloria Steinberg was quickly moving on, perhaps too quickly. A little mascara running down her cheeks or swollen eyes might have been nice, but her outward nonchalant demeanor might be nothing more than a lack of maturity.

Dan thanked her for her time, gave her his business card, and asked her to call him if she could think of anything important, especially the significance of the number fourteen. As Dan left for his next appointment, he thought about handing out his business card and asking the person to call if they could think of anything important. In all his time as a detective, he could only recall one return call in all those years, and that was from his wife Sally; and that might have been something more than just the desire to pass on information.

Dan looked at his watch. He would be a little late for his next appointment with Ralph Jones

Ralph it turned out was Bryce's best friend. They played beach volleyball together at North Avenue Beach. Ralph looked a little more in mourning than Gloria.

He said, "And to think we all had dinner together just two nights ago. Man life is so cruel. Bryce told me it was a horrible death. I feel so sorry for Bryce, and Carol's parents must be devastated."

"They are Ralph. I had to break the news to them early yesterday morning. It's hard to lose a child, and she was an only child. How long have you known Carol?"

"I guess just over a year. Bryce and I used to come to the bar after volleyball games, and then we just started adding people and soon it was like a habit. We meet every Thursday after work, have dinner, and watch whatever games are on TV."

"Did Carol have any enemies?"

"Hard to imagine. We all liked her man. Bryce was one lucky guy to find her. Bryce is taking it pretty hard, isn't he?"

"Yes Ralph. I'm sure he'd appreciate your friendship right now."

"I know. I promised I'd see him after you and I met."

Ralph Jones could add nothing to what Gloria had already said. It seemed Carol McCowen didn't have any enemies. It was hard to imagine anyone could be such a goody two-shoes, but perhaps Carol was one of those rare people who everyone liked.

As Ralph left to see Bryce, Dan paid an unannounced visit to Jeffrey Smothers. Dan walked up to the third floor of the crime scene and knocked on the door. Dan recognized an Aaron Copland piece playing a bit too loud. He knocked again, a little louder to be heard over the music.

Jeffrey Smothers answered the door dressed in workout clothes. He seemed to recognize Dan and blocked the doorway with his body. Dan said, "Mr. Smothers. I hope I've caught you at a good time. I have some questions regarding the murder of Carol McCowen."

Smothers, with a pained expression on his face, led him into the living room. Jeffrey Smothers was a minimalist. The layout of the room was designed for a single person to sit in the middle of the room and listen to music.

Dan certainly wasn't an audiophile, but he could recognize expensive equipment when he saw it, and the 7.1 surround sound system was certainly worth megabucks.

As an icebreaker, Dan said, "I love Copland; he has a way of capturing the American spirit."

Smothers replied, "Appalachian Spring is my favorite next to Fanfare for the Common Man."

After turning down the amplifier volume, Smothers asked, "What can I do for you tonight detective?"

"Mr. Smothers, I'd like to review everything you did Thursday night. Maybe you'll be able to think of something that can help us on the case."

This was just a nice way of getting Smothers to account for his whereabouts on the night of the murder.

Smothers smiled, obviously recognizing the real purpose of the question. "As I told you detective, I heard nothing and didn't know she was murdered until you told me."

"I appreciate that, but please just tell me what you were doing that night."

"I arrived home about seven o'clock. I had dinner with a business associate. We were trying to figure out some software glitches with our main server at work. The system is always crashing during peak usage periods."

Dan interrupted, "And where do you work Mr. Smothers?"

"Bank of America over on LaSalle Street. Anyway, I got home around seven and listened to music until eleven o'clock. Then I went to bed and got up at six o'clock. You knocked on my door just as I was leaving for work."

Dan asked, "What music were you listening to?"

"Tchaikovsky, the Fourth Symphony, and then Swan Lake. I like Swan Lake; I listened to it twice."

Dan asked, "Carol McCowen opened the door to her apartment but left the security chain locked. That means she probably knew the killer, but he wasn't a real friend. Any idea who that person might be?"

"No detective, as I said Thursday night, I hardly knew her. Sometimes our paths crossed at the mailbox, but that was about it."

The interview was getting nowhere, so Dan got the name of Smothers' business colleague, thanked him for his time, and left. Dan looked at his watch. He toyed with the idea of asking Emma Phillips if she remembered whether Smothers was listening to Tchaikovsky that night, but decided to go home instead.

Dan headed home without any new leads in what was becoming the toughest case he had ever worked on.

Chapter 12

Dan was up at six o'clock; he wanted to get an early start at work. He sat at the kitchen table with a bowl of Rice Chex and bananas. He pulled the Chicago Tribune out of its protective plastic wrapper and scanned the headlines. A quick read of the lead story, and he knew he was in trouble. The banner headline read "Gory killing in Bucktown." Dan wasn't sure how the story leaked, but it was all there: the victim tied to the bed, her belly slit open, and of course the perceived confusion within the police department who were always viewed as totally incompetent. There was even a quote that the lead investigator, Detective Dan Lawson, had no comment.

Luckily there was no mention of the number slit in the victim's forehead. Dan tossed the paper over to Sally who appeared in a bathrobe. "The shit's hit the fan. You'll probably be watching me tonight on the local news."

Sally quickly read the article and smiled. "At least they didn't call you an incompetent idiot. You should consider yourself very fortunate."

Dan left for the office and thought about what he would say at the news conference Joey would certainly be forced to hold. By the time he reached the office, he had no real idea of what to say and decided to just wing it.

Before he could get to his desk, Joey intercepted him and held up the newspaper. "Lucky you, I've set up a press conference for ten o'clock, and you're going to be the star of the show."

"Gee thanks Joey; you're one hell of a guy."

"You bet your sweet ass I'm one hell of a guy, and the best boss in the police force and don't you forget it." He turned to the dozens of cops who had overheard the comment and raised his arms pleading his case. "Ain't that right guys?"

A chorus of *yes boss* echoed throughout the precinct. Joey threw the paper on Dan's desk and retreated to his office.

As he sat down at his desk, Amy looked up from her paperwork with a smile on her face. "He's really a nice guy once you get to know him. He's just getting hassled from up above."

"I know it's like the third law of plumbing, *shit flows downhill*, but why am I always at the bottom of the hill?"

"That's why you get paid the big bucks Lead Detective Lawson, so you can catch all the shit, but don't you worry, I'll be in the room with you, and I know you'll do a great job."

"Thanks. By the way, how did you do on the court order?"

"I had girl to girl talks with the DA and Judge Wilson, and got the order signed. I contacted her bank, Visa, and Verizon and the records should be arriving this afternoon. How about you; what did you learn from her friends and Jeffery Smothers?"

"Not much. It seems Carol McCowen had no enemies, and Bryce Collier and Carol McCowen were in love with no apparent hint of the relationship turning south. And they all confirmed Bryce's account of the evening. Smothers says he knows nothing, but he's one weird dude. So at the end of the day, we know diddly-squat."

"I'm sure diddly-squat will not be your comment at the press conference."

"Maybe that's exactly what I should say. Sometimes the truth is therapeutic.

The press conference started on time. It must have been a slow news day because the small auditorium was filled to overflowing. All the major TV and news services were there. Joey led off the event with a quick introduction of Dan, who he introduced as the senior homicide detective on the case. That was it, a twenty-three second stint, and then he moved to the back of the stage after nudging Dan up to the microphone.

"Good morning ladies and gentlemen. Let me spend a few minutes bringing you up to speed, and then I'll answer any questions you have."

Dan looked down at some notes he had scribbled at his desk. "At 3:07 a.m. on Friday morning our precinct received a call concerning a homicide at 1476 West Cortez Street. The police arrived on the scene at 3:11 a.m. The victim was pronounced dead at 3:46 a.m. We have interviewed witnesses on the scene and have begun the process of gathering evidence central to the investigation.

Our office is committed to solving this case at the earliest possible date.

"Now I'll be happy to answer any questions you have."

The Channel 9 reporter who had confronted him at the crime scene shouted from the back of the room. "What was the victim's name and who found the body?"

"The victim was Carol McCowen, and the body was found by her fiancé."

A reporter in the front row asked, "Do you have any leads?"

"As you can appreciate, we're still in the very preliminary phases of the investigation, and we're still gathering evidence."

Another reporter asked, "Why wasn't the victim taken to the hospital?"

"It was clear from the onset that the victim was dead when the police arrived on the scene."

"Could you elaborate?"

"I'm going to leave it at that. From the condition of the body, it was obvious the victim was dead."

"Is it true that the victim's belly had been slit open?"

"No comment."

"Are there any Persons of Interest?"

"At this time we have no Persons of Interest. As I pointed out, we are still in the very early stages of the investigation."

One of the seasoned veteran reporters asked, "How many resources have been allocated to the case?"

Joey stepped to the microphone before Dan could answer the question. "Detective Lawson is our most senior detective. Any resources he requests will be provided. Our department is committed to the early resolution of this case."

Another reporter asked, "Do you know the motive for the killing?"

"As I have already explained, we're in the early stages of the investigation, and we are exploring all possible motives for the homicide."

The questions went on for another ten minutes, and Dan finally ended the news conference with a request that anyone with information on the case should contact the Chicago Police Department, and he repeated the telephone number for his precinct.

Chapter 13

Joey corralled Dan and Amy inside his office for a post-mortem. "You did good Dan. Anything new yet?"

Before he could answer, Jackie Sherman, Joey's assistant burst into his office. "I just got a call from the Seventeenth Precinct. They received a call about an hour ago about a homicide over in Wrigleyville. The beat cops say it looks just like the McCowen killing."

Dan said, "Tell them we'll be there in twenty minutes."

He and Amy left Joey's office, and they took Amy's car, which was the closest one in the garage. Amy drove while Dan thought about the newest development. "I'm thinking serial killer, but let's wait to see what we've got."

The location of the homicide was a single family residence close to Wrigley Field. The tranquility of the tree-lined residential street had been rudely interrupted by the presence of several of Chicago's finest. Dan recognized the license plate numbers of Amber's medical examiner's van and Julie's crime scene SUV. It definitely looked like a repeat performance.

The street was lined with onlookers who were observing the activity with a little more than casual interest. The security of their street had apparently been violated. Dan and Amy spoke with the beat cops who were standing outside the crime scene ensuring privacy for the people inside. Dan introduced himself to the guy apparently in charge. "What you got?"

"It's bad, very bad. The victim looks just like the case over in Bucktown. The cop pulled out some notes. "Woman in her late-twenties; name's Emily Farrow; belly slit open; blood and guts everywhere. The body was discovered by the cleaning lady. She's inside in shock."

Dan said, "I want you to look for security cameras all along the street and in the alley. Talk to the onlookers and the neighbors. Let me know if anyone saw anything out of the ordinary this morning. Let me know what you get."

As Dan and Amy walked through the front door, a Channel 9 news truck screeched to a stop near the end of the street. Dan yelled out, "Amber, where are you?"

A voice from upstairs answered, "Up here in the master bedroom."

As Dan and Amy entered the master bedroom, they once again smelled the terrible aroma of death; shit and a coppery smell from the blood splattered room. Amy who hadn't seen the first body took one look and walked out of the room. Dan had prepared himself for the worst and wasn't disappointed. Amber, who was bending over the corpse said, "It's the same M.O. and there's a number fourteen cut into her forehead, and she was slit open from the vagina to the sternum with one long stroke."

Dan looked closely at the body. The young woman's arms and legs were bound to the corners of the bed with duct tape. She lay on her back without any clothes, and her glazed wide-open eyes expressed the horrid pain inflicted by the killer as her belly was slit open. Her mouth was taped shut, and there it was, the number fourteen cut into the victim's forehead. Even a bad detective didn't have to think twice about concluding the same person had killed both victims.

The obvious question was whether there was some relationship between these two women, something that had made them both targets of the demented person who had done this, or was this some random act by a serial killer acted out against society in general or young women in particular.

Amy walked back into the room. "Are you okay?" Dan asked.

"It's the worst I've ever seen. I knew it was going to be bad, and I still wasn't prepared for it."

Amber said, "A rough estimate on the time of death is 9:00 a.m. The weapon is probably the same or at least the same type."

Dan looked around the room and noticed a square area, void of blood near the master bathroom. Probably the same type of tarp was used to remove all of the blood stained clothes of the killer.

Dan had never worked on a serial killer case before. He had studied them in one of his criminology courses at college, but had never seen anything like this first hand. He called Joey and briefed him on the crime scene. "Joey, I need three things. First, we're going to have to increase the resources on this. Second, I want to bring in the FBI, and third, I want you to find the best profiler at the University of Chicago Crime Lab and get him or her down to the precinct as soon as possible."

Joey, because he was actually a great boss, didn't argue at all. "You've got it. You call your friend Jimmy Davis, and I'll take care of the rest. I'll try to set up a meeting for first thing tomorrow morning."

The beat cop entered the bedroom and spoke to Dan. "My guys are still getting you the information on the security cameras and neighbors, but the husband just walked into the house. I told him to wait downstairs. He knows what happened. One of the neighbors called him at work."

Dan said, "I want extra resources on the case right now. Have your Precinct Captain call Joey Capelli in the Thirteenth Precinct. I want everyone who lives on this block interviewed, absolutely everyone. Did anyone see anything unusual this morning between seven and ten o'clock?"

As the beat cop left on a new mission, Dan walked downstairs and found the victim's husband sitting at the kitchen table. Why did people gravitate to the kitchen in times of crisis? It must have something to do with the fact that it's the most lived-in part of the house; there's comfort and familiarity in the surroundings. You don't sit in the living room because living rooms are for show, not living.

The husband, probably around thirty, was staring at the kitchen stove, just totally focused on the upscale range. "She loved that thing. She loved to cook, and when we bought the house she insisted on buying that expensive stove, and the things she created on it were beyond delicious. Just this week, she made a wonderful chocolate soufflé."

His name was George, and he started to cry. Dan had a hard time dealing with a crying man, especially one who had just lost his wife. He never knew whether to put an arm around the guy or leave him alone. In the end, he just decided to sit down and wait.

George eventually looked up and said, "I want to see her."

Dan answered, "I know you do, but I'm not going to let you see her."

"Why not?"

"Because seeing her now will fill your heart with a pain and hurt far beyond what you're dealing with now. I'm sure your wife, if she could reach out to you now, would forbid you from seeing her."

"How did it happen?" he asked.

"We don't know yet. Our crime scene people are here now, and as soon as they're done, I'll have a clearer picture."

"Next week we were going to celebrate our third anniversary."

It was a statement of finality; recognition that whatever joy in life they had experienced together, it was all over now. There would be nothing now but memories.

"Mr. Farrow, if you could answer one question for me, it would be very helpful. Did you or your wife know a woman by the name of Carol McCowen?"

George Farrow tried to process the question. Maybe he was just being thoughtful but more likely he didn't understand the need for answering the question. In any event, he answered no. "I've never heard the name. Should I know her?"

"Just a few days ago Carol McCowen was the victim of a homicide, and the circumstances were very similar. I was hoping there might be some connection between your wife and the other victim."

"I'm sorry detective; I wish I could help you, but I don't know anything about the other person."

"The killer left the number fourteen at the crime scene. Do you have any idea what the number might mean?"

Farrow thought for a long time. He wanted to know the significance but finally answered no.

"Mr. Farrow, can you tell me about what happened this morning from the time you got up?"

"It was just like any other day. The alarm went off at seven. I shaved and showered. Emily was still asleep. She always stayed up late and slept in. I fixed myself breakfast and left for work about eight o'clock. She was still asleep when I left. I never even had a chance to say goodbye."

That last realization pushed him over the edge again and George Farrow put his head in his hands and once again began to cry. Dan left him to grieve in private and looked for Julie Westerman. She was dusting the front door for fingerprints.

"What you got?"

"Nothing yet, but it looks like the same M.O. as the McCowen killing: the body, the tarp to collect the bloody clothes, the blow to the back of her head. It's got to be the same guy."

"Any signs of a break-in?"

"Nope, it looks like she probably just let the person in."

Dan thought about that. The victim was hit over the head so she could be tied up on the bed, but the killer probably didn't drag the victim upstairs after hitting her over the head. To confirm this fact, Dan walked upstairs and looked carefully at the upstairs hallway carpeting. There were no drag marks on the carpet. Maybe the killer just carried her upstairs, but that didn't seem likely.

So once again we're probably dealing with someone who knew Emily Farrow. The front doorbell rings. She answers the door and lets him in because she's not afraid of the person. Then somehow the killer gets Emily upstairs and hits her over the head while they're near the bed. Maybe the killer threatened her with a gun or knife. The killer did use a knife after all to kill her. This was obviously a well thought out and well planned killing. The killer was probably waiting outside until George Farrow left for work.

Dan walked into the master bedroom and found Amber still taking detailed pictures of the victim. Amy was in the bedroom closet. She looked up and said, "I doubt the victim answered the door without any clothes. That means that once again the killer took her clothes off and put them away in the closet. A robe is on a hanger, and everything is put away."

Dan thought about the implications. "What we've got is a killer who is an orderly person, someone who is compelled to put everything in its proper place. That kind of compulsive behavior fits in with a person who is a meticulous planner, and the guy who did this is all of those things."

It was time to bring the FBI into the case.

Chapter 14

Jimmy Davis was the head of the FBI's Chicago Office and Dan's best friend. They roomed together in college, and both received degrees in Criminology. Dan tapped in Jimmy's private number on his smartphone.

"Hey Bro, I just saw you on TV. I loved the no comment parts, but you need to work more on your smile. The smile disarms the bad guys and makes the questions a lot easier."

"Thanks buddy, I can always count on you for the best advice."

"How's my Goddaughter?"

"She's progressing from waddling to actual walking. It's fun to watch her grow up. Listen, we're going to need your help. We've just had another killing just like the McCowen case, and it looks like we've got a serial killer prowling the streets of Chicago. Can Amy Green and I come down to your office for a meeting this afternoon?"

"Alice is in my office right now. Let me find out if she's available."

Thirty seconds passed before Jimmy got back on the phone. "Alice is going to switch an appointment. What time do you want to meet?"

"Let's make it four o'clock."

"See you then Bro."

Dan walked back into the kitchen and sat down next to George Farrow who had recovered and had poured himself a glass of water. Dan patted him on the back and with a tear in his eye said, "I promise you, we'll find the person who did this. I will never give up until we find the person who did this."

George Farrow, also with tears in his eyes, looked at Dan and nodded in grateful understanding.

Dan brought his emotions back in control and said, "George, did you see anyone out in front of your house waiting for you to leave this morning?"

"No, I left by the back alley. I didn't see anything out of the ordinary."

"The person who did this has taken two lives. These could have been random killings, but I don't think so. I'm certain whoever did this knew your wife and the other victim. There's some common link between your wife and Carol McCowen, and I'm going to need your help in trying to figure out what the common link is."

It must have registered with the grieving husband. He looked at Dan with a new sense of purpose. "Detective Lawson, I'll do anything to help you catch the person who did this, anything; just let me know what I can do to help."

"Do you have a place to stay tonight?"

"I guess I can spend the night with the next-door neighbors."

"Tomorrow I want to spend time with you walking around the house. Together, we may be able to find some clue that will help us find the link between these two women. Give me your cellphone number, and I'll call you in the morning."

Dan also gave George his business card with the usual request to call with any information that might help. He then left to find Amy, who was in the library gathering evidence.

Amy said, "I'm making a pile of the evidence here on the desk."

Dan could see the victim's purse and a printout of contacts from the Farrow's computer in plastic evidence bags, but not much else. He looked at his watch. They needed to leave if they were going to make the meeting at FBI headquarters by four o'clock. "I set up a meeting with the FBI in Jimmy Davis's office for four o'clock. We'll need to leave in five minutes if we're going to make it in time."

Chapter 15

Dan was all too familiar with the FBI Head-quarters building on West Roosevelt Road. He and Sally had been asked to assist the FBI on several occasions, and he actually carried FBI identification as a Special Agent. Walking into the building was always a series of hugs and hand-shakes as he made his way up to Jimmy Davis's office.

Alice Folkman and Jimmy were waiting in Jimmy's conference room. Dan gave Alice a kiss on the cheek and Jimmy a hug, and he then introduced Amy Green. It took Dan and Amy almost an hour to brief the FBI agents.

Jimmy asked, "How many detectives is Joey going to put on the case?"

"I'm not sure yet, but knowing Joey, he's going to get a lot of pressure from the Mayor's Office, and that's going to mean a full-court press. I'll know more tomorrow morning."

Just then Joey called on Dan's cellphone. Dan explained they were meeting with Jimmy and his people so Joey called back on Jimmy's upscale conference call system.

Jimmy said, "How's it going Joey? Looks like you've got a tough one here. Dan and Amy just finished briefing me. What resources are you going to need from us?"

"Probably the more the better. I just called Dan to let him know I called the University of Chicago Crime Lab, and they're going to have their best profiler, Dr. David Sugarman, meet with us at tomorrow morning's meeting. Dan, I want you to give him a call and brief him on the case just as soon as you can."

Joey rattled off the doctor's phone number and then excused himself, claiming he had to get to a meeting with the Mayor to brief him on the two cases and what was sure to be a feeding frenzy by the press.

Jimmy said, "I know Sugarman; we use him all the time. He really knows his stuff."

Dan looked at his best friend. "So you and Alice will be at the ten o'clock meeting?"

"You bet, wouldn't miss it for the world."

As Amy drove them back to the precinct, Dan called Dr. Sugarman and did the total data dump. The doctor had already talked with Amber Carlson and Julie Westerman, and by the time they arrived at the precinct, Sugarman was up to speed on all the facts.

Amy stopped at Dan's car and the two split up for the night. On the way home, Dan thought about the implications of the second killing. This killer was sending a message, something beyond the brutal mutilations of the two victims. It was his job to understand the message, because an understanding of the killer would help lead to his being apprehended.

Dan tried to consider the killer's motive. The number fourteen obviously had implications. Dan wasn't a psychiatrist, but the actual killing of the victims with the weapon being inserted into the women's vagina must have great significance. Something sexual might be at the heart of this and Dan was surprised Julie's group hadn't found any evidence of sperm in the victims or around the bed. He was hoping Sugarman would have some answers.

The au pair was feeding Debbie, who gave her daddy a big grin while trying to stuff a cut-up hot dog into her tiny mouth. Dan wished he could enjoy his dinner tonight, but the reality was that after seeing the most recent victim, he doubted he'd be able to keep any food down.

Sally showed up a few minutes later, and Debbie repeated her big-time grin and held out both her little arms to Sally. Dan once again realized where he stood in the pecking order. Hopefully he was ahead of the au pair.

Chapter 16

The conference room was filled to capacity. Joey had received an unmistakable message from the Mayor; *get this killer before any more people are killed.* The morning newspaper had only reinforced the Mayor's demand. The banner headline was descriptive: *Serial Killer on the Loose! Young Women Beware!*

Joey stepped up to the podium and started the meeting by introducing Dr. Sugarman, Jimmy and Alice. Then he turned to the mayor's demands. "You're in this room this morning because each of you is going to help apprehend the demented killer who murdered these young women. The Mayor wants a full-court press. No resources will be spared in trying to catch this guy. Insufficient resources will not be tolerated as an excuse. If you need something, ask for it, and you will receive it.

"The FBI has been asked to assist us. Many of you know Jimmy Davis and Alice Folkman. Alice, who is the senior agent in the Chicago office, will be assisting our team on this case, and Jimmy Davis has assured me that if other FBI resources are needed, we'll get them."

Dan couldn't remember a meeting where all of the attendees were actually paying attention. Somehow the cops in this room understood the seriousness of this investigation. Perhaps they could each imagine their own wives or daughters being viciously attacked by this killer, and they all knew it could happen.

Joey continued, "I don't think any of us were around for the last serial killer case in our precinct. That was back in 1976. So I've asked Dr. Sugarman, a Forensic Psychologist with the University of Chicago Crime Lab to give us a profile of what makes this kind of crazy tick. Welcome Dr. Sugarman."

The expert profiler stepped up to the microphone. He was a plump middle-aged prematurely grey-haired man with an out of control goatee. He was dressed like a professor in college, that is to say, kind of without a common theme. Nothing matched: a plaid beige-colored blazer with leather elbow patches, a green and black striped bow-tie, an orange shirt, new blue jeans, and Nike gym shoes.

"Ladies and Gentlemen, my summary profile is being passed out as I speak. You may wish to reference my thoughts in the future."

Joey's Administrative Assistant was circulating the doctor's information. After waiting for the sheets to be passed out, Sugarman continued. "What is a serial killer? A serial killer is a person who kills victims in succession in a series of homicides. There're usually a minimum of three to four killings, and sometimes there is a cooling off period in between. Serial killers usually have a sadistic urge to dominate and control their victims. They're not doing it for monetary gain but rather the psychological satisfaction derived from the killings. Most serial killers are white males, in their late 20's to early 30's. They usually come from lower middle-class families, and they have above average intelligence."

Sugarman looked around the room, pausing for effect. "There are two types of serial killers, the psychotic and the psychopath. The psychotic killer is legally insane. Many times they hear voices commanding them to take certain actions. They may see visions or have hallucinations just before committing their murders.

"Now the psychopath is a different kettle of fish. They do not have hallucinations, and most importantly, they know the difference between right and wrong, but they just don't care whether what they're doing isn't right. These people are in touch with the real world. These psychopaths lack one important trait; they do not have a conscience. They do not feel guilt, and they certainly aren't sorry for their actions. And of course in very rare instances you can have a person who is both psychotic and psychopathic."

The good doctor had everyone's attention. He was definitely on a roll. "There are many theories regarding what causes people to become a psychotic or a psychopathic killer; some say environment others say genetics. I believe it's probably a combination of the two factors.

"Psychopathic killers have the ability to blend into society, but underneath their persona lies a person who is sexually abnormal with a consuming need for power. Killing gives them pleasure. They do it because they want to and because they enjoy doing it."

Dan looked around the room, and everyone was processing the doctor's words, probably trying to compare his analysis to their own personal experiences.

Sugarman continued, "Now let's get to this specific series of murders. I find several things that are very interesting. First, the number fourteen cut into the victim's foreheads. I'm being obvious, but the number has special significance to the killer. The question is whether the number has any significance to the victims. If it does, then these are not random killings but rather the killer is Mission-Oriented. That is to say, he targets a specific group of people he believes are unworthy of living and without whom the world would be a better place."

Dan thought about Sugarman's words. He would definitely need to focus on whether the number fourteen meant anything to both victims. That might very well be the key to understanding what was really going on.

"The fact that the knife was inserted into each woman's vagina at the beginning of the death-stroke clearly demonstrates strong sexual motives here. Perhaps the killer had relationships with each of his victims. There was no semen found within, on, or near the victims. Many times if the killer doesn't rape the victims first, he masturbates on the victim after the killing. The lack of semen is certainly unusual; however, I am convinced the killings have some sexual basis."

Doctor Sugarman went on for a few more minutes and then asked for questions. One of the younger cops asked, "If we ran into him on the street, how would we know it was him?"

"Ah, an interesting question officer. The simple answer is you probably wouldn't, but let me tell you a little bit about the killer. He's most likely considered quiet by his friends, but he probably has few real friends, merely acquaintances. People would consider him kind because of his quiet demeanor. He's probably very immature and prefers to stay around people much younger than he is. All of his relationships would be superficial. He's probably not married, and any relationship with the opposite sex would be very short-lived."

The questions went on for another ten minutes. It was clear everyone was trying to better understand the bizarre psyche of the killer. Dan spoke to Amy who was sitting next to him. "This is going to be a tough nut to crack."

"You're right and when the doctor talked about the knife being inserted into the women's vaginas, I could feel it between my own legs. It sent shivers down my spine."

"I felt it too, and I don't even have a vagina."

Amy just shook her head like a mother mildly scolding her son without ever saying a word.

The meeting with Dr. Sugarman finally broke up and Jimmy, Alice, Dan and Amy met privately in Joey's office. Joey looked at Dan. "Okay you've got all the resources you'll ever need, what do you want to do with them?"

Dan had been pondering the same question. "We've got to focus the resources into two areas. First, what does the number fourteen mean; and second, we need to interview anyone who knew either of these victims to see if they also knew the other victim. Of course if these are just random killings, then I don't know where to begin."

Joey chimed in. "There's no way these are random. I'd bet my career on it. The guy who's doing this had some grudge against these two women. The only thing these two women appear to have in common is they're roughly the same age. The problem is we don't know the connection yet, but you can be sure there is one. Even Jack the Ripper, who killed randomly, always chose prostitutes who he picked up on the street."

Dan continued, "Alice and I will check out the two victim's houses again and interview Bryce Collier and George Farrow again, and then we should interview the parents of both the victims. All the rest of the resources should focus on interviewing all of their friends at work or anyplace else where people knew them. Can any of their friends see a link between both victims? Amy should coordinate all of this work. Let's also set up a daily briefing at nine o'clock for everyone to share information."

Jimmy added, "Dan, you and Alice should do the press conferences together. We need to get the press on our side. At some point we may get a clue on the guy who did this, and we may need their help in getting the public to be our eyes and ears."

The others agreed, and with the senior team's assignments set, the meeting broke up. Jimmy put his arm around his best friend's shoulder. "Good luck man; call me if you need anything."

Chapter 17

Dan called George Farrow immediately after the meeting and set up an appointment at the victim's house. As Dan and Alice pulled up to the Farrow residence, a number of cars were parked in the victim's driveway. George Farrow met them at the front door and ushered them past a group of people grieving in the living room and into the library where he closed the French doors.

Dan introduced Alice Folkman and explained the FBI was now involved in the case. George seemed pleased. "Do you guys have any leads?"

"The murder of your wife and the other woman appear to have much in common. I asked you when we last talked about the number fourteen and what it might mean. Have you given any more thought to what the number might have meant to your wife?"

"Detective Lawson, I've spent hours trying to think of any connection to the number, and I just can't think of any."

Dan showed him a picture of the first victim. "Do you recognize this woman?"

"George Farrow stared at the picture and started to cry. "Detective I'm truly sorry. I know this is important, but I can't remember ever seeing this woman before. I have a lot of family and friends out in the living room. Would it help if we showed them the picture?"

"That would be a great idea George. Let's do it together."

Dan and Alice followed George Farrow into the living room. He addressed his family and friends. "This is Detective Dan Lawson and FBI agent Alice Folkman. They want to ask you some questions."

Dan passed the picture of Carol McCowen around the room. "Do any of you recognize this woman? It's very important to our investigation."

Each person looked for a long time at the picture. They were really trying to think hard about whether they had ever seen this woman. An elderly woman started to cry after she studied the picture. George Farrow introduced Dan and Alice to his mother-in-law, Ruth Bannon.

She stared at the picture. "I'm not sure. I think so, but I'm not sure. Maybe not recently though; maybe sometime in the past."

As Alice continued to pass around the picture, Dan brought Ruth Bannon into the library. "Mrs. Bannon, I know this is hard for you and I wish I could let you and your family grieve in private, but we need to do this for your daughter."

The lady held up her hand to silence Dan. "Detective Lawson, my daughter was the youngest of our three children. I miss her more than you can ever know, but you need to catch the horrible person who did this and the sooner the better. So don't you worry about me. You just ask your questions so you can catch this person."

Alice walked into the room with the picture of Carol McCowen. She handed the picture to Ruth Bannon. "Nobody else recognized her."

Mrs. Bannon looked at the picture again, trying to place the face within the context of how her daughter might have known the woman. She was quiet for a long time thinking about the picture, and then she smiled, "I've seen her face in another picture; somewhere around my house, but I just can't picture where."

Dan interrupted, "Can we drive to your house and take a look around?"

Mrs. Bannon stood up trying to fight the arthritic pain. She was on a mission now, a mission to help find her daughter's killer. Dan explained to George Farrow where they were going.

Chapter 18

Amber Carlson looked down at the body of Emily Farrow lying on the stainless steel autopsy table. She had finished her report and yet there was a mystery still needing to be solved. It was about the weapon used to slice open this young woman. What was there about the wound that kept on bringing Amber back to this table?

It was certainly the most unusual wound she had ever seen, and the uniqueness was in the length of the cut. What could slice a person open from vagina to sternum in one vicious cut? She looked again at the wound with a magnifying glass attached to her forehead. It was clear the killer had started the cut by inserting the blade into the victim's vagina, and then with what must have been a forceful stroke, the blade was brought rapidly upward. Amber once again closely examined the wound. She was certain the cut was made with a single slice.

What were the implications of a single cut? She thought about the question as she continued to study the exposed woman's innards. Either the person who did this was very strong, or the blade was incredibly sharp, almost like a razor.

She examined the beginning of the wound where the blade had been inserted into the woman's most intimate area. The deepest penetration point was interesting. It almost seemed flat, and a flat endpoint meant the tip of the blade wasn't pointed. And perhaps this was at the very heart of the mystery, because Amber just couldn't think of a weapon as sharp as this must have been, but without a pointed tip. What weapon had the sharpness of a razor but lacked a pointed tip?

Amber moved back to her desk and began an internet search, not that she expected to find a knife meeting the constraints but rather out of professional curiosity. Finding the knife that fit the wound might be instrumental in helping to solve the case.

Chapter 19

Ruth Bannon lived in a small two-story all brick home about ten minutes from the Farrows. She unlocked the front door and led the way into her house of memories. Mr. Bannon had died of cancer five years earlier, and Mrs. Bannon was at the age where memories in the form of pictures formed the basis of her life.

Scattered among the few works of art hanging on the walls were hundreds of pictures ranging from her ancestors, who had immigrated to the United States many years ago, probably from Eastern Europe, to pictures of her three children, many grand-children, great-grandchildren and all their families. Pictures of vacations, pictures of Christmases' past, pictures of her husband in a World War II uniform, pictures of a son serving a tour in Iraq or Afghanistan. Hundreds of photographs, hundreds of memories.

Dan and Alice followed the elderly lady as she walked slowly down memory lane. She paused longer than necessary at some pictures, obviously soaking in some thoughts about the persons in the photograph. It took almost ten minutes to view the pictures on the first floor. A picture of her youngest daughter Emily resulted in some tears and an explanation of that wonderful day at the Lincoln Park Zoo where the picture was taken.

With great difficulty, Ruth Bannon climbed up the stairs to the second floor, and shuffled into a small room at the top of the stairs. "This was Emily's room," she said.

Starting at the door, they worked their way around the room, looking at each photograph of Emily and her many friends. Toward the back of Emily's dresser, Ruth Bannon stopped and reached for a picture of a much younger girl. She held it close and smiled, "This is the one."

She handed the picture to Dan who was shocked at what he saw. It was the same picture he had seen a few days before in Carol McCowen's scrapbook. The picture was of a group of young girls at a summer camp. Ruth Bannon pointed to her daughter in the first row and a young girl in the second row who did indeed look like the older woman in the picture she had been shown.

Alice asked, "Mrs. Bannon, what is this picture?"

"Emily went to summer camp when she was fifteen years old. This is a picture of the girls who were in her cabin."

Suddenly excited, Dan asked, "Do you have the information on this camp Mrs. Bannon?"

"I think so; let me look."

Ruth Bannon opened Emily's closet and turned on the light. She asked Dan to reach up onto the shelf and pull down two large photo albums.

Dan allowed Mrs. Bannon to open the albums and move from page to page. Finally, she turned to a page focusing on Camp Greenwoods. A brochure from the camp was taped to the page along with a dozen other pictures of life at the camp. Dan's eyes wandered the page and his eyes stopped at a picture of a group of girls, the same ones who were in the picture on the dresser, standing in front of a large cabin. What captured his attention were not the girls but the sign above the cabin's front door. The number fourteen stood out in bold black painted numbers. It was as simple as that. The number fourteen cut into the foreheads of the victims clearly meant cabin fourteen at Camp Greenwoods.

Dan asked Mrs. Bannon if he could keep the book. She readily agreed, and as they walked slowly down the stairs, Dan asked, "Did Emily ever talk about any of her experiences at the camp, something that happened there that might have caused someone to hold a grudge against her?"

"I can't think of anything like that. She loved her time at the camp, and she was always talking about the good time she had."

Questions from Alice and Dan about Emily's experiences at the camp continued, but Mrs. Bannon couldn't think of anything shedding light on the motive for the killings. She offered to talk to her two other children to see if they could remember anything Emily might have told them, and Dan encouraged her to do so.

They drove Mrs. Bannon back to the Farrow house, and once alone in their car, Dan said, "What a fool I've been. There's a picture just like this one in a photo album back in the Evidence Locker. The same exact picture in Carol McCowen's apartment, the same exact picture."

Alice tried to provide some comfort, "We were focused on recent history. Who would have thought these killings were the result of some events over ten years ago?"

"I should have Alice. I wasn't thinking outside the box."

"Okay, but that's in the past; what's next?"

"It seems obvious the killer knew these two women at the summer camp. Something happened back then that really pissed off the guy who did this, and it took all these years before he acted. I think we need to pay a visit to this camp and talk to the owners to see if we can figure out what happened back then and who the killer might be."

Alice added, "And we need to warn these other women, because whoever the killer is, he probably isn't finished."

Back at the precinct, Dan and Alice reviewed the latest information with Joey. Jimmy listened in on the conference call. Joey said, "Sounds like Mrs. Bannon has literally a photographic memory. I would never have picked up on the likeness between Carol McCowen now and ten years ago."

Alice said, "She was grieving Joey. We could tell she was the kind of elderly lady whose entire life is wrapped up in the memories of what the stories in those pictures throughout her house told. I wouldn't doubt that after her daughter's death she studied all the pictures of her daughter to remember the good times. We got a lucky break, and now we need to take advantage of the lead."

Jimmy said, "Which brings me to the question of what are the next steps."

Dan answered Jimmy's question. "We need to contact this camp and focus on two things. First, we need to get the names of all of the other girls in this picture and warn them. They may be next on the killer's list, and just as important, the other girls in the picture may be able to provide some explanation regarding what happened that summer. Second, we need to talk to the owners of the camp and find out what they know about what happened.

"Alice and I should go up there, while the team tries to find these other girls. We'll call the owners right away and get the names of the girls. Protecting them is the highest priority."

Joey thought for a moment and said, "Do it! Get me the names as soon as you can, and I'll get the team to warn them."

Chapter 20

The brochure for Camp Greenwoods had turned a yellowish-white over the years, but the phone number was still clearly visible at the bottom of the advertisement. Dan turned on the speaker-phone in an unused conference room and dialed the number.

After five rings an answering machine recording came on. "Hello, you have reached Camp Greenwoods. We're unavailable right now, but please leave a message, and we'll get back to you just as soon as we can."

"This is Detective Dan Lawson with the Chicago Police Department. I'm with FBI Special Agent Alice Folkman. We have an emergency situation we need your help resolving. Please call back as soon as you can to the following number."

Dan gave out his cellphone number and then hung up. Meanwhile, Alice had found a website for Camp Greenwoods. It was located up in Minocqua, Wisconsin. The website was one of those amateurish attempts to enter the digital age.

A review of the pictures and text revealed a camp for girls between the ages of ten and eighteen. The camp was run by Kate and Bill Barker. The camp seemed rustic, that is to say old but well maintained. It was located on the picturesque shores of Lake Tomahawk in Oneida County. The pictures on the website showed girls of various ages all having fun: swimming, horseback riding, playing volleyball, and doing a variety of arts and crafts. Dan thought it was the kind of place Sally and he might want to send Debbie to when she got older.

Dan's cellphone rang. It was Bill Barker returning his call. Dan turned on the speaker and set the phone down on the conference table. "Mr. Barker, Special Agent Folkman and I are working on a number of homicides in Chicago that seem to be the work of the same killer. Two women have been killed, and the only connection between the two seems to be that both attended your summer camp ten years ago."

Dan paused and there was silence on the other end. Mr. Barker was probably thinking of those horror movies with the guy in the hockey mask, or more likely he thought his business was about to come to an unfortunate end. "Mr. Barker, are you still there?"

The man cleared his throat and answered, "I'm sorry Detective Lawson. I was thinking about the implications. What can I do to help?"

"The names of the two women who were killed are Carol McCowen and Emily Farrow, although Emily's maiden name is Bannon. They were both in cabin fourteen the summer they were there. Here's specifically what we need. We want you to go back into your records and find the names and addresses of all of the girls who were in cabin fourteen that summer. We need to warn them. Also, Agent Folkman and I would like to drive up to see you tomorrow. We need to find out what might have happened that summer and who might have wanted to kill both these women."

"We should have the information. My wife and I will e-mail you the names and addresses in a couple of hours. We're about eight hours drive from Chicago. You can find the directions on our website. We'll do everything we can to help you find the person who did this. What time do you think you'll be here, and do you need a hotel for the night?"

"If you can make a reservation for Agent Folkman and me, we'd appreciate it. Something close to the camp would be good, and we should arrive in the early afternoon."

After the call, Dan and Alice found Amy, and they walked down the street to the local coffee shop. It was early afternoon and the officers of the thirteenth precinct were out in force getting their afternoon caffeine fixes. Dan ordered a double espresso. If there had been a quadruple espresso on the menu he would have ordered it. They briefed Amy on their phone call to Camp Greenwoods.

Dan thought back to Dr. Sugarman's presentation earlier in the day. "Sugarman said it was sexually motivated because of the knife being inserted into the victim's vagina."

Amy and Alice unconsciously crossed their legs in revulsion as Dan continued. "I'm thinking there was some guy who worked at the camp or had access to the camp who had sexual relations with these women. Maybe the experience wasn't very good and the guy carried a grudge against these women for years. The guy's a little nuts, so it just kept festering in his mind, and finally ten years later, he decides to take action, to seek revenge. The scenario fits the profile Sugarman was portraying."

Alice and Amy agreed with Dan's assessment. Alice said, "I went to a girl's camp when I was twelve. There was a boy's camp on the other side of the lake. Once a week our camp put on a dance with the boy's camp. It was kind of ridiculous. Most of the boys were too shy to want to dance, but there were a few boys who were sexually advanced who saw the dance as a golden opportunity to get some action; and there were plenty of girls who eagerly snuck out with those guys into the woods behind the building, and the girls were more than willing to brag about what they had done. Keep in mind it may be a male camper. So when we get there, we need to find the young boys who were sexually aggressive at any nearby camps."

Dan laughed, "I'm sure you were one of those lucky girls."

Alice produced the glare of a thousand daggers. "No fucking way man. I was a good girl. In hindsight I wish I had been one of the chosen ones, but I was too young to realize what I had missed."

That was the advantage of Alice and Dan being such close long-time friends. They were both more than willing to confide some of their closest secrets to each other.

When they arrived back at the precinct, Dan had an e-mail waiting. The Barkers had sent a list of seventeen names. In addition to the names, they sent the home addresses and telephone numbers and emergency contacts for each of the girls. Of course the list was now ten years old, and the chances were good that most of the women couldn't be found at these addresses. People move, people die, and women get married and change their names. At best they might get lucky and be able to locate half of these potential next victims.

Amy took the list and headed off to muster the rest of the team and start locating as many of the women as possible. Alice and Dan left for home to pack and get ready for their trip. They flipped a coin to see who would drive and Dan lost. "I'll pick you up at six o'clock," he said, "That way we'll avoid the rush-hour traffic.

Chapter 21

Alice dozed off once they merged onto Interstate 94 and headed north. Just after entering Wisconsin, they stopped for breakfast at Castle Cheese, a famous roadside combination store and restaurant specializing in slabs of smoked bacon and a variety of Wisconsin cheeses. This was cheese-head country after all.

Dan decided on the truck-driver special, and Alice, who always looked fit, duplicated the order. As they waited for their meals to arrive Alice shared some personal information with her long-time friend. "I think I found the right guy."

Dan almost choked on his coffee. "My God Alice, how did this happen. I thought you were going to stay single forever?"

"It sort of snuck up on me. I met him at my fitness club. His name's Bob Winters. We have the same workout schedule, and one thing led to another, and we started going out for coffee and then dinners, and then you can probably fill in the blanks."

"What happened when he saw you load your pistol in your shoulder holster?"

"That's the good part. He saw my gun from the very beginning, and it didn't bother him. He told me it makes him feel secure knowing I'm packing heat."

"So when are Sally and I going to meet him?"

"Soon, real soon. Shall we do the double date thing?"

Dan leaned over and kissed her on the cheek. "That sounds like a plan. I can't wait to meet him."

Back in the car, they continued north on the highway and switched over to Interstate 39 just north of Madison. They stopped for lunch in Wausau, Wisconsin and then switched onto Route 51, a two-lane highway leading to the northern lakes region of the state.

Camp Greenwoods was located on the western shore of Lake Tomahawk, just south of Minocqua. Dan turned off onto Camp Minocqua Trail, an oil-coated gravel road, and headed toward Lake Tomahawk. The road split and they took the right-hand fork, and a minute later they passed an old wooden sign confirming they had indeed arrived at their ultimate destination.

The main office was easy to find. It was just past the main entrance and had a large wooden sign above the door. The camp was basically empty. It was late spring, a few weeks before the end of the school year and the beginning of the summer camp season.

Dan and Alice approached the front door to the office and rang the doorbell. A minute later an elderly man emerged from a large shed near the office and approached them. He had probably been working on some large equipment because he was wiping off oil from his hands with a towel.

Dan asked, "Mr. Barker?"

"Yes, but please call me Bill."

After cleaning his hand he extended it in a muscular handshake. The man, at least in his early seventies, looked like he was in great shape, not from working out in a gym, but by putting in long hours keeping the campgrounds in tip-top shape. Alice, no slouch in the fitness department matched his strength on the handshake.

Bill reached for his walky-talky. "Kate and Joyce, Detective Lawson and Special Agent Folkman are here."

The walky-talky screeched two responses. Both women were on their way. Bill said, "Let's go into the office. We can meet there, and that's where we have most of the records."

Bill led them through a beat-up screen door. The hinges squeaked in protest as he opened the door. "Got to oil those hinges," Bill said. "Want some water or a soda?"

Alice and Dan both accepted a glass of ice water from their host. An elderly lady and a woman in her thirties arrived as the glasses were set down on the table. Bill introduced his wife and their youngest daughter Joyce. Both ladies went to the fridge and pulled out Diet Cokes.

As soon as everyone was seated at a long pine planked table, Dan began. "Agent Folkman and I really appreciate your cooperation on this case. We received your list of the girls who were in Cabin Fourteen that summer, and our people back in Chicago are trying to establish contact with each of them as we speak."

Kate Barker asked, "What actually happened Detective Lawson?"

"Carol McCowen and Emily Farrow were killed a few days ago. I don't need to get into the details, but suffice it to say both of their bodies were mutilated in a sexually perverse way.

The only thing these two women seem to have in common is they were both here ten years ago attending summer camp, and apparently they were both staying in Cabin Fourteen."

Bill said, "That's the Roses Cabin."

After seeing Dan's and Alice's expression, Joyce clarified. "We name all of our cabins for flowers. Cabin Fourteen is named Roses. Others are named Tulips, Sunflowers, Geraniums; you get the picture."

After shaking his head in understanding, Dan continued, "Since there were sexual overtones to these killings, we think the person who did this might have had relations with these two girls or some other experience that created a deep desire for revenge taking ten years to express itself in the killing of these two women."

Kate Barker said a little too defensively, "Our girls don't have sexual relationships with boys at this camp. We don't allow that."

Joyce Barker rolled her eyes as she looked directly at Dan. Dan and Alice took note of the look and knew they needed a private meeting with Joyce Barker.

Dan said, "Mrs. Barker, I'm sure you run a really nice camp here, and you take all types of precautions to ensure your girls are protected, but the fact remains that something happened here result-ing in two women being murdered."

Mrs. Barker continued. "Maybe it's because of something that happened in Chicago. They both live in Chicago don't they?"

"That's true Mrs. Barker, and we've consid-ered the possibility, but there appears to have been no contact between these two women after they left camp that summer. Is it possible for us to get the names of all of the males who were working here that summer? From the size of your camp, you must have quite a few people who you employ during the season."

Bill stood up and walked over to a grouping of old grey file cabinets. He opened a drawer and pulled out a folder from ten years ago. The file con-tained a number of Government documents. He passed three pages of information over to Dan. "These are the people who were getting paychecks here that summer. Most are college girls who were acting as Cabin Counselors, but we had a couple of men who helped out."

Dan and Alice looked at the list of people. There were a total of seven men on the list. Dan asked, "What can you tell us about each of these men?"

Bill Barker took the papers and adjusted a pair of reading glasses. He began going down the list in alphabetical order. "Jake Barker is my nephew. He worked for us each summer until he graduated from college."

Alice asked, "Where's he living now?"

Kate Barker answered, "He's a nice boy. He's married and he lives out in California. I'm sure he had nothing to do with any of these killings."

Bill said, "Now Kate. You can understand they have to explore all the possibilities. Just let me get through the list."

Bill looked down at the pages again. "Lester Dunlop, he lives in Minocqua now, but he's confined to a wheel chair. Bruce Barlow's got a landscaping business in town. He's been here every day for the last week working on the camp grounds. When did you say the killings occurred?"

"Both in the last week Mr. Barker. It sounds like Mr. Barlow couldn't have done it."

Bill Barker continued down the list. "James Hill, he's our cook. He's worked for us for over twenty years. He's in his seventies now. He lives in the area. I saw him at the local hospital three nights ago. He has diabetes, and he had a leg amputated.

"Mark Miller, he also worked in the kitchen back then, but he died last year."

Alice said, "I think we can rule Mr. Miller out."

"Josh Relder, he was our chief mechanic; everything is always breaking down. He quit here six years ago, and moved out of town. I have no idea where he is now.

"Freddie Taylor is one of our waiters. He's been with us for over twenty years. He lives in town, and he's single. I haven't seen him for a couple of months."

Dan said, "We're going to need more information on some of these men."

Bill answered, "I have some of their addresses and telephone numbers in another file. I'll get them for you. The last guy on the list is Jack Weiner. He was fired halfway through the summer and then left town."

Alice asked, "Why was he fired."

I caught him stealing money from our commissary. I fired him the same day."

Joyce Barker said, "Dad, why don't I show Detective Lawson and Special Agent Folkman around the camp while you get the information on the men on the list."

Bill smiled, "Good idea Joyce. Show them everything including the Roses Cabin."

Chapter 22

As Joyce Barker led them toward a large play-field, she apologized for her parents. "You need to understand; they've had this place for over thirty years. In the beginning the girls who came here were different; they weren't sexually advanced for their ages. Things changed when the boy's camp opened up twenty years ago."

Alice interrupted. "I was at a girl's camp when I was twelve, and there was a boy's camp across the lake. I don't think the owners had a clue how much heavy petting was going on."

"It's the same here. The girls are basically good kids, but once a month we host a dance with the boy's camp, and let me tell you, the hormones are flying. We have to really watch the girls over thirteen. I know you're focusing on the male workers here, but I wouldn't be surprised if one of the kids at the boy's camp did this."

After crossing an open field, they entered a lightly wooded area with the lake in the background. "We've got nineteen cabins. The older the girls, the higher the cabin numbers."

As they stopped in front of Cabin Fourteen, Dan could smell the deep fragrance of the tall pine trees surrounding the building. He was struck by the incredible tranquility of the place. Looking out over the lake, Dan could see a lone eagle flying over the shoreline hunting for a meal. Close to shore he could see fish jumping near the protection of the boat dock. It was the tall majestic pine trees, however, that defined the setting. Many were close to one-hundred feet tall, and they were everywhere. Other than a few homes spread out along the shore, the trees dominated the landscape.

When Debbie grew up, he would want her to go to place like this. When you live in the city, you need to break free of Urban America and spend time in a place like this.

Joyce led them through the cabin's front door and let them get a feel for the place. Dan counted eight double bunk beds and a single bed near the bathroom. Enough space for seventeen kids. Dan asked, "Who gets the single bed?"

"The cabin counselor gets the single. They're usually college kids who have spent several summers here."

Dan took out his picture of the Cabin 14 girls and showed it to Joyce. "What do you remember about these kids?"

"Becky Rheems was the counselor back then. She probably took the picture." Joyce stared at the picture trying to recall anything of importance. "None of them were bad girls. We keep records of the girls who are disciplined for any reason. I looked at the record book this morning, and there weren't any comments about this cabin back then. Most of the problems were in Cabin Seventeen that year."

"What kind of problems?" Alice asked.

"Most were for the girls sneaking out during the night."

Dan asked, "For what purpose?"

Joyce laughed, "For sex with the older guys at the boy's camp."

Alice laughed at Dan, "You know Dan, for a smart guy you really have no clue. Guys don't understand that when the hormones start flowing and you're fourteen or fifteen all you think about is boys and sex. The bold ones are already into heavy petting, and a few are even going all the way. Why do you think they're so many teenage pregnancies?

"I don't know Alice. When I was that age, I don't think anyone was having sex."

"You're such a romantic!"

Alice then asked, "So where's the make out spot?"

Joyce laughed again. "It's called *Virgin Rock* by the kids. Come on, I'll show you where it is."

The three left the cabin and walked down to the edge of Lake Tomahawk. A wooden dock extended out into the lake, and a large wooden raft was anchored about forty feet out from the dock. A dozen canoes and a few row boats were lined up along the shore and turned upside-down to keep them dry. A speed boat, probably used for water skiing, was tied up at the end of the dock.

Joyce led them along the shoreline to the edge of the woods, and then began walking along a dirt trail leading into the woods. The winding path finally led into a clearing, and there in the middle of a grassy area sat a huge flat bolder, probably pushed hundreds of miles from up north by an advancing glacier back in the last ice age. Dan could picture virgins being sacrificed by some ancient religious cult. Certainly *Virgin Rock* was an appropriate name.

Joyce pointed toward the lake. "The boys from the camp across the lake sneak out at night and come over here in canoes. This is the meeting place."

Alice laughed again. "It's the ideal spot for the sacrifice of the virgins."

Joyce laughed, "And not just girls but the boys too."

As they walked back to the camp area, they could hear the unmistakable sound of a large lawnmower. Joyce pointed to the man driving the equipment. "That's Bruce Barlow."

Dan asked, "Joyce, if you were to guess, who from the boy's camp might have been having sex with these girls back then?"

Joyce Barker didn't hesitate for a second. "That would be Donny Stanton. He was here for a couple of summers and was trying to screw everyone. We kept on telling the owner of the boy's camp that he had to control him, but his father was always donating a lot of money to the camp. Money always talks."

Dan said, "We're going to need to speak to the owner of the boy's camp."

Joyce Barker pulled out her cellphone and punched in a number. "Ed, it's Joyce. The FBI is here. Two of our girls who were here ten years ago were murdered. The connection seems to be our camp. They want to talk to you."

Joyce listened and then replied. "I'll bring them over on our boat."

She turned to Dan. "It's a ten minute boat ride and almost an hour by car."

Five minutes later they were speeding across the lake. Off in the distance, they could see what must have been the boy's camp. The lake was perfectly calm. A few motorboats were positioned off a large island in the middle of the lake, and Dan could identify several fishermen doing their thing.

Joyce was indeed correct; a ten minute high-speed boat ride brought them to a long pier stretching out into the water. Joyce threw a line to a man who had come out to the end of the dock. He tied the boat up and welcomed the three as they stepped up onto the wooden pier.

"Ed Tipton, this is Detective Dan Lawson with the Chicago Police Department and Special Agent Alice Folkman with the FBI. Is Sarah in?

"She's in the kitchen."

"I'll be up there with her until you guys are done."

Joyce Barker walked away and Ed Tipton said, "Let's go up to the office. We can talk up there."

Dan wasn't an expert on camps, but the layout seemed very similar to the Barker's camp. In Tipton's office, Dan picked up a brochure advertising the camp; *Camp Tipton, a place for young men to grow up.* Dan read it and thought to himself, *and a nice place to screw girls*. It took Dan and Alice a few minutes to bring Ed Tipton up to speed on why they were here. Dan finally got to the heart of the matter. "Mr. Tipton, as we alluded to earlier, there appears to be a strong sexual aspect to the two girls murdered, and the fact of the matter is the only connection we can make between these two women is the summer they spent here. It seems likely there must be a connection between these girls and the killer. Naturally, with a boy's camp so near the girl's camp, the potential for teenage sex seems fairly high."

"And I'm sure Joyce reinforced your perception. She blames us for every sexual encounter the girls have, as if no other boys live within ten miles of the girl's camp."

"Mr. Tipton, let's dispense with the accusations. Frankly, Special Agent Folkman and I don't have time for it. The facts in these cases are consistent with these two deaths involving a killer who is probably in his late twenties or early thirties. So if these sexual encounters occurred ten years ago, the person who did this would have been in his late teens. We need to see the list of boys who were here that summer, and let's consider only those who were older than fourteen at the time."

Tipton gave a snort and trotted off to a grouping of file cabinets at the back of the office. He pulled out a file and walked over to a copy machine in the corner. Ten minutes later Dan and Alice were looking at a three page listing of all the boys at the camp older than fourteen.

Dan found Donnie Stanton's name. "Tell me about Donnie Stanton."

Ed Tipton glared at Dan. "So that's the game here. You think Donnie Stanton did this. Is that it?"

"We were told that Donnie Stanton was fairly active sexually with the girls that summer."

It didn't take a rocket scientist to see Ed Tipton was really pissed. He finally spoke. "Donnie Stanton was indeed sexually active. He would routinely sneak across the lake to play around with the girls, but let me tell you, those girls weren't innocent at all. Whenever we would hold dances or other functions with their camp, the girls were competing to see who could get in his pants."

"We're going to need Donnie Stanton's home address and the addresses of these other campers as well."

"Sure, but just to warn you, his father is Arnold Stanton the head of Stanton Industries."

Alice and Dan knew the name. Stanton Industries was a big name in the Chicago area. The company specialized in high-tech metallurgy for the aerospace industry.

Ed Tipton copied the address and telephone numbers of all the campers, including Stanton's information, and handed Dan the list of names. "Just remember this information is ten years old. It may not be accurate anymore."

Sensing a general lack of cooperation from the head of Camp Tipton, Dan and Alice decided to return to Camp Greenwoods. Ed called Joyce on her cellphone and told her he was bringing Dan and Alice to the dock. Ed Tipton silently led the way back to the pier, where Joyce was already waiting in her boat.

After a quick goodbye, and the passing out of their business cards, Joyce started up the boat's engine and slowly pulled away from the dock. She waited until they were clear of the dock and then shouted over the roar of the twin engines, "Did you get any useful information?"

Alice answered, "We did, but it seems Mr. Tipton isn't on the best of terms with you."

"Gee, really; I had no idea." Joyce laughed. "He's of the opinion that boys will be boys."

Chapter 23

Bill Barker was waiting in his office. He had collected Social Security Numbers, home addresses and telephone numbers on all of his male employees. Everything was stacked in a neat pile next to him. Everyone sat down at the large table, and Kate Barker poured them all cups of coffee.

Joyce said, "I showed them around, and they wanted to see Ed Tipton so I drove them over in the boat."

Bill answered, "I know, we could hear the boat pull away from the dock. You drive too fast."

Dan could relate to the parental reprimand. Even though Joyce Barker was thirty something, she would always be their little girl. Such was life. It was probably the same even in China.

Bill said, "We made reservations for you at the Northwoods Lodge. It's in Minocqua on East Milwaukee Street, just on the right as you pass through town. It's not the best place, but it's got a great location, and you can walk to a dozen restaurants. Are you guys going to need our help with anything else?"

Dan looked at Alice and they both indicated they had gotten everything they needed and would head back to Chicago the next morning. They thanked the Barkers and handed out six business cards, three from Dan and three from Alice. Then they got in Dan's car and left Camp Greenwoods with a lot more information than when they had arrived earlier in the day.

The ride into town took all of fifteen minutes, and just like Bill promised, the Northwoods Lodge was the first place they noticed as they approached East Milwaukee Street. It was definitely vintage, but it looked well maintained and had recently received a fresh coat of light-green paint.

The person behind the counter welcomed them both with a smile, and after signing them in and scanning their credit cards, she directed them to their rooms on the second floor of the three-story lodge.

After dumping an overnight bag in her room, Alice walked next-door to Dan's room and they called Jimmy Davis. Jimmy had his administrative assistant find Joey and soon the four were linked into a conference call. It took Alice and Dan almost twenty minutes to bring them up to date on what they had found out.

Dan said, "Jimmy we need you to locate four people for us. At this point they're all just Persons of Interest: Jay Barker, Josh Relder, Jack Weiner, and Donnie Stanton."

Dan then gave Jimmy all of the information he had on the four men. Joey asked, "Is Donnie Stanton related to Arnold Stanton?"

Alice answered, "He's his son. You may not have to talk with Arnold Stanton. I'm betting his son has moved out of the house. Let's not spook him.

The best thing would be to locate him without contacting the father."

Jimmy answered, "We'll try to trace him through his Social Security number. We'll only contact the father if all else fails. Right now it sounds like Donnie Stanton is your lead suspect."

"You're right Jimmy," Dan said, but that's only because we really don't have any good suspects."

Alice said, "Tomorrow morning before we leave, we'll interview Freddie Taylor. He's a waiter for the camp and lives in town."

They wrapped up the conference call, and then Dan voted for dinner and hitting the sack early. It had been a full day.

The person behind the counter recommended Paul Bunyan. She claimed it was famous and within walking distance. It was certainly close; just on the next block. There was a large wooden statue of the famous lumberjack holding a huge axe in front of the place.

It was a bit early for the summer tourist season, so getting a table without a reservation wasn't a problem. The patrons were a mixture of local families, single males who probably had no place to go for a good meal, and a few old geezers who might have been the local fishing guides. There was a table of five of them. They looked like they hadn't shaved in a couple of years, and their plaid flannel shirts and wide suspenderes were every color imaginable. They were arguing about something; between loud comments and some aggressive pounding on their table, they each were making their own opinions known to everyone in the restaurant.

A nice middle-aged brunette gal named Beth with a wonderful smile on her face, brought their menus and announced the specials for the night. Dan asked for a recommendation. "You look like tourists, so I would recommend the Cracker-Crumb Walleye. The cook does a really good job on all our fish. It comes with a choice of two sides"

Alice and Dan agreed on Beth's recommendation, and with that settled, they both ordered a local beer. While waiting for their salads, Dan asked Alice what she thought about the case.

"The more I think about it, the more I'm convinced this is all about sex. I think with both these girls, there was a sexual experience with the guy who did this, and it went very bad. Maybe he couldn't perform, maybe he was humiliated, and maybe they dumped him; who knows. Anyway, these experiences festered in his head for ten years, and all that time he was planning his revenge. You can tell he's a detailed planner. These were definitely not impulsive killings."

Beth interrupted Alice's assessment with the bottles of beer. She filled their glasses and left."

Dan continued, "What I'm worried about is there're going to be more killings. If there're two girls who had a bad experience with this nut, why not three or four or a dozen. To hear Joyce Barker tell it, the nights were one sexual orgy after another. Where was the supervision? That's what I want to know?"

Alice laughed, "Dan, you're living in a dream world. I can tell you from my own experiences at camp, when you bring boys and girls together in an environment like this away from parental supervision and the counselors are college age girls, the only question would be how many girls were getting screwed each night."

"Maybe, but I'm thinking of my little Debbie; and I keep on thinking what she would do in this situation."

"Dan, it's the peer pressure versus what her understanding of right and wrong is. Parents can do a lot to teach what's right and wrong, but they can only do so much."

Dan would do anything to protect his young daughter, but Alice was right. At the end of the day it would be about Debbie's friends. Perhaps the most important thing was to help her pick the right friends.

Alice said, "We need to consider one more fact. If it's all about sex, then why only Cabin Fourteen. Maybe the first two victims are Cabin Fourteen and then the guy's going to move onto Cabins Sixteen, Seventeen, and Eighteen. We should consider warning all the older girls."

Dan considered Alice's comment. "I hope you're wrong, but I'm thinking the number fourteen etched into their foreheads makes Cabin Fourteen something special. I'm thinking the guy has a thing for Cabin Fourteen."

Dan downed a half glass of the beer without really tasting it. Alice looked at him with some concern. "What's wrong?"

"Alice, I almost quit when I saw the first body. It was so mutilated, and the guy who did this; of course he must be sick, but to kill a person that way. And then I thought about how she must have suffered, and how the guy must have wanted her to suffer. What could she have done to justify what he did?"

Alice took a long sip from her glass. She reached out to her good friend and held his hand. "I know this sounds hokey, but people are counting on us to protect them. We're the good guys, and without us the world would turn to shit. I saw the pictures; I know what you're going through, but when we catch this guy, you'll look back at this as just a bad memory. The parents of Carol McCowen and the Farrows are counting on us, and we can't let them down, because without us, who do they have?"

Dan raised his glass in a toast. "Here's to the best friend a detective ever had, and may we solve this case before more women die at the hands of this creep."

Alice smiled at her friend as they clicked glasses.

Chapter 24

After an early breakfast of bacon and eggs in the hotel's restaurant, they headed over to the home of Freddie Taylor, the camp's waiter. His place wasn't too difficult to find. It was a small white clapboard bungalow at the end of a street overlooking a small lake. A guy in a shabby bathrobe answered the door. Alice held out her FBI badge for Freddie's inspection.

"I was expecting you. The Barkers called last night and told me you might be stopping by."

So much for the shock value of an unexpected visit from the FBI. Alice introduced herself and Dan, and Freddie led them into his small home. Dan was prepared for what a middle-aged bachelor's pad might look like, but he underestimated the clutter. The place smelled from week-old pizza and beer, and a half-eaten sausage pizza and five empty cans of Miller Lite sat on a TV tray in front of a small television in the living room.

After sitting down at his tiny kitchen table, Freddie, who was already sweating, said, "I didn't do it. I've been in town every day for the last twelve days. I've been painting the Dorfman's house. You can check with them."

Dan said, "We'll do that Mr. Taylor, but actually, we're here to ask you about what you remember about that summer ten years ago when both those victims were at the camp."

Dan showed him the picture of the girls in front of Cabin Fourteen. Freddie looked at it and asked, "Which were the girls who were killed?"

Alice pointed to the two victims. Freddie finally said, "You have to remember it was ten years ago. Some of these faces look familiar, but I don't remember anything special about these two."

Alice asked, "Tell us about what you do at the camp."

"I'm in charge of all the boats during the day. I take the girls on canoe trips and run the water skiing boat, and during meals I'm the waiter. That's about it, and if I have any spare time, I help out with other chores."

Dan asked, "We think there may be a sexual connection between these two victims and the person who killed them. You must have been aware of some of the stuff that was going on over there."

"Sure there was stuff going on. I'm not blind. I have ears. The older girls were always coming on to me. God they were horny."

Freddie looked at Alice and apologized, but Alice laughed, "It's alright Mr. Taylor; I understand the concept of young girls being horny. Back in the day, I was actually a young girl."

They all laughed and Freddie Taylor began to relax. "I didn't dare do anything. I have a good job, and I knew if I played around with any of the girls, Bill would fire me. I needed the money."

Dan asked, "But there was sexual stuff happening?"

"Sure, but it was mainly with the boys at Camp Tipton. I heard from the girls that the boys would sneak over at night, and the girls would meet them in the woods."

Alice asked, "Who told you that?"

"All the girls were constantly talking about it. It's amazing what you can overhear on a quiet lake in a canoe. The girls would brag about who got laid and by whom."

"Do you remember any of the boy's names?"

"The only name I remember was Donnie. I forget his last name."

Alice asked, "Donnie Stanton?"

"Yes, that was his name. He was at the boy's camp for a couple of summers, and he must have been getting it regular because all the girls were talking about him. I never met him, but he must have been one lucky kid."

Their conversation continued for another half-hour but no additional useful information was forthcoming. Freddie gave them the address and telephone number of the Dorfmans, and Dan handed Freddie Taylor his business card as they left his home.

Back in Dan's car, Alice contacted the Dorfmans and confirmed Freddie Taylor was indeed in the process of painting their house and had been there every day for the past twelve days. Of course the Dorfmans might be covering for Freddie, so Dan found the Dorfman's address on his Tom Tom navigation system and drove over to their house.

The Dorfman's house was located on a street overlooking a large lake. They had several acres of land and a beautiful home. Most importantly, it was clearly in the process of being painted. Ladders were on the grass alongside of the house, and you could see a definite change between a yellowing white and the bright white color of the fresh paint. From the number of outbuildings on the property and the size of the main house, it was clear the process of painting the entire property would take well over two weeks.

Satisfied with Taylor's story, Dan punched in his home address into the navigation system and headed back to Chicago. Alice immediately fell asleep as Dan retraced their route from the previous day.

About an hour north of Madison, Jimmy called. "Listen guys we've got some news for you. The LA Office is checking into Jake Barker. He lives in Orange County, and an agent will contact him today. We still haven't located Jack Weiner, but we have located Donnie Stanton. Actually it was pretty easy; we googled him. He's an attorney living in Atlanta. He works for the law firm of Kendall, Morgan, and Hamilton."

Alice said, "Jimmy book us on a flight to Atlanta tonight. Don't get the Atlanta Office involved. I want to talk to him face to face."

"I've already anticipated that. You're both booked on an eight o'clock flight out of O'Hare. I called the Atlanta Office and briefed them, but they'll stay out of it unless you need their help. I've already called Joey and updated him."

After hanging up, Dan asked, "Do you need fresh clothes?"

"I'll make due; how about you?"

"If you can put up with the smell, I'm okay."

Dan called Sally on the Bluetooth and briefed her on their change of plans. Alice and Sally talked for a few minutes and then Dan explained that Alice had a significant other. This information resulted in Alice explaining her new romantic status, and Sally insisting on meeting him as soon as possible.

They made it into the O'Hare Field parking garage two hours before the flight's scheduled departure, and found time to have dinner at the American Airlines Food Court. While they waited for their Wolfgang Puck's pizzas to cook in the oven, Dan said, "I'm thinking we should interview Stanton at his home, not at the office."

Alice agreed and immediately called into the office. A moment later she was talking to her best friend at work, Benny Cannon. She explained the need to find Donnie Stanton's home address. For most people, such a task would mean several hours of work on the computer, but not for the best techno-geek in the FBI. Benny asked her to hold on while he got the information. Five minutes later he was back on the phone. "Okay here it is; I found it by checking his IRS tax filings."

Alice just shook her head; she had no desire to know how he was able to get hold of the information without a Search Warrant. So much for security at the IRS. She wrote down the information. It was about a twenty minute ride north of the Atlanta airport in Marietta, Georgia.

Alice looked at her watch. It would be after midnight before they could get to Stanton's house, so she and Dan agreed they would try to talk to him in the morning before he left for work.

Alice located a Holiday Inn Express in Marietta, and she made two reservations.

Chapter 25

Amber Carlson was busy in the morgue. Between a recent gang fight and the usual deaths requiring an explanation, her team was busy doing their thing, meaning the instruments of her trade were in short supply. She needed a special device to crack open a sternum without generating debris from a saw blade, but it was being used by one of her colleagues. She walked over to a large storage cabinet and pulled out a new set of specialty tools from a medical supply company.

As she searched the array of blades, her eyes were suddenly attracted to a little used specialty knife in the corner of the clear plastic pouch. What caught her eye was the knife's unusual tip. It was rounded, not pointed, not blunt, but totally round.

Amber took the razor-sharp knife from its protective pouch and examined the blade. It was exceptionally thin, about three centimeters wide and eight inches long. The stainless steel knife was actually a beautifully crafted instrument, at least from a pathologist's perspective. She ran her fingers along the blade's razor-sharp edge. It was incredibly sharp, really a beautiful piece of steel. Amber walked over to the refrigerators storing the bodies. She opened Carol McCowen's drawer and slid her body out of the storage locker. After gloving up, she removed a protective shroud from the body and carefully placed the knife inside the exposed body cavity. The eight inch knife fit perfectly into the beginning of the fatal cut, and the bottom of the incision matched the rounded tip of the blade.

Amber repeated the process on Emily Farrow's body and once again the unusual pathology knife fit the profile of the cut perfectly. Amber returned the bodies to their death chambers. She then pulled off her gloves and washed up at the sink, all the while trying to understand the implications of what she had discovered.

Back at her desk, she thought about what must have been the weapon used in both murders. Could the killer be a doctor? This specialty knife was available online to anyone who wanted to buy it, but who other than a pathologist at a morgue would need or want such a knife?

The conclusion was obvious. Whoever killed these women probably had access to this unusual knife, meaning the knife most likely came from a morgue or other medical facility. Could someone not having a medical background buy the knife? Sure, but highly unlikely. It wasn't like you go on the internet and google knives and this blade would suddenly appear. No, you would have to google pathology knives. To prove the point, Amber googled pathology knives, and after an extensive search, she found only three manufacturers of the unusual blade.

Of course the killer might also work at one of the companies making the knife, but two of those companies were in Germany. The killer might also work for a medical company, maybe in an animal research lab where autopsies might be necessary. One thing was clear, this wasn't the kind of knife a crazy serial killer might consider purchasing.

Amber took out her cellphone and sent a text message to Dan. *I think I've identified the weapon. Call when you have a chance.* Amber sat back in her chair with a smile on her face. A huge weight had been lifted from her shoulders. She had been struggling for several days with trying to understand what unusual weapon the killer might have used, and it felt good to finally solve the problem.

Chapter 26

Dan met Alice in the hotel's self-service breakfast area as soon as it opened. They wanted to confront Donnie Stanton before he left for work. It took three attempts before Dan was able to get a decent waffle from the so-called automated machine. At least the coffee was good. By 7:15 a.m. they were in their rental car, and twelve minutes later they were parked in front of Donnie Stanton's upscale apartment building.

Alice dialed his apartment on the telephone system in the lobby. A call from a woman was always less threatening. Stanton answered the call, and Alice announced the arrival of the FBI. The buzzer sounded, and they took the elevator up to the seventh floor. Donnie Stanton was waiting at his doorway with a perplexed look on his face. Alice had seen the look a thousand times. It was the *what would the FBI want with me look*. Most of the time the look was justified, but sometimes the person knew exactly why the FBI wanted to talk to them.

Stanton, who was in his late twenties had that look about him. No doubt women swooned over his politician's smile and good looks. At a little over six feet in height, he was built like a person who liked working out in the gym, and his smile was captivating. He might have been an actual descendant of Casanova.

They had caught him in the middle of breakfast. He evidently lived alone, which was just as well. It was hard to explain to a spouse or girlfriend why the FBI wanted to talk. Stanton offered them both some coffee which they accepted. Stanton broke the ice as he poured the coffee. "It's not every day I get a visit from the FBI. What can I do for you?"

Dan was looking for a tell-tale sign; something that might indicate Donnie Stanton knew exactly why the FBI was making a house call, but there was nothing, just an honest look of surprise.

Dan started the conversation. "Mr. Stanton, during the last week, two women were brutally murdered in Chicago. There are two common elements to these killings; both were mutilated in a similar fashion, and both women attended Camp Greenwoods in Minocqua, Wisconsin ten years ago.

"There are clearly some sexual aspects to these cases and after discussions with the Camp Greenwoods people, we have been interviewing people who worked there, and also talking to people who worked at or attended Camp Tipton. We understand you were at Camp Tipton the same summer as these women."

Stanton interrupted, "Wait a minute Detective Lawson. Do you think I had something to do with these homicides?"

"I'm not saying that Mr. Stanton, but others who we have talked to indicated you were sexually active that summer."

Stanton interrupted again. "You say these murders all took place in the last week. Well I've been in court for the past two weeks on a very complex civil case."

Stanton pulled a day planner from his suit's pocket and turned to the past week. He handed the calendar over to Dan. "As you can see, I've been in court during the days and meetings with my clients every night. I've had nothing to do with these killings."

Dan passed the day planner to Alice. She took out her smart phone and took pictures of the important pages. Dan felt the wind leave his sails as he continued his questioning. If his story checked out, Donnie Stanton had nothing to do with these killings.

Donnie Stanton, knowing he had the perfect alibi, felt comfortable in speaking more freely. "Look Detective Lawson, I admit to some pretty aggressive sexual activity at the camp. It was no secret. The girls loved me; I was in demand. I've got nothing to hide. What can I do to help you on the case?"

Dan took out his picture of the Cabin Fourteen girls and identified the two victims. Stanton looked at the picture. "I never had sex with either one of them." He pointed to another girl. "I had sex with her but these girls were a little young. I spent more of my time with the older girls in Cabin Seventeen."

Alice sensed Stanton's pride in explaining his sexual adventures. He was certainly a person who was in love with himself. She asked, "Tell us about that summer Mr. Stanton. What was it like?"

Donnie Stanton considered the question. He was trying to recall his time at the camp. He finally looked at Alice and said, "It was the best summer of my life: sports during the day and sex at night. At first I couldn't believe how easy it was to get girls in the sack, and then I realized they wanted it just as much as I did. At night I used to sneak over to their camp in a boat and meet them at this rock in the woods. One of the girls told me they used to draw straws to see who would get to come to the rock. A few who came got scared and decided not to do anything more than heavy petting, but most were eager to go all the way."

Dan asked, "Did you know any of the men who worked at Camp Greenwoods?"

"No, never met any of them."

Alice asked, "Were there any men who worked at your camp who might have been involved in these killings?"

"There was one weird guy. I don't remember his name, but he was always telling us stories of his sexual exploits. I never believed him though. He was too much of a dork to ever get laid."

Dan asked, "Was there anything else unusual about that summer? Any incidents having sexual aspects?"

Donnie Stanton looked at Dan with a sardonic grin. You guys don't have a clue, do you? You really don't know."

"Know what?" Dan said.

Donnie Stanton looked like a kid with a choice piece of gossip to tell his friends, and it turned out to be a key piece of information. "These two girls who were victims. They and two others were close friends. They did everything together.

They were known as The Four Roses because they lived in the Rose cabin.

"Anyway one day The Four Roses caught two girls in the woods having sex. They took a picture with their smartphone. I guess they snuck into the camp's office and got on a computer. They printed pictures of the girls having sex and underneath the picture were the words *Sam does it for the first time.* Then they stuck the pictures on all the cabin doors.

"The counselors quickly took down the posters, but the word spread all over the camp, and our camp too. I can't believe you don't know about this."

Stanton held Dan's picture of the girls and pointed to a girl standing in the second row on the end. "That's her!"

Dan knew her name. "That's Samantha Johnson," he said.

"Everyone called her Sam."

Dan asked, "Who was the other girl?"

Stanton answered, "I don't know."

Alice asked, "What happened after the incident?"

"It was the last week of camp, so nothing much happened that I know about. Everyone just left for home, but I can tell you this; that's all everyone talked about the last week. They never admitted to doing it, but everyone knew it was The Four Roses."

Alice asked him to point out the other Four Roses. Stanton identified Barbara Batten and Kim Tuttle, and he was certain they were the other two.

Dan and Alice left their business cards and headed back to the Atlanta airport. Dan was almost in shock. He had jumped to conclusions. It was so obvious a man had done this. He hadn't even thought about the possibility of the killer being a woman. It was all about preconceived notions. Doctor David Sugarman had said it was probably a male between the ages of 28 and 35, which had only reinforced the mistake. Women didn't do things like this, just men. As if there were no female serial killers in the world. Of course there were some, just not many.

Sugarman had said the killer might very well be on a mission, and Dan could easily understand what the mission was all about: getting even with the four girls who had ruined her life. Samantha Johnson was on a mission to kill, to exact revenge on The Four Roses, the girls who had embarrassed her and made her the brunt of jokes throughout the camp.

Alice broke the silence. "I know what you're thinking and I'm as guilty as you. How could we have immediately discounted a female serial killer? We're trained to never jump to conclusions, and that's exactly what we did. We jumped to conclusions and lost almost a week in the investigation because of it. That's bad investigative work, and we're both guilty of the error."

Dan looked at Amber's text message and immediately called her. Amber explained what she had discovered after Dan explained what they had uncovered. "A female serial killer! How's that for a shocker. Listen, I'm going to try to find out about who might have bought this type of specialty knife in the Chicago area. I'll let you know what I find out."

Alice added, "I'll have Jimmy call you. Our FBI people can help out with the search."

"Thanks Alice, I'll expect his call."

Alice then contacted Jimmy who set up a conference call with Joey. They were still talking when they arrived at the Atlanta airport, and they parked by the side of the road to finish the call. Only three of the Cabin Fourteen girls had been located. Samantha Johnson was no longer living at home, and her father had no idea where she was living. Kim Tuttle's parents had recently died, and their daughter's whereabouts were a mystery. The Battens must have moved out of town, and none of their neighbors had any idea where they might be living.

The search for all of the girls was still ongoing. Dan knew it was only a matter of time before everyone in Cabin Fourteen was located, but time seemed to be a luxury in short supply.

With the probable killer identified, Jimmy and Joey promised they would focus on trying to locate her. Dan filled everyone in on Amber's discovery, and Jimmy said he would give her a call and put some resources on the lead.

After the call, they returned the car to Hertz and booked the earliest available flight back to Chicago.

Chapter 27

Sam Johnson waited in a rental car outside the home of Barbara Batten Wilson. It had taken almost seven years to locate her. She had finally been successful by talking to Barbara's parents and claiming to be an old friend from Camp Greenwoods. She had received her new address, and learned Barbara was living on Long Island and married to a doctor she met at college.

Last year Sam had spent two weeks on the island tracking Barbara's daily habits. Her husband, who was a Resident at Long Island Jewish Hospital, left home each morning, except Wednesdays and weekends, at five o'clock. He returned at various times but always after four in the afternoon. Barbara had a young son, probably a little over one year old. By observing the boy's bedroom with binoculars, Sam knew the child always napped just after lunch. Simple logic indicated the ideal time to strike was while the young toddler slept.

Samantha had a custom magnetic sign printed that she could attach to the side of her rental car. The advertisement indicated the car had come from Long Island Florists. She had purchased a beautiful bouquet of white roses, fitting for the job at hand. Ten minutes after junior's naptime, she placed the florist sign on the side of her car. She then repositioned the car in front of the Wilson residence with the sign facing the front door.

She held a pistol in her hand hidden by the bouquet. Barbara opened the door after looking through the door's sidelight. A woman holding the flowers provided reassurance that the visit was in no way a threat. She opened the door with a smile on her face and was immediately confronted with a gun held against her face.

Barbara stifled a scream as Samantha forced her way into the house. "Don't scream or I'll kill your son."

It was a threat Barbara believed. Samantha placed the glass vase holding the flowers on a near-by table. "Take me to your bedroom."

Barbara Batten Wilson didn't recognize Sam Johnson. Her focus was on the gun and protecting her young son's life. The two walked upstairs and entered a rather large master bedroom. Sam then hit Barbara on the back of the head. After hitting people over the head a few times, she had become skilled at how hard a blow to deliver to render a person unconscious but still able to awake after a few minutes.

Barbara fell onto the carpet beside the bed. Sam gloved up and removed a roll of duct tape from her pocket. She dragged her next victim to the edge of the bed and holding her under the arms, was able to lift the young mother onto her bed.

Sam carefully undressed Barbara and then using the duct tape tied each of her four limbs to the four corners of the bed. She placed another strip of tape over her mouth and then carefully placed all of her victim's clothes on hangers in the closet or in a dirty clothes hamper in the bathroom. Then she walked out to the rental car and removed a large valise from the trunk and brought it into the house.

She repositioned the glass vase containing the roses onto the kitchen table and wiped away any fingerprints. After checking to confirm the toddler was asleep, she sat down in a master bedroom chair and waited for Barbara to awaken.

You might think waiting for the victim to wake up was an exercise in restraint but it was not the case. Sam used the time to relive the fateful day ten years ago which had changed her life forever. Revisiting the day was actually therapeutic.

It took almost twenty minutes for Barbara Wilson to awake. First there was stirring, then eyes were opened, and finally as she realized she was tied down to her bed, she struggled to free herself. She finally noticed Samantha Johnson, but still had no idea of who this woman was.

Samantha looked at her with enjoyment, not pity for what she was about to do, but complete anticipation over the upcoming event. "You don't know who I am, do you?"

It was a simple question, one she had asked each of the women before she had killed them, and none had recognized her. Did they really not know what they had done, or was it some ploy to prevent their death?

Barbara Wilson, shaking with terror, shook her head no. Sam smiled at the predicted answer. "Does the name Samantha Johnson mean anything to you?"

Suddenly recognition formed in Barbara Wilson's eyes, and she struggled with her bindings with renewed vigor. Sam knew she recognized the name and surely knew what that meant.

The ritual began. For Sam it was always the same; the telling of the story, the analysis of the cruelty of it all, the showing of the instrument of death, the taunting of the victim, and finally the actual act of revenge.

She took out a scalpel from her bag and as Barbara squirmed, she cut a small breathing slit in the duct tape covering her mouth. "Who was the ringleader Barbara? Who decided to ruin my life? Who was it?"

Sam moved close to Barbara's mouth so she could hear the words as Barbara struggled to answer the question. The word Kim was uttered, not clearly because of the duct tape, but nonetheless clearly enough for Sam to recognize the name. It was the same name given by the others, and that was why she was saving Kim Tuttle for the last victim.

Sam sat down on a chair near the bed and began retelling the story. "I was so young then. It seems like ages ago, but it was only ten years. She took me to Virgin Rock. I had never been there before, and she wanted to show me. We sat down on the rock next to each other, and she told me how pretty I was, and she kissed me on the lips. I had never been kissed on the lips before, and it felt so good, so natural a thing to do, and she said she loved me. Can you understand all of that?"

Sam really didn't expect an answer, so she never even looked at Barbara. Instead she remained in a trance-like state. She paused for almost a minute before she continued. "We took off our clothes and lay down on the rock. I thought we were alone, but obviously we weren't. You Four Roses must have been hiding in the woods. She told me what she wanted, and I let her do it. I didn't know what to expect, but it seemed like the right thing to do. She was the only person who ever said they loved me."

Barbara Wilson, almost anticipating what would happen to her, once again tried to free herself, but without success.

Samantha Johnson stood up and looked down at her victim. "None of you understood the cruelty of what you did. You just thought you were having fun, but that picture changed my life. Everyone from the oldest girls to the youngest laughed at me and taunted me. You have no idea of how it affected me. I cried myself to sleep every night, and who could I take comfort from? Nobody, every person at that camp was cruel. If it wasn't the last week of camp, I would have left early, but I tolerated the extra couple of days of scorn and ridicule. Do you understand the cruelty of what you did?"

Barbara shook her head yes and Sam could hear her trying to say she was so sorry. So sorry! What bullshit. They all said the same thing. The great confession before the death sentence is passed. They were all weak and deserved to die for what they had done.

Sam reached down into her bag of tricks and removed a blue plastic tarp. She spread it on the carpet near the bathroom. Then she slowly took off her clothes and carefully placed them on the back of a chair far away from the bed. Barbara looked on in fascination, not really understanding what was about to take place. Sam took out a disposable plastic jumpsuit she'd taken from work and slowly put it on. She zipped it up and then put on disposable overshoes and a plastic hair wrap. Only her face was exposed.

She reached into the bag again and took out the eight inch pathology knife she had stolen. Now for the fun part. She showed Barbara the knife. She held it close to her face and moved it back and forth. Do you know what I'm going to do to you Barbara? I'm going to stick this knife into your vagina and then in one vicious cut, I'm going to slit your belly open from the sexual thing between your legs all the way up to your heart. You're going to try to scream, but nobody will hear you. You're going to die a slow violent death, the type of death you deserve for what you did to me.

At this point Barbara Batten Wilson lost control of her bowels. She defecated onto her bedspread, and strained against her bindings. The duct tape cut into her wrists and legs but held tight. Tears ran down her cheeks and snot dripped from her nose.

Sam was almost in a euphoric state as she inserted the blade slowly into Barbara's most intimate body part, and then with one quick movement of her hand, slit her belly completely open. The blood liberated by the single cut flew out of her body in all directions. Sam stepped back from the withering death dance and watched as the blood and other bodily fluids splattered around the bedroom.

Sam's heart was racing as she watched the effects of her actions play out on the bed of her third victim. After the death throws had subsided, Sam reached into her bag again and removed her scalpel.

She stood over the now limp body of her victim and carefully cut the number fourteen into Barbara's forehead.

Samantha's racing heart finally returned to normal as she stood over her victim admiring her work. Three down and one to go, and the last one on the list was the one who would pay the biggest price. Sam stepped over to the blue tarp and carefully removed her disposable clothing and placed the garments on the tarp. She walked into the bathroom and found a clean washcloth. After wetting it, she removed most of the blood from her face. She placed the bloody washcloth on the tarp and then dressed in her original clothes.

Carefully rolling up the bloody tarp, she took a large black garbage bag out and slipped the tarp inside the bag. Tightening the ties on the bag, she left the bedroom, careful not to step in any of the blood on the floor, and then wiped the front doorknob to remove her fingerprints.

Back in her car, she removed the magnetic advertisement from the side of the car and drove slowly down the street toward the airport. She found a dumpster in a Denny's parking lot, and after confirming there were no witnesses, she threw the garbage bag and sign into the dumpster.

She took her time driving. She had four hours before her flight left for Chicago.

Chapter 28

A flight attendant interrupted Dan and Alice. "Detective Lawson and Special Agent Folkman?"

Dan answered yes. "We have an urgent call for both of you. We can patch you in at the back of the plane."

The flight attendant led the way to the galley in the aft section of the plane. There were two phones on the wall next to the attendant's seats. "The call is on channel three. You'll both be able to hear it."

The call was from Jimmy and Joey. Jimmy said, "I just got a call from the New York Office. There was a homicide on Long Island a few hours ago. It's the same M.O. as the Chicago murders. The Woman's name is Barbara Wilson, but her maiden name was Batten. It looks like Samantha Johnson got the third person."

Dan looked at Alice and received a return glare. They had failed to prevent another killing. "Alice and I need to fly out there!"

Jimmy answered, "We anticipated that. You've both got reservations on an American Airlines flight leaving O'Hare at 4:09 p.m. One of the New York Office agents will meet you at the airport and drive you out to the crime scene."

Dan said, "Joey, I want Amber Carlson to contact their medical examiner and confirm the killings were done with the same knife."

Joey answered, "I'll get on that right away."

Alice insisted in a demanding voice, "You guys have to find Kim Tuttle before Samantha Johnson finishes the job."

Jimmy and Joey answered in unison, "We know! We know!"

Back at their seats, Alice said, "We're losing this one Dan; we're losing this fight. I wish we were in Chicago trying to locate Tuttle before it's too late."

Dan looked at his watch. They would be landing in Chicago in less than one hour, and would have plenty of time to make their connecting flight. Alice was right. They were losing this one, and it was mainly because of errors he had made. Assuming the killer was a man was a rookie mistake, and one he hoped he would never make again.

Suddenly, Dan had a thought. He used the plane's passenger communication system to call Jimmy. "Jimmy, Samantha Johnson might not live in New York City and she probably used her real name to book a flight back to wherever she lives. Maybe we can get lucky and pick her up when she gets off the plane."

"Thanks pal, I'll get right on that."

"Good. Also, I think we need to hold a press conference tomorrow and ask for the public's assistance."

"I'll talk to Joey about that. We can make it a joint meeting with the FBI and the police."

Dan placed another call to Sally. She understood the need to go to New York. While Dan was on the phone with Sally, Alice was talking to someone else. After hanging up, she said, "We had a dinner date for tonight. I told him I wasn't going to make it."

Dan smiled, "I hope he's an understanding guy?"

Alice laughed, "If he isn't and our relationship is for real, then he soon will be or it's never going to work.

Chapter 29

Immediately after hanging up, Jimmy called Benny Cannon. "BennyMeister, I have an emergency job for you. A woman by the name of Samantha Johnson is probably trying to fly out of New York as we speak. Find out what flight she's on. Maybe we can catch her when she lands."

"I'm on it right now."

The BennyMeister was an expert among experts. He knew there were only fifteen domestic airlines with flights out of New York, and he knew how to hack into each of their databases.

He called Jimmy back in less than ten minutes. "She's on a Southwest Airlines Flight. It gets into Midway at 3:47 p.m., flight 3106."

Jimmy didn't bother to say thanks. The plane would be landing in three minutes. It would be close. He called Joey. "Joey, Samantha Johnson will be landing at Midway Airport in three minutes, Southwest Flight 3106."

Joey screamed, "I'm on it."

Joey immediately looked in his computer and found the number for Midway Security. "Midway Security, Officer Melborn speaking. How may I help you?"

"This is Lieutenant Joey Capelli with the Thirteenth Precinct. We have a homicide suspect, Ms. Samantha Johnson, who will be arriving on Southwest Flight 3106. The plane is scheduled to arrive at 3:47 p.m. We need the suspect apprehended."

"Do you have a picture of the suspect?"

"Yes, I'll Fax it to you as soon as you alert your people. Prevent the plane from disembarking."

"Hold the line!"

Joey could hear the woman talking into a communication system. "Attention all officers. Immediately move to Gate H6. Prevent the passengers from disembarking. We need to apprehend a passenger, a Ms. Samantha Johnson. A picture of the suspect will be arriving shortly. I will bring the picture to the gate as soon as it arrives."

The woman then spoke to Joey, and gave him her FAX number. Joey warned the picture was ten years old and asked the woman to call back. He took out a picture of the Cabin Fourteen girls, circled the picture of Samantha Johnson, and Faxed it to the telephone number he had been given.

He sat back at his desk and waited for a call. With luck, the suspect would be apprehended, but they were cutting it close, and the flight might have already unloaded its passengers.

After Samantha Johnson deplaned, she decided to make a pit stop. As she exited the bathroom, she noticed a group of cops running toward her gate. As the last officer ran past her, she tried to disappear into the crowd. She fell in line next to a family of four and just tried to blend in with the crowd. Her heart was racing as she stayed in the center of the herd moving slowly toward the baggage claim area.

She was certain they were after her, but how could they know she was on that plane? She considered the possibilities and quickly settled on the one making the most sense. Someone must have noticed her rental car and taken down the license plate number. That's how they traced the car to her name, and then they somehow found out she was on that plane. She was certain the cops hadn't found the connection between all these women that were being murdered. That was just too improbable.

She followed the crowd down an escalator to the baggage claim area. Cops were milling around the baggage carousel checking the baggage claim ticket of everyone who picked up a piece of luggage. She couldn't chance picking up her one bag. She had to leave now and get back into the city. Once again staying close to a group of people, she headed for the exit marked rapid transit.

She took the moving sidewalk to the train entrance, used her Metra pass at the turnstile, and boarded the next train leaving for the city. A cop was standing on the platform, but seemed to be paying no attention to anyone. Just to be safe, Samantha moved to the back of her car in an enclosed area sometimes used by engineers.

Her heart was still racing as the train left the airport terminal. It had been close, too close. As the train moved toward the city, Samantha Johnson considered her situation. What did the police know? They must know her name, and if they knew her name, then they could trace her credit card purchases. She watched enough police movies to know this was how they traced people. She needed to move to cash transactions, and that meant immediately withdrawing her savings from the local bank. The bank would be her first stop. As for where she lived, she wasn't worried. She paid cash at a low-end boarding house and had registered with another name.

The real issue was whether the police suspected Kim Tuttle was next on the list. She immediately discounted the notion; she doubted anyone would understand the connection between these three victims. She would just need to be extra careful in the next few days, and then she didn't care what happened to her; her mission would be completed and her pounds of flesh extracted.

Chapter 30

"We just missed her," Joey said, "but we did get her luggage. The knife was inside the bag along with some clothes and toiletries. Forensics has the knife, and there were some traces of blood on the blade. We'll do a DNA match with the victim's blood. Benny says she flew out to New York two days ago. So she was gone for only a couple of days. We're finding out where she lives and getting her credit card and bank information. With any luck we'll be able to pick her up in a few days."

Dan and Alice listened to Joey's report as they waited to board the flight to New York. Dan felt it would be a wasted trip. What would they accomplish anyway? They needed to be in Chicago searching for Samantha Johnson and Kim Tuttle. But Dan knew procedures called for both he and Alice, the lead investigators on the case, to talk to the New York police and see the crime scene. With any luck, they would be back in Chicago late tonight.

Alice said, "She never picked up her bag. That means she knows that we know that she's killed that woman; but she doesn't know that we know that she wants to kill Kim Tuttle."

Dan smiled at all of the *knows* and answered, "She might know, but I think you're right. I'm sure she believes we haven't figured out the Camp Greenwoods connection."

"What if she has?" Alice asked.

"I don't think it will change anything. She's on a mission, one she believes is justified. I don't think she gives a shit whether we catch her, as long as she can kill all four women."

Their flight was called. They both wheeled their carry-on bags onto the plane and settled down in emergency isle seats. The extra legroom would be the only comfort on their flight into Kennedy.

After reaching cruising altitude, Alice stopped turning the pages of the onboard shopping magazine and tapped Dan on the arm. "You know, in all the years I've been doing this, I've never been able to understand the mindset of these killers. Well, maybe the psychotics, because they're just crazy, but not the psychopaths. They're not crazy, at least not legally nuts; they know exactly what they're doing. How does a person like Samantha Johnson come to believe that killing these four women for something that happened ten years ago is justified?"

Dan thought about the question and finally turned to her and said, "You know, I really don't have a clue. Just between us, I think she must be crazy too, maybe not legally nuts, but definitely a nut case."

Chapter 31

Special Agent Jack Donovan met them at the gate. Mere mortals couldn't get past security without a ticket, but terrorists, FBI agents, and cops had no problem. He was holding a sign with their names, and after quick introductions, they proceeded to his car parked just outside the nearest exit. He waved to a beat cop on duty, a signal of thanks and confirmation that they were vacating the prime real estate.

"Be prepared for the worst crime scene you've ever seen."

Dan answered, "We've already seen the same scene twice, so nothing's going to surprise us. Is the woman slit open like a fish from top to bottom?"

"Yep, and the number fourteen is cut into her forehead."

Alice said, "It's the same killer; a woman if you can believe it."

Donovan said, "I've never heard of a female serial killer, except in the classroom."

Dan said, "This woman's on a mission. This is number three. We're pretty sure she wants to kill four. It all dates back to something that happened ten years ago."

Dan summarized the historical background on the case as they drove. Jack Donovan white knuckled the steering wheel as Dan brought him up to speed. He was silent for the rest of the trip to the crime scene on Long Island.

At the crime scene Forensics was just wrapping up. Jack introduced them to Becky Borden the agent in charge and Detective Phillip Morgan. The body had already been removed by the medical examiner, but Agent Borden had taken a few pictures with her smartphone. She sent them to Dan and Alice, and as they all looked at their own phones, Agent Borden walked them through the crime scene.

The body had been found by the victim's husband, a Resident at Long Island Jewish. He was waiting in the kitchen to be interviewed by Dan and Alice.

The victim's husband was just sitting at the table staring off at a piece of artwork on the kitchen wall, no doubt something of special significance to both of them.

Agent Borden made the introductions, and they all sat down at the kitchen table. Dan said, "Doctor Wilson, I know this is a very difficult time for you, and both Special Agent Folkman and I offer our most sincere sympathy. We're both from Chicago. Two other women were murdered in the last few days, and all appear to be the work of a woman by the name of Samantha Johnson. Apparently your wife, as well as the other three victims, spent the summer at the same camp in Wisconsin ten years ago. They became close friends and were known as The Four Roses."

Doctor Wilson listened carefully to Dan who was offering an explanation of why this might have happened. He had been struggling all afternoon since he discovered the body to try to understand the why, and finally someone was offering an explanation.

Dan continued, "Apparently, your wife and her three friends discovered Samantha Johnson having sex with another woman. They photographed the incident, made a poster, and circulated it to all the other campers. We believe Johnson is taking revenge against the four girls who did this."

"Are you telling me my wife was killed because of some teenage prank ten years ago at a summer camp?"

"Yes sir, that's exactly what we're telling you. We've been trying to find your wife to alert her to what was happening, but with her changing her name and leaving the state, we were not successful in locating her."

"So you guys are telling me if you had done a better job my wife might be alive today?"

Dan apologized because he knew the doctor was right. "We did the best we could. We had dozens of cops and the FBI trying to locate her, and we've still not been able to locate the fourth potential victim."

Wilson grabbed his head with both hands and started to cry. Dan and the others could offer nothing to soothe his grieving. In fact, they all knew this was a necessary part of the process. He finally clutched a box of Kleenex, wiped his eyes, blew his nose, and looked around the table.

Dan continued, "Did your wife ever mention anything about Samantha Jonson or what happened that summer at the camp?"

Wilson answered, "Never, I've never heard the name before and Barbara never even mentioned she spent a summer at a camp in Wisconsin. Believe me, I wish I could help you, but I can't."

After talking to Doctor Wilson for a few more minutes, the combination of agents and cops walked upstairs to the victim's bedroom. Dan pointed to the area where the tarp had been placed near the bathroom and explained their theory on the sequence of events leading up to the vicious mutilation of Barbara Wilson.

"We just missed catching her at Midway airport when she returned to Chicago," Alice said.

It almost sounded like Alice was making excuses, but Dan knew she wasn't. It was merely a statement of fact. Dan, after looking around the room, said, "I want to talk to the medical examiner."

Detective Morgan took out his cellphone, and after reaching a person, passed the phone over to Dan. "Hello Doctor Billings. I'm wondering whether Amber Carlson, our medical examiner back in Chicago has been in touch with you."

"Yes Detective Lawson, I spoke with her about an hour ago. She explained her theory about the murder weapon and sent me a picture of the possible weapon. We have one of those same blades in our morgue, and I can tell you with some confidence, the cut seems to be consistent with that type of knife."

There really wasn't a need to spend any additional time at the crime scene or interview witnesses. Dan and Alice would leave that to the local agents and detectives. They exchanged business cards and Jack Donovan drove them back to the airport.

The FBI office had been able to book them on a late-night flight into Midway, and around 2:00 a.m. Dan slipped into bed next to Sally who provided some first class snuggling.

Chapter 32

The morning meeting at the precinct started on time. Jimmy had brought in his key people, and along with all of the detectives assigned to the case, the conference room was overflowing. Amy Green started off the meeting by sharing what the team had learned about Samantha Johnson.

"We used security cameras to follow her into the city. We know she got off the train at the Roosevelt station and then transferred onto the Red Line; and then we saw her head west after getting off at the Bryn Mawr Station. Joe is passing out the pictures we took of her transferring to the Red Line at the Roosevelt Road Station."

As Joe handed out the only recent picture of Samantha Johnson, Amy continued. "We recovered the bag she checked in at the airport. She must know we're looking for her, and she decided to abandon her luggage. The only item of interest was the apparent weapon she used on Long Island." Amy showed a picture of the weapon on the large screen in the front of the room. Amber Carlson has confirmed it's the exact weapon she had suspected was used in all of the killings. We're doing DNA testing on the blood found on the weapon and checking for fingerprints."

Amy showed a series of pictures of the bag's contents. There was nothing unusual, just what you might expect a person to take on a short trip: a couple of changes of clothes, and the usual type of personal items a young woman might take on a trip.

We were able to get a fairly broad Search Warrant early this morning, and we've been able to determine Johnson stopped at the Bank of America branch near the Bryn Mawr Station last night where she withdrew all the money in her checking account."

Dan asked, "How much did she withdraw?"

Amy looked at her notes. "Just over $42,500; $4000 in cash and the rest in a cashier's check."

She continued, "The address she used to get her driver's license was the same as her father's. She's not living there anymore. We found that out when we thought she might be one of the victims. So as of right now, we have no clue where she might be living."

Jimmy interrupted, "Benny, I want you to work with Amy. We need to find out where she lives."

Benny said, "You got it boss."

Joey asked, "Have we been able to locate the whereabouts of Kim Tuttle?"

Amy looked defeated as she said, "Not yet."

Jimmy said, "Benny, you can add a search for Ms. Tuttle to your tasks."

Benny wrote down her name in his notebook.

Alice and Dan then summarized their findings over the last two days. There were a number of questions, but it was clear everyone was thinking about the future and how to capture Samantha Johnson before she added a final victim to her tally.

Joey walked up to the podium and looked at everyone with one of his *you better get your asses in gear* stares. "We need to pull out all the stops. Jimmy and I have scheduled a press conference in a few minutes. We're going to focus all of the combined FBI and police resources on finding Samantha Johnson and Kim Tuttle. I want Dan and Alice to find Kim Tuttle before she dies, and Amy, you work with your team to locate Samantha Johnson. Resources will not be a problem. I repeat, resources will not be an excuse for lack of performance. If you need something, anything, just ask for it."

The meeting broke up on a somber note. Everyone had something to do, and they each began their assigned tasks in an effort to bring closure to this horrific crime. The senior team met in Joey's office. Joey said, "We need the newspapers and TV newscasts to help us on this one. Dan, I want you to summarize the status of the case and ask for their help. We've got pictures of Samantha Johnson and a younger Kim Tuttle from ten years ago. Someone out there must recognize one of these two."

Jimmy said, "We're running out of time on this one. My gut tells me if we can't find Tuttle in the next two days, it will all be over. Benny, I don't care how you do it, but you've got to find her."

Benny said, "I need her Social Security Number. If I have the number, I can find her."

Joey looked at his watch. "Let's get down to the press conference. We're late already."

Chapter 33

The senior team entered the conference room from the back of the small auditorium. The vultures from the press quickly took their seats, and an anticipatory silence fell like a curtain of gloom. Dozens of microphones were set up at the lectern. Dan recognized all of the evening news show celebrities in the front row. He had been thinking about what to say, and more importantly what not to say.

"Good morning everyone. My name is Detective Dan Lawson, the lead investigator on these cases. I would also like to introduce Special Agent Alice Folkman, the senior investigator at the FBI's Chicago Office. I want to summarize the facts on this case as we presently know them, and then I'll open the meeting to questions.

"As most of you are aware, there have been two homicides in the last few days in the Chicago area. However, you're probably not aware of another homicide on Long Island yesterday, and it appears to have been committed by the same person. These killings have one common theme. Each of these three women attended the same summer camp ten years ago in northern Wisconsin.

There was an incident that summer at the camp. We have reason to believe a woman by the name of Samantha Johnson is the person who committed these murders. We have a recent picture of Ms. Johnson available at the back of the room following this briefing.

"A fourth woman by the name of Kim Tuttle is also being targeted by the suspect in this case. The FBI, in conjunction with the Chicago Police Department, are trying to locate both the suspect, Samantha Johnson, and her next intended victim Kim Tuttle.

Ms. Tuttle may have married in recent years, so her name may have changed. We are requesting that you show pictures of Samantha Johnson and a picture of Kim Tuttle taken ten years ago on your evening newscasts. Please request any person having knowledge of the whereabouts or other information regarding these two individuals to contact either the FBI or the Chicago Police Department."

Dan then read off the appropriate telephone numbers and e-mail addresses. "I'll now open the meeting up to any questions."

A feeding frenzy began. It was clear none of the press were aware of the recent killing in Long Island. Dan's favorite Channel 9 reporter asked, "Was the victim in Long Island slit open and mutilated like the other two victims?"

Dan answered, "I'm not going to get into the nature of the crime scene at any of the homicides."

A national CNN reporter asked, "Why haven't you been able to locate the suspect or the possible next victim yet?"

"The suspect was identified only yesterday, and the information normally used to locate a suspect was out of date. The same is true for trying to find the next victim. All we have to go on is a name from ten years ago. Both of her parents are dead and her whereabouts are unknown. That's why we're asking for your help in getting the word out so we can apprehend this suspect and prevent another killing."

An unidentified person in the back of the room shouted, "What was this incident at the camp?"

"At this point we don't want to release that information. It's not relevant to the task at hand of trying to prevent another homicide."

Another question from the back of the room. "What's the name of the camp in Wisconsin?"

"I'm sorry, but we're not going to release that information at this time."

"Why not?"

"Because we don't want you contacting the camp."

The questions, mostly repeats of the other questions went on for another half hour. What don't people understand about the police not releasing information? Then a bizarre question was asked. "Why isn't the FBI heading up this investigation?"

Jimmy to the rescue. He leaped to the front of the stage and introduced himself. "Detective Lawson has a long history of working with the FBI, and has helped us solve important cases over the years. Special Agent Folkman and Detective Lawson have worked together on many cases. This isn't about who's in charge. This is about finding these two people as soon as possible."

Jimmy's answer to the nasty question seemed to put an end to all the questions. As the reporters ran to the back of the room to pick up their pictures, the investigative team left the room.

Joey's phone rang as they walked into his office. It was Mayor Becklin. Joey listened for a minute and then put the mayor on speaker. "I want you to know if there's anything my office can help with just let me know. The city's counting on you to solve these heinous crimes before the next victim is killed. The city can't afford another killing."

What the mayor really meant was his popularity couldn't withstand another killing. A vicious serial killer loose on the streets of the Windy City was not good for tourism let alone incumbent politicians seeking reelection.

Chapter 34

Dan, Alice, Amy, and Benny decided to find some quiet time at a nearby restaurant. They needed to prioritize Benny's time. His was a resource they all needed to make use of, and there were only so many hours in the day even for the BennyMeister.

Benny stated his dilemma. I need her Social Security Number. Her birthday might also help. With a name and a birthday I can search Motor Vehicles databases in each state to try and find her, but that approach is going to turn up thousands of names.

Alice said, "While we're getting you that number, maybe you should work with Amber Carlson and try to locate who bought the knife. Amber said it's used in autopsies, and you may be able to find out how Samantha Johnson got hold of it."

Benny answered, "I've already started on it. There are three companies worldwide who sell the knife. I examined the weapon, and it was bought from a U.S. company. I've already contacted them and asked for a list of everyone who purchased the knife in the last six years. I sent them a picture of the knife and they confirmed the model has only been on the market for four years. They promised the information by tonight."

The group turned to Amy Green. How was she going to locate Samantha Johnson? "I've got to talk to her parents. They're divorced, but maybe one of them knows where she's living. Our Search Warrant is broad so we can search their homes if we don't get their full cooperation."

Locating someone who was off the grid wasn't the easiest thing in the world, especially if they weren't using credit cards. Samantha Johnson may have only had enough cash to last a couple of months before she needed to cash the cashier's check, but right now it seemed they only had days not months before she would take her final victim.

Alice added, "The best bet may be to trace her movements starting with when she left home. If not her parents, then her friends might know where she went after leaving home."

Amy agreed to follow Alice's advice, and the team now looked at Dan and Alice. How would they find Kim Tuttle in time?

Dan said, "The good news is Kim Tuttle isn't trying to hide from us. We may get lucky if somebody sees her picture on the news, but let's face it, the picture's ten years old, and who knows, she may be living in another state just like Barbara Wilson. I'm guessing Samantha Johnson already knows where Tuttle lives. She probably didn't start on this rampage until she had identified where all of her victims were living. I'm thinking our best bet is to go to Madison Wisconsin where she grew up and talk to people she might have known. Her parents are dead now, but maybe some neighbors know where she's living now."

Alice added, "We can check at the local school. They may have records, maybe even a Social Security number, and she must have had friends at school. Girls know where their friends go. They keep track of them."

Finally they sorted things out and had a plan. They each left on their assigned tasks, and they all knew time was a luxury they didn't have; only one or two days at most.

Chapter 35

Amber Carlson had been stewing over the problem for almost a day. Benny was working the knife company angle, but during the night Amber had awakened from a restless sleep and suddenly had an idea. Her morning coffee had resurrected the notion and now, sitting at her desk, she pulled out her personal contact list and phonebook and began calling all of the morgues in the area.

With almost one hundred hospitals in Chicago and the surrounding suburbs it was going to be a long day, but she was hoping to locate where the missing knife had been taken from. Of course it could have been an online purchase by the killer, but Amber doubted that approach. The killer somehow knew about this type of knife, and it wouldn't have been mere chance. Amber was betting on the knife being stolen by the killer from the place where she worked, and a hospital's morgue seemed like the place to start.

With each call, her approach was always the same: give a quick summary of the case, send a picture of the knife to the person's smartphone, and ask them if that type of knife was missing from their inventory. A missing knife would somehow link the morgue with the killer.

Amber hit pay dirt on her eleventh call. Her friend Doctor Thomas had looked in the instrument cabinet and had returned in an agitated state. "Ours is missing, and I remember we had another one stolen two years ago. It's the kind of instrument that doesn't get misplaced. So you think the killer works here?"

Amber answered, "Yes, works there or has some affiliation with the hospital. I'm going to get this information to the police. Thanks Doris, this might be the big break on the case."

Amber immediately called Joey Capelli. "Joey, it's Amber Carlson. I've just been in contact with the Cook County Morgue. A person I know there, a Doctor Doris Thomas, confirms the kind of knife we've been looking for is missing from their inventory, and not only that, the same type of knife went missing two years ago."

Joey was no rocket scientist, and he didn't need to be to understand the importance of Amber's lead. "Amber, you're a honey. I'll let Detective Green know right away. We'll have someone there within an hour. Thanks again; great work!"

Amy Green was in her car when she got the call from Joey, and it took her less than thirty minutes to reach the Cook County Morgue over on West Harrison Street. The morgue and the medical examiner's office shared the same sterile single story concrete building. It looked like a prison for the dead. Amy wasn't sure if the thick concrete walls were meant to keep the dead from escaping or the necrophiliacs from breaking in.

Doctor Doris Thomas was a striking figure. At well over six feet in height, she towered over most of her colleagues, and as the facility director, she ruled the roost with an iron hand.

It took Detective Green almost thirty minutes to bring Doctor Thomas up to speed on the case. The doctor listened without interrupting, but Amy could see the doctor was listening and thinking at the same time. Amy showed her a picture of Samantha Johnson. Thomas studied the picture for some time and finally said, "She doesn't work here, but I know I've seen her before. I just can't place her."

Doctor Thomas stood up and said, "Follow me."

Amy was led through a number of tall metal doors that opened automatically as Doctor Thomas approached. They wound up in a large laboratory consuming almost a third of the building. With hundreds of body coolers lined up along the wall like filing cabinets for the dead, the room looked imposing.

Thomas walked to the center of the room and shouted for all to here, "I want everyone to drop what they're doing and come here."

A moment later, she was circulating the picture of Samantha Johnson to her crew who were dressed in surgical attire and dripping with blood and other bodily fluids. "Do any of you recognize this woman? She's a suspect in the serial killings."

A worker lifted her plastic surgical mask and said, "I've seen her late at night. I think she works on the cleanup crew."

Two other workers agreed. It was the break in the case Amy was hoping for. Doctor Thomas led Amy back into the office area where they barged into the office of the facility administrator. "Gail, I need your help. What's the name and address of the cleaning crew?"

The administrator walked over to a file cabinet and began thumbing through the files. She found what she was looking for and removed the file. As she walked over to the copy machine she said, "It's Acme Cleaning Services. They're located over on West Cermak Road."

The administrator handed the copy of the information to Doctor Thomas who passed it to Detective Green. Amy thanked the two for their help and ran out to her car in the parking lot. She called Joey with the good news. "Do you need any help?" he asked.

"No, I'm only five minutes from their office. I'll call you as soon as I get more information."

Amy thought about the lucky break. Samantha Johnson had access to the morgue and probably stole the first knife two years ago. Then, when her bag was confiscated by the police, she probably returned last night to get a second weapon. The morgue was the ideal place to stock up on all of the disposable gowns and tarps she would need for the killings. The morgue would never miss a few disposable gowns.

Chapter 36

It took Dan and Alice a little over three hours to reach the outskirts of Madison Wisconsin. The Tuttle residence from ten years ago was located about a mile west of Lake Mendota in Middleton, a middle-class single-family neighborhood just off Route 12.

Kim Tuttle's old neighborhood house was situated on the corner of Maple Street and Hubbard Avenue. The single story ranch looked like it had been built in the fifties, but it was well maintained and fit in nicely along the tree-lined street.

Dan and Alice were confronted by a young girl riding a bike with training wheels in the front yard. In Chicago a responsible parent would never allow a young child to ride their bike alone, but this was not Chicago and you could sense the tranquility of the neighborhood and the sense of security the neighborhood provided. Predators were a big city problem, not a problem in Middleton, Wisconsin. Dan thought *don't worry; your time will come.*

The girl with curly red hair looked at them like she owned the street which she probably did. "What do you want?" she demanded.

Alice took out her FBI badge and knelt down next to the little girl. "Hi," Alice said, "what's your name?"

The little girl studied the badge. She was probably too young to read, but she had seen enough TV to recognize the mark of authority. "My name's Tina and my mom's inside. Did she do something wrong?"

Alice answered, "No honey nothing wrong, but we think she might be able to help us solve a mystery."

"I like mysteries. I see them all the time on the Mickey Mouse Club. Tootles always helps Mickey solve the mystery. Do you know Tootles?"

Alice had no clue what the little girl was talking about, but played along. "We're hoping your mom can be just like Tootles."

They left Tina on the front sidewalk and rang the doorbell. A young woman dressed in jeans and a white sweatshirt opened the door. Alice showed the woman her badge. Alice said, "Tina is a good guard. She demanded to know what we wanted."

The woman introduced herself as Margaret Mead and led them into the living room. "Does this have something to do with the people who lived here ten years ago? The Chicago Police called two days ago asking about them."

Dan answered, "Yes it does Mrs. Mead."

They wanted to pick Margaret Mead's brain, and to do that, they would need to spend a little time feeding her enough information to convince her to help. It took Dan a good fifteen minutes to fill Margaret Mead in on the background.

"Like I told the people who called two days ago, I really have no idea where Kim Tuttle may be now. We bought the house from the Wilmots last year, and I think they bought it four years ago after the Tuttles died in a traffic accident."

Alice said, "We know that, but we're here to talk to some of the Tuttle's neighbors who might know where Kim Tuttle is living now."

Margaret Mead thought for a few seconds. "The Bigalows across the street have been here forever, and the Franklins live two doors down. I think they probably knew the Tuttles."

It wasn't much of lead, but it was the kind of response they were hoping for. One of these neighbors might know Kim Tuttle's whereabouts. They thanked Margaret Mead for her time, handed out two business cards with the usual message to call if anything came up, and left by the front door. Tina Mead was still peddling her bike and followed them down two doors to the Franklin's house.

Mrs. Franklin opened the door and Tina screamed, "They're with the FBI."

The elderly Mrs. Franklin smiled and said, "Thank you Tina. You've been a big help." Mrs. Franklin looked like everyone's aging mother. In her late seventies or early eighties, she was dressed in a calf-high skirt and matching jacket that might have been fashionable twenty years ago but looked a little dated.

A visit from the FBI evidently didn't faze Mrs. Franklin in the least. She ushered them into her kitchen and asked if they would like a cup of coffee. She told them it was fresh, and a coffee break seemed like a good idea.

Sitting at the kitchen table sipping their coffee, Dan once again provided Mrs. Franklin with the background on the case. At the more gruesome parts, she held her hand up to her mouth as if to stifle a shock induced scream. Dan finally got to the question. "Mrs. Franklin, as you can imagine, we're desperate to locate Kim Tuttle and save her from becoming the killer's next victim. Do you have any idea where Kim is living now?"

"I'm sorry Detective Lawson. We lost contact with Kim after her parent's death. She sold the house as soon as she could, and we never saw her again."

Alice asked, "Can you tell us about the circumstances surrounding her parent's death."

Mrs. Franklin took a few moments to compose her thoughts. "I'll never forget the day. I was sitting in the backyard when the police came to the door. They were looking for whoever lived in the Tuttle house. There was a terrible car accident over on Route 12, just a few miles from here. Cynthia and Ralph were both killed instantly. A truck jackknifed and rolled over their car. They had no chance. I told them Kim was away at school."

Dan interrupted, "What school was that Mrs. Franklin?"

"Why the University of course. Ralph worked there, and he got a special tuition discount. She was a junior when her parents died. The police tracked her down and gave her the bad news. My husband and I helped her the first night. It was just terrible, absolutely terrible."

Alice asked, "Do you remember where any of her other family members lived?"

"No, I'm sorry; I don't remember any of that."

After half an hour of discussion, the only lead they had was Ralph Tuttle worked at the University of Wisconsin, and Kim Tuttle attended college there. Actually the lead might be useful. It might allow them to find her Social Security Number.

Mrs. Franklin confirmed the Bigalows were the only other family on the block who might remember the Tuttles. The neighborhood had substantial turnover in the last few years. Dan and Alice thanked Mrs. Franklin for her time, handed her their business cards and with Mrs. Franklin pointing the way to the Bigalow house, they walked across the street.

Mr. and Mrs. Bigalow were both home, both in their eighties, and both a little short on the memory thing. They did, however, remember the terrible day when the Tuttles died with great clarity. Unfortunately, they had no idea of where Kim Tuttle might be living. As they were leaving the Bigalow house, Dan had a sudden thought. They walked back to the Franklin house, and when she answered the door, he asked her a simple question. Mrs. Franklin, do you remember what bank the Tuttles used?"

The elderly Mrs. Franklin thought for a moment. "I think the First National Bank of Middleton. Just about everybody around here has used it for years."

Dan received directions to the location of the bank and thanked Mrs. Franklin again for her help.

As they drove to the bank, Dan said, "Hopefully the Tuttles had a will, maybe even a trust for Kim Tuttle. If they did, then the trust would have to have filed income tax returns, or maybe the trust paid a monthly income to Kim Tuttle. Either way, if the bank managed the trust, then they probably have Kim Tuttle's Social Security Number. Who knows, we may even find Kim Tuttle had an account at the bank, which might lead to a Social Security Number."

Alice agreed. It was certainly worth a few minutes of their time. The First National Bank of Middleton must have been one of the few banks left in the country not yet absorbed by one of the large multinationals. Their FBI badges allowed them quick access to the president of the bank, a Mr. Harlan Frank. He greeted them with a visible amount of apprehension.

"What can I do to help you today?"

Dan spent a few minutes explaining their need, and Mr. Frank asked them for their Search Warrant. Dan produced the certified copy of the document, and Mr. Frank scrutinized it carefully. "This is about the broadest Search Warrant I've ever seen. It just about gives you the right to access any information."

Dan replied, "Mr. Frank the urgency of our problem certainly justifies the broadness."

"Well let me have you work with Jeff Cousins. He's our database person, and if anyone can help you, it's going to be him."

Frank dialed a number and a minute later Mr. Cousins walked into Frank's office. Frank explained both the urgency and importance of his locating the desired information, and then Alice and Dan left with Cousins. He led them back to his small office in the bank's basement.

"I've only been with the bank for two years, so I don't remember the Tuttles, but we keep our records in the computer, so we should be able to find something if they in fact did their banking here."

Cousins worked the computer behind his desk while Dan and Alice sat on the other side. Finally Cousins spoke. "Okay, Ralph and Cynthia had a checking account and savings account at the bank. It was closed out six years ago. Now let me check out something else."

Cousins worked the database for a few more minutes. "Aha," he said smiling, "I've got what you need."

His printer began printing a stack of papers. Cousins then placed the printouts in front of both of them. He guided them through the stack. "This first document is a personal profile of Mr. and Mrs. Tuttle. This next document is the form closing out their account, and this next document is the Power of Attorney proving Kim Tuttle is the legal heir and executor of their trust. This final form is the wire transfer used to transfer the funds to Kim Tuttle's bank at the University of Wisconsin, and this is your lucky day because the amount of the transfer required the IRS identification number, i.e. her Social Security Number. So my friends, here's the number you've been looking for."

Alice said, "Mr. Cousins you have no idea what a help you've been. Because of the information you've been able to find, we just might be able to save this women's life."

Jeff Cousins was all smiles as he escorted Dan and Alice to the front door, and he had good reason to be proud.

Out in the car, Alice called Benny and gave him the Social Security Number. "I'll get right on this. It's going to take me a couple of hours to get her address, but you'll have it by the time you get back to Chicago."

Dan looked at his watch. It was almost two o'clock. Time was running out.

Chapter 37

Amy Green had no problem finding the Acme Cleaning Services' office. It wasn't anything more than a small storefront in an aging strip mall, but the nature of the business didn't require anything more substantial. The entire business consisted of a receptionist, a fair-sized waiting area with a half dozen cheap plastic chairs, and a manager's office.

Luckily, the person behind the desk confirmed Mr. Gilbert, the owner was in, and would see her. A call into the closed-door office alerted Mr. Gilbert to the presence of the police. He opened the door and greeted Detective Green. After the introductions, she quickly got to the point. "Mr. Gilbert, we're looking for a person by the name of Samantha Johnson."

She passed a picture of the suspect to Mr. Gilbert who confirmed she worked for the company as a part-time worker and she was responsible for providing nightly janitorial services to the Cook County Morgue. "What did she do?" he asked.

"We believe she is implicated in some recent homicides."

"You mean the person who slices the victims from bottom to top."

"Yes, that would be the person. Do you have an address for where she lives?"

"Of course," he said.

He walked over to a file cabinet and pulled out a folder. He opened it on his desk and put on his reading glasses. "Here's what we've got. She lives at 3015 South Canal Street, and her telephone number is 312-787-0668."

"What can you tell me about Ms. Johnson?"

Gilbert looked again at the folder. "She's a reliable worker. She's only missed work twice in the last year. She's taking a two-week vacation now, and she's expected to go back to work next Monday. We did a satisfaction survey last year, and the morgue rated her as an excellent worker."

As Amy Green left Gilbert's office, he asked, "Can I expect her to return to work on Monday?"

"Probably not Mr. Gilbert. I wouldn't count on it, but if she does, here's my business card. Call me immediately."

Detective Green quickly contacted her boss. "Joey, I've got her address. She lives over on South Canal Street. I want a backup squad to meet me on the corner of 28th Street and South Canal."

"You got it. They should all get there in ten minutes."

Amy Green turned on her blue lights but kept the siren turned off. She made the three mile trip in seven minutes, and there were already three of Chicago's finest waiting at the meeting point. Soon there were a dozen cops standing beside Amy on the side of the street. The gathering was already attracting a crowd of onlookers. Amy decided not to wait for additional reinforcements. Surprise would probably be on their side, and time was of the essence.

Amy had slowly cruised past the house on her way to the meeting point. Samantha Johnson lived above a small neighborhood grocery store. Amy divided up the responsibilities. She would advance through the front door with six other officers while the remaining group of eight would surround the sides and back.

The team left their cars and walked quickly to the address. A few cops prevented the crowd of onlookers from following. After everyone was in position, Amy gave the go order to the team. Amy Green rang the doorbell on the side of the storefront. A female voice answered, "Who is it?"

"The Chicago Police Department. Please let us in immediately."

The buzzer sounded and three officers led by Detective Green ran up the flight of stairs leading to Samantha Johnson's apartment with their guns drawn. A woman who didn't look at all like Samantha Johnson was waiting at the top of the stairs. She seemed totally bewildered.

Amy demanded, "Where's Samantha Johnson?"

The woman, suddenly flushed with color, shouted, "I don't know. She moved out last week." The cops quickly spread out through the two-bedroom apartment, and immediately confirmed another person was not hiding inside. As the woman had stated, the second bedroom looked vacant. Whoever had lived there had left quickly, leaving many personal items behind.

Amy asked, "Was she your roommate?"

"Yes, she lived here for about five years. We shared expenses. She decided to move out like I said last week, and she didn't give any notice; she just packed up and left. Now I'm looking for another roommate."

"Do you know where she moved?"

The woman now in tears said, "No, she wouldn't tell me."

Green told the woman. "You're going to have to come down to the station for questioning."

"Why, I haven't done anything wrong."

"Because we're going to need your help. It seems Samantha Johnson is the main suspect in the recent homicides."

"My God," the woman said, "she actually did it. You mean she's the one who killed those women?"

"We believe so."

They allowed the woman, Janie Fuller, to get some things and then led her out to a car brought to the storefront. As Ms. Fuller was driven off, Amy called Joey and briefed him on what had just happened.

Chapter 38

Samantha Johnson sat in her car outside Kim Tuttle's house in Rockford Illinois. She had been waiting all day for Kim Tuttle to return home from an unexpected shopping trip. Her husband had left at his usual time, just after eight o'clock, but Kim had left in her car ten minutes later.

Samantha Johnson had planned on killing her final Rose at ten o'clock, just enough time to ensure her husband didn't return unexpectedly from work and long before he returned home at the end of the day.

Sitting in her car, she reflected on the last twelve hours. What did the police and FBI know, and when did they know it? She still felt safe. How could they know about the Camp Greenwoods connection? It happened too long ago. In any event in a few hours it would all be over. She couldn't contemplate what would happen then. She knew she couldn't go back to work. She was sure the police now had her name. She was off the grid now, operating on cash, but the cash would eventually run out. She needed a long-term plan, a place to go, and a way to make a living; and to be honest, she had never given much thought about how to disappear. She just was so focused on taking her revenge, the next steps never crossed her mind.

The voice within helped her think about her options. She could probably flee to Mexico, and from there, go further south. Working for cash in South America seemed like a good option. Unfortunately, she had learned French in high school, and she wasn't aware of any country in South America speaking French. Maybe a few places in the Caribbean, but not in South America.

If nothing else, Samantha Johnson was an obsessive planner, and even though her end-goal might be to flee to South America, she knew she wasn't going to just be able to drive across the border, not in her present car and with no false identification. For sure the immigration people would be on the lookout for her. She needed a short term place to hide after taking care of business.

She thought about how close she had come to being captured at the airport. She had seen enough TV programs to know her picture had probably been taken by several security cameras as she left the airport, and knowing the police, her picture would be on the local news in the next few hours. With that in mind, she had stopped by a Walmart after stealing a new knife from the morgue and purchased a Vidal Sassoon Pro Series product, a color called Extra Light Cool Blond. She always wanted to be a blond.

Last night she had transformed her hair from a dark-brown color into her new look, and had also cut her long flowing ponytail into a shorter style. Staring into her bathroom mirror, she had laughed at her new look, and knew she should have become this sexy blond years earlier.

She looked at her watch. It was a little after three o'clock. She hoped her last victim would get home soon or she might have to risk waiting until the evening and that meant probably shooting Kim's husband in order to have enough time to end Kim's life, with enough pain and suffering. Only then would her revenge be complete.

A metallic ice-blue SUV turned the corner and headed for the Tuttle house. She recognized the color and sure enough it was Kim Tuttle returning from her day's adventure, the last outing of her life. The car turned into the driveway, and as soon as the garage door opened, Kim Tuttle pulled in and closed the garage door after removing several large shopping bags from the SUV's trunk.

Samantha bought a dozen long-stemmed roses from a florist on the way to the Tuttle house. Now she held a single red rose close to her face, kissed it, and took in its strong magnificent fragrance. It was a smell she would cherish for the rest of her life.

Ten minutes later Samantha left her car with a gift of flowers. What woman would not open her door for a dozen beautiful red roses? She walked across the street and rang the front doorbell.

A smiling Kim Tuttle opened the door. Flowers, next to diamonds, were a girl's best friend. "Kim Monroe?" Samantha asked.

"Yes, oh my God, Flowers. Are they from Luis?"

"I'm sorry mam, I don't know who they're from, but you'll need to sign for them."

Kim allowed Samantha to step through the doorway and into the foyer. She set the flowers down on a nearby table and handed Kim a receipt to sign. As Kim Monroe signed the paper, Samantha pulled out her small caliber pistol from her pocket and held it up against Kim Monroe's face.

Surprise and then fear registered on Kim's face. "I have a surprise for you Kim from a good friend, Samantha Johnson."

Kim couldn't immediately place the name. It was ten years ago after all. "Camp Greenwoods," Samantha blurted out. Why couldn't these girls even remember her name? You'd think they'd be able to remember the name of a girl whose life was destroyed forever.

Samantha knew the layout of the house, having cased it out for many years. She marched Kim Monroe up the stairs to the master bedroom, and just as with her other victims, she hit her over the head with the butt end of the gun when she stood next to her bed.

Samantha took out a fresh roll of duct tape, and after lifting her next victim onto the bed and stripping off her clothes, she bound Kim's arms and legs to the four corners of the large king-sized bed. Samantha placed a final piece of tape over Kim Monroe's mouth, cut a slit in it, and then quickly walked out to the car to retrieve her instruments of death.

As she was hanging up Kim's clothes in the closet, Kim regained consciousness. A general awareness suddenly transformed into genuine fear as Kim realized she had been bound to the four corners of the bed. Only when she tried to scream did she realize tape had been placed over her mouth. A muffled sound of terror was all she could produce. She struggled in vain to break free from the bed.

Chapter 39

Benny's call found Dan and Alice just south of Beloit, Wisconsin heading south on Interstate 90. "Good news," Benny said not waiting to offer a greeting. "I found what you need in the IRS database. Kim Tuttle married Luis Monroe three years ago. For the last two years, they've been living in Rockford, Illinois. The address is 3279 N. Trainer Road. Their telephone number is 779-355-4758.

Alice said, "Got it darling, I'm going to give you a great big kiss as soon as I see you again."

Alice punched in Kim Monroe's telephone number and waited for someone, anyone to answer. After the fifth ring, the call transferred over to an answering machine. "You've reached the telephone number of Kim and Luis Monroe. We can't answer the phone right now. Please leave a message and we'll get back to you just as soon as we can."

Alice's message left little room for doubt. "This is Special Agent Alice Folkman with the FBI calling. We have reason to believe a woman by the name of Samantha Johnson is trying to kill you. As soon as you hear this message, go immediately to the nearest police station. Do not, I repeat, do not stay in your house. When you arrive at the police station, have the police call the FBI at the following number."

Alice rattled off the phone number of the Chicago FBI Office and then hung up. She turned to Dan. "I hope we're not too late."

Dan responded by turning on his car's siren and pushed the petal to the metal. Luckily, the road was mostly empty and the car easily reached 110 miles per hour. Alice punched Kim Monroe's address into the Tom Tom. The device responded with critical information. They would reach Monroe's house in eighteen minutes, but that was adhering to the posted speed limits, and Dan had no intention of obeying any traffic signs.

It took Alice five minutes to contact the right person in the Rockford Police Department. Five minutes of being shuttled around finally led to a 911 desk. Alice quickly explained who she was, and the police needed to get someone out to the Monroe house as soon as possible. The lady on the phone explained the State Police had jurisdiction in the area, but she would immediately contact them and get them to the house as soon as possible.

Chapter 40

Samantha Johnson listened to the message with obvious alarm. How could they have figured out Kim Monroe was her next victim? She looked at her watch. The call probably came from Chicago. Even if the FBI alerted the Rockford police, it would still take them more than fifteen minutes for the police to reach the Monroe house. After all, the house wasn't within city limits and Johnson knew the closest police station was at least twenty minutes away. She figured she easily had ten minutes to finish her work and escape without any problems.

Samantha Johnson had thought about her plans for Kim Tuttle for too many years. She wasn't about to be denied ultimate revenge just because the cops might be alerted. She took out her scalpel, and moved it slowly in front of Kim Monroe's eyes.

"You still don't know who I am, do you?"

Kim Monroe shook her head.

"Let me remind you. Ten years ago, you and three other girls took a picture of me at Camp Greenwoods and posted that picture all over the camp."

The name finally registered with Kim Monroe and she began to violently pull against the duct tape. She now realized who this woman was and what might be happening to her.

Samantha slowly moved the scalpel back and forth in front of Kim Tuttle. Kim followed it with her eyes. "If you move your head, this is going to hurt."

Kim's head still jerked back and forth, the fear running through her mind trumped the warning. Samantha jumped onto the bed and placed her knees on both sides of Kim's head. With Kim's head immobilized, Samantha held the scalpel against Kim's forehead and began cutting the number fourteen into the space above her two eyes. The pain was excruciating, and Kim screamed a muffled scream into the duct tape. Blood began flowing down her forehead and into her eyes.

When Samantha Johnson finished, it wasn't a very pretty number fourteen, but then again the others had been cut after the victims had died. Blood flowing from the wound burned Kim's eyes. She continued to try to pull her arms free of the duct tape but with no success. Cut wrists were the only result. Blood was now dripping into her mouth and the salty metallic copper taste of the blood created even more despair.

The distant sound of a police siren quickly grew in intensity. Samantha looked at her watch. How could they be here so soon? She looked out a front window as Dan and Alice pulled into the Tuttle's driveway. Should she kill her now or kill the police first? Samantha knew the answer because she would not be denied the final enjoyment of torturing Kim Tuttle. She would kill these cops and then finish the final chapter in her long overdue revenge.

She looked for a place to hide. Behind the door was too obvious and inside the closet prevented her from getting a clear shot. She settled on the corner of the room behind a large upholstered easy chair. She pulled her autopsy knife from her bag and hid behind the chair with her knife in one hand and her pistol in the other. She lowered herself to the carpet and looked at the bedroom door through the small space below the chair. She waited and knew she couldn't waste any bullets. She would need to kill whoever walked through the door with a single shot.

Chapter 41

Dan and Alice quickly identified the license plate number on Samantha's car as they approached the house. They had her trapped, but to wait risked Kim Tuttle's death. Without a spoken word, they both knew they would have to get in the house as soon as possible to prevent another killing.

They ran up to the front door, but it was locked. There was no need to ring the doorbell. Samantha Johnson had obviously heard the siren from their approaching car. She would be waiting for them. Dan said, "Wait here, I'll break in the through the backdoor."

Dan drew his pistol and ran to the back of the house. The backdoor was locked, but he broke a small window pane in the door with his gun and reached in to unlock it. He advanced slowly into the kitchen, swinging his weapon from left to right. He peeked into the foyer and looked quickly into the living room and then the library. With the coast clear, he walked to the front door while keeping his eyes focused on the upstairs' hallway.

He opened the front door and Alice quietly slipped inside. Dan pointed upstairs and Alice nodded. They silently advanced up the stairs, listening carefully for any sounds. Dan knew Samantha's M.O. and knew she would be in the master bedroom, certainly armed and probably waiting for them.

At the top of the stairs, Dan looked left and then right and decided the master bedroom was probably on the right. The room beyond the door certainly looked big enough to be the master bedroom. Side by side, they advanced down the hallway. Dan signaled to Alice; he would move to the right and she should move to the left. Alice nodded in agreement. Dan looked into the room and saw Kim Tuttle tied to the bed, her face covered in blood. She was squirming, still alive and trying to break free from her bonds, and desperately trying to speak through the small slit in her taped mouth.

Dan couldn't see Johnson, but he sensed her presence. She was definitely hiding in the room, just waiting for them to enter. Dan looked at Alice and nodded. They both burst into the room, Dan moved to the right and Alice to the left. Two shots rang out in rapid succession.

Alice fell to the ground as a bullet struck her in the chest. Dan was hit in the right arm by the second shot. His gun fell from his hand as his body twisted to the left. He went down on one knee, temporarily stunned by the bullet.

Samantha Johnson could hear the faint sounds of police sirens in the distance. She had to change her plans. She suddenly jumped from behind the chair in the corner and lunged toward Dan. With a crazed look in her eyes, she swung her knife at Dan's right arm as he desperately tried to reach for his gun. The blade sliced through his forearm all the way down to the bone. Blood squirted from his wound. Samantha Johnson kicked Dan's gun away from his body. She stared at Kim Tuttle and then shot her in the stomach.

Samantha Johnson was certain she had killed Kim Tuttle. Now it was all about trying to escape before reinforcements arrived. She looked quickly at the two cops. The guy was withering in pain and rapidly bleeding out on the beige carpeting. The woman was not moving and lay in a growing pool of blood.

Escape now, she had to escape now. She ran into the hallway and down the stairs. The sounds of police sirens grew louder. It took her less than thirty seconds to get in her car and drive away. It hadn't ended the way she had dreamed about, but Kim Tuttle was dead, and at the end of the day, nothing else mattered. She drove down the street with no plans other than to get away from the Tuttle's house as quickly as possible. She made her way onto Interstate 90 and headed north.

Meanwhile, Dan struggled to his feet. His focus turned from capturing Samantha Johnson to saving the two women in the room. He took a look at half his forearm exposed down to the bone, with blood flowing down his hand onto the floor. He felt dizzy and sick to his stomach, but he reacted instinctively. He removed his belt and used it to tie a tourniquet around his arm just above the knife wound. He pulled his cellphone from his pocket and dialed 911. After identifying himself, he asked for ambulances and police to come to their aid.

He staggered over to Alice and turned her onto her back. Blood was all over the front of her blouse. She had been hit in the chest, and the bullet was still lodged inside her body. He felt for a pulse. She was still alive but unconscious. Kim Tuttle was also hit in the stomach but just a grazing wound, and she was still conscious. Dan removed the duct tape from her mouth. Kim Tuttle screamed, "She tried to kill me. My God, she tried to kill me. She was crazy."

Dan replied, "Don't talk now. Help is on the way."

In fact, Dan could now hear police sirens. He collapsed onto the same chair Samantha had been hiding behind and waited. As he heard cops enter the house, he screamed, "We're up here."

The cops ran into the room with guns drawn. "I'm Detective Dan Lawson with the Chicago Police Department. FBI Special Agent Alice Folkman has been hit in the chest with a small caliber bullet. Kim Tuttle is on the bed and has been shot in the stomach. Samantha Johnson did this. She left here about five minutes ago in her car, Illinois license plate number 23L4163. Put out an APB. I've already called in ambulances."

That was all Dan could muster before he collapsed back onto the chair. Within minutes there were dozens of cops and medics crowding into the small bedroom. Dan, on the edge of consciousness, saw the medics free Kim Tuttle's arms and legs and place her on a gurney. Alice was removed and Dan lost consciousness as he was wheeled out of the house. The last thing he noticed was a crowd of onlookers gathered around the ambulances watching the bodies being loaded.

He thought he could hear the sound of the ambulance as they were rushed to the nearest hospital, and then there was nothing: nothing to see, nothing to hear; just absolute silence, a serene absence of reality, like floating in a dark abyss, floating in a soup of darkness.

Chapter 42

A voice called to him. It came from far off in the distance and grew in loudness and clarity. "Open your eyes Detective Lawson. Open your eyes."

Dan willed his eyes open and a haze lifted slowly before him. A woman in a surgical mask was looking at him. "You're going to be all right detective. The surgeon had to repair a bullet wound in your arm and a vascular surgeon fixed the terrible cut in your arm. You've lost a lot of blood, but you're going to be okay. Do you understand me?"

"Dan, with slurred words answered, "I'm okay. What about the other two women?"

Dan looked at the nurse with hope. "The young woman is going to be fine. The older woman is just out of surgery. The bullet was lodged alongside her descending aorta. She lost a great deal of blood. She's stable, but it could go either way. We'll know more in the next twenty-four hours."

Dan drifted back into a state somewhere between reality and darkness. He felt something rubbing his arm. It wasn't demanding; more of a presence. Nonetheless, he felt its comfort and warmth and love. He opened his eyes, and as a mental fog lifted, Sally appeared before him. "Well, I hope you've enjoyed your rest. You've been asleep for hours. I talked to the surgeons. You'll be fine."

"What about Alice?"

"She'll make it, but it was close, very close. Jimmy's with her now. She's not awake yet, but I've seen her chart. She'll make it."

"And Kim Tuttle?"

"She's fine. Her husband is with her now."

"Did they catch Samantha Johnson?"

"No, she got away. There aren't any signs of where she went."

"How's my daughter?"

"She's at home with the au pair."

Sally fed him some chicken soup. Dan's grandmother had extolled the virtues of chicken soup. He had always believed it to be a myth, but with every sip his energy seemed to double, and soon, with Sally's help, he was sitting up inspecting the two bandages on his right arm. As he regained his strength, his mind cleared as well. He lifted the sheet and looked at the catheter between his legs. "I guess I don't have to worry about getting up to take a leak."

"No, that will come tomorrow when they take it out."

Jimmy suddenly appeared at the doorway. "You dumb shit. Why did you go and get yourself shot? Don't bother to answer. I'm just glad to have you back from the dead."

Dan's best friend leaned over and gave him a gentle hug. "Do you feel up to giving me a quick summary of what happened?"

Dan did just that. He tried to recall all of the details of yesterday's ordeal. Jimmy listened to the story in silence, smiling at his good friend from time to time. At the end he said, "You did good Dan; I'm proud of both you and Alice. You saved the last woman from becoming the next victim. So where do you think Samantha Johnson is going to go?"

Dan tried to clear the cobwebs but without much success. "I can't think right now."

Sally admonished, "It's the anesthesia Jimmy. It's going to take a couple of hours for the drugs to clear his system."

Jimmy stood up from his chair and began pacing. "Her picture hit the news services last night. It was all over the local news. It even made the Tribune. We're bound to get some leads after people see her picture. If she lives in the city, we'll find out. Her last roommate knew nothing, a real idiot. The girl had no idea Johnson was into anything."

Jimmy continued to pace back and forth across the room. Dan interrupted Jimmy's walk to nowhere. "I want to see Alice!"

Sally said, "You're too weak; you need to rest."

Dan looked her in the eyes. She had seen the look only a few times in their marriage, and she knew there was no denying his request. "I'll talk to the doctors."

She left the room and returned ten minutes later with a middle-aged man wearing a stethoscope wrapped around his neck and a grey lab coat with his name embroidered on the front. Dr. Greyson said, "I understand you want to take a trip down the hall to see your friend. Dr. Lawson tells me she's a very good friend. Here's the thing Detective Lawson, you're too weak to get into a wheel chair and you've got a catheter and urinary drainage bag to contend with. I'm sure you can see the problem."

Dan stared into the man's soul. "I want to see my friend. Do you understand doctor? I want to see my friend now!"

Dr. Greyson spoke quietly to Sally off to the side of Dan's bed. Greyson returned to Dan's side. "Here's what we're going to do. These rooms were originally designed for two patients until we decided to convert them into single rooms. How about if we move your bed into Special Agent Folkman's room. It's a bit irregular to have a man and a woman in the same room, but it sounds like it might benefit both your recoveries. Is that acceptable?"

"Doctor Greyson, that sounds like a very practical solution to the problem."

It took a nurse and two orderlies to move Dan's bed. He looked on as his bed, I.V. pole, monitoring equipment, and a urinary collection bag were wheeled down the hall toward Alice's room, with a full entourage following the parade.

Alice had dozed off but was awakened by the clatter of Dan and his accessory equipment moving into the room. A smile crossed her peaked face. Dan reached across the gap between their beds and squeezed Alice's extended hand.

Jimmy, with tears in his eyes said, "Okay, are we all done with the kumbaya moment? Because if we are, then we've got some serious investigative work to accomplish."

Alice nodded off to sleep again and Dan just stared at Alice, just surprised and thankful to see her alive.

Sally said, "Jimmy, let them regain their strength. I'll watch them both tonight."

"Okay, but I'll be back tomorrow with the group. We're going to have a meeting right here in this room."

With Doctor Sally promising to provide continuous medical monitoring, Jimmy left for the ninety minute trip back to Chicago.

Chapter 43

Samantha Johnson sat in her car in the parking lot of the Janesville Oasis. She had arrived at the rest stop a little after five o'clock. While eating at the McDonald's, she had seen her picture on the Channel 9 evening news. It had been taken at Midway airport and she now knew she had absolutely no chance of returning to Chicago. That old bitchy manager would probably recognize the picture and call the police.

She began shaking and suddenly felt cold and alone. She had no real friends and none of her acquaintances would provide any help. She was a loner and she knew it. One thing for sure, the cops would be looking for her car. She had an idea.

She moved her car to a remote section of the parking area, near a pickup truck towing a small camper. She found a screwdriver in the trunk of her car, and after looking around the parking lot, she switched license plates with the Illinois plated car. The cops would be looking for her license plate. Hopefully the owner wouldn't notice the change.

After repositioning her car at the other end of the parking area, she waited for the owner of the truck to return. It didn't take very long. A family of four walked out to the truck and drove off without noticing anything.

Samantha needed a plan. She had been thinking about heading south into Mexico, but the more she thought about the idea, the more she knew she needed to wait before attempting the border crossing. She knew nothing about the border area between the United States and Mexico, but knew the local authorities would be heavily guarding the border.

How do you cross the border without getting caught? She needed a safe place to hang out, a place where she could plan in detail how to do it. Both her divorced parents offered no possibility of help; she had burned those bridges many years ago. She knew only one person in the world who might provide sanctuary. It was certainly worth a phone call.

Chapter 44

Things began moving rapidly after the evening newscasts. For the last twenty-four hours the calls came in like clockwork. There were the usual bunch of kooks. There always were. Some people just wanted an opportunity to seem important to themselves, but amongst the hundreds of calls, there were a few good leads. Amy Green was now following up on the best, a woman who ran a boarding house in the Lakeview area was certain the suspect was renting a room with cash on a day to day basis.

Amy walked up to the aged brick building with its back right up against the Red Line elevated train tracks. The noise of the passing trains was more than enough to frighten off all but the poorest and those hard of hearing. The building held several dozen single room efficiency apartments, actually forty-eight by a count of the keys hanging on the wall behind the manager's desk.

Detective Green introduced herself to Martha Stewart. The elderly lady was quick to point out she was not the same Martha Stewart of celebrity fame; as if anyone would think they were the same person. Amy showed her the picture of Samantha Johnson. "Yep, that's her alright, but she registered as Janice Fuller. She's up in Unit 24B, but I haven't seen her since yesterday morning, and you can see her key is still on the board. Her stuff's still up there, and now she owes me for two day's rent."

"Can I have a look in her apartment?" Amy asked.

"Sure, I'll take you up there myself."

Martha Stewart locked up the manager's office and led Amy up to the second floor. She opened a squeaky door to apartment 24B. The place looked like it hadn't been cleaned since the Chicago Fire. In the corner of the room five assorted suitcases were filled to the bursting point.

Amy looked around the room and was immediately attracted to the small bathroom in the back of the unit. The empty bottle of Vidal Sassoon colorant and strands of long black hair in the sink hinted at what Samantha Johnson had probably done after her identity had been discovered.

Amy Green turned to the manager and said, "Ms. Stewart we're going to have to declare this a crime scene. I'm going to station a police officer here just in case Ms. Johnson comes back."

"What about my rent? Who's going to pay the rent? I can be renting out this room in a day. This place is in demand."

"Really Ms. Stewart. How many rooms are unoccupied at the moment?"

"Not many, I can tell you that."

"Well I'll tell you what. As soon as all of your other rooms are occupied, I'm sure the city will be willing to reimburse you for the time the apartment might be rented. Is the front door the only entrance to the apartment complex?"

"We've got emergency exits on all the floors, but you can't enter the building through them. Everyone's got to pass the front office to get their keys."

Amy returned to her car and called Joey. "I've located her apartment. It looks like she's bleached her hair and cut it shorter than her picture. I've told the landlord it's a crime scene now. Get Forensics down here to go over the place. I'll wait for them, and then we'll look through all of her belongings. Just in case she comes back, send one of the rookies over here to guard the place."

"Good work Amy. I'll let Jimmy know. He may want his people down there as well. Do you think she'll be coming back?"

"If she does, it will probably be in the next few days, but I think she's on the run. After she blew the Tuttle killing, she'll think twice before trying to get her things."

Chapter 45

Dan looked around his hospital room with a new-found clarity. Sally was asleep on a recliner, and Alice was stirring in her bed. With a clear mind, he thought about the previous day. What should he have done differently? Would the outcome have changed if they had waited for the police? What if they had called to Samantha Johnson from the street and ordered her to surrender? It was the woulda, coulda, and shoulda game. A lot of what ifs, but one fact remained; they were dealing with a crazy woman who was cornered. In every scenario the outcome seemed to be the same, Kim Tuttle would be dead, Samantha Johnson captured and Alice and he wouldn't be in the hospital.

He knew the answer. They had reacted in the only way they could to save a life, and if that meant Samantha Johnson was still free, then so be it. It had been the right choice.

A med-tech arrived to draw some blood, as if he had any to spare. The young lady looked at the two patients in the same room and asked Dan, "I hope that's your wife?"

Dan smiled, "My wife's in the recliner, but the other patient is a very close friend."

"But we have rules against that."

""We were granted special papal dispensation."

The woman shook her head as if to say *what has this hospital become*. She withdrew some Vacutainer supplies from a basket, and reached for his nearest arm. After withdrawing blood, she rolled the supply cart over to Alice's bed, waking Alice from her peaceful rest. "Ms. Folkman, I have to draw a blood sample."

Alice stirred and before she even had a chance to push away the cobwebs, the med-tech had grabbed her arm, placed a tourniquet, and drew her sample. A moment later she was gone. The noise of the cart awakened Sally, and after rubbing her eyes, she sat down on Dan's bed and gave him a much-needed good morning kiss. She looked at Alice and then back at Dan. "Well, don't both of you look better this morning."

Sally couldn't resist being a doctor. She took a stethoscope from her purse and proceeded to check out both patients. "I looked at your charts a couple of hours ago, and if the blood work comes back okay then things are looking pretty good. Alice, you're one lucky lady. The bullet just grazed your descending aorta; a millimeter to the left and we'd be attending your funeral."

Alice opened her hospital gown and analyzed the dressing covering her twelve inch scar. "I guess I'm never going to wear a bikini again."

"Consider yourself lucky to be able to swim again," Sally replied.

Alice demanded the full detailed explanation of what had happened at the Tuttle house. Dan's own recollection was spotty at best, so the story ended with the arrival of the ambulances. Alice reflected on the information. "I never saw her hiding behind the chair. I was looking to the left when I went down."

Alice was silent for a long time. She was thinking how lucky she was to be alive. Like Dan, she was angry at herself for having failed to capture Samantha Johnson, and like Dan, she was processing through all the other scenarios they might have employed with a better outcome. But just like Dan, after analyzing the possibilities, she also concluded Kim Tuttle would have died. She finally looked at Dan. "We did the right thing you know. Any other way and Kim Tuttle would be dead."

Dan answered, "I came to the same conclusion. By the way speaking of Kim Tuttle, how's she doing?"

Sally answered, "She's down the hall. Physically she's doing fine, but emotionally, I'm not so sure. They called in a plastic surgeon to repair her forehead, and the lacerations on her wrists and ankles will eventually heal. Luckily, the bullet just nicked her. I think they'll release her today."

Dan said, "We need to talk to her. We need to find out what really happened at that camp."

Sally answered, "I talked to her last night. She said she wanted to talk to both of you as well. She's got a lot on her mind. She wants to thank you both and confess her sin from ten years ago. I'll set the meeting up after you've both had breakfast."

A few minutes later, two doctors arrived and began talking to Sally. They then introduced themselves as the two surgeons who had repaired their wounds. They each moved to their respective patients. A group of nurses arrived and Dan's surgeon gloved up and began removing the dressings on Dan's right arm. Sally looked over his shoulder. Dan guessed it was a professional courtesy thing.

Dan looked down at the bullet wound and then at the slice that had followed the bullet. Bullet wounds were something Dan was very familiar with; it was the knife wound that surprised him. It looked fine now, but Dan could imagine what his arm had looked like when the doctors had first seen it.

Doctor Smith said, "Dan, if you hadn't put the tourniquet on yourself, you'd be dead now and resting in the morgue."

"Thank you for the pleasant thought Dr. Smith. It was the only thing I could think to do."

"Do you feel any numbness or tingling?"

"Just some local pain over the wound and a slight tingling."

"Well that's to be expected. The tingling is from the nerve endings cut by the knife. I'm afraid you'll be living with the tingling for some time. We're pumping you up with antibiotics. The only risk now is going to be infection, but things look good right now."

"When can I be released?"

"Well normally I would say in another two to three days, but since your wife is going to be your caregiver, and if there's no signs of infection, then I think we can make it happen tomorrow morning. No promises you understand, just a guess."

Doctor Smith then drew a curtain between the two beds and proceeded to remove the urinary catheter from Dan's middle leg. Dan looked down in disbelief as the mile-long plastic tube was withdrawn. The momentary pain was more than offset by the immediate sense of freedom of being removed from that terrible thing. The doctor said, "You'll probably be peeing blood for about a day. That's normal."

Alice's doctor was a bit more conservative, and given the nature of her wound, he stated in no uncertain terms that she would be in the hospital for at least a week. Alice was too tired to argue, and knew her doctor was right.

As both doctors headed out with their nurses, some people brought in their breakfasts. Sally said, "I took the liberty of ordering breakfast for both of you."

As Alice and Dan ate their full trays, Sally nibbled at some of the food on Dan's tray. When Dan complained, she said, "I ordered enough for both of us."

After eating a few muffins and a cup of coffee, Sally retreated to her recliner and began making some calls. The first was to their au pair, and after confirming Debbie was doing fine, she explained Dan's status to Susana and how he might be released tomorrow. Then she called into the emergency room at Northwestern and talked for almost ten minutes to her colleagues who wanted to know how Dan was doing.

After her calls, Sally got up from her chair and headed over to Kim Tuttle's room. Alice looked at Dan. "You're one lucky dude; never let that woman go."

"Alice, if I could get out of bed, I'd give you a great big kiss. We're both lucky to be alive and now we owe it to ourselves to capture that bitch before the trail gets too cold."

Sally returned, "She'll be here in ten minutes. They're going through the discharge papers now."

Alice wanted to borrow Sally's cellphone. "I need to call Bob," she said.

Alice punched in a number she knew by heart. "Bob, it's me. Listen something happened yesterday. I got shot trying to apprehend a suspect."

Silence, then, "No, no, I'm fine, really I am."

Silence again, then, "The hospital's in Rockford; I have no idea where. Wait, I'm going to hand the phone over to Sally Lawson. I've already told you about Sally and Dan. She can tell you where the hospital is."

Alice passed the phone over to Sally. "Hello Bob. Nice to talk to you. Alice is at Rockford Memorial Hospital, It's just west of the Rock River; the address is 2400 North Rockton. It's at the corner of Rockton and Bell."

After a moment of silence Sally said, "She's doing fine and unless she tries to jump back in her car and catch the person who shot her, she'll be just fine. She's no longer in critical condition."

More silence and then, "I'll be here. Dan and Alice are sharing rooms; isn't that romantic."

Sally handed the phone back to Alice. Alice wiped away tears and said, "I love you too Honey. I'll be expecting you."

Alice hung up, and Sally sat down on her bed and gave her a gentle hug and kiss. "He sounds like a wonderful caring person."

The special moment was interrupted by a knock on their door. All three looked up to see a wheelchair being pushed through the doorway and into the room. Kim Monroe, looking in good shape except for a large bandage across her forehead and bandages on her arms and legs, had a smile on her face. A man pushing the wheelchair also seemed extraordinarily happy. It didn't take too much effort to figure out the man was Kim's husband.

Sally backed away to a corner of the room and let Kim move between the two beds. She was clearly struggling with where to start. "This is my husband Luis. I don't know what to say except thank you. I know if you hadn't burst into the room when you did, I would be dead right now. I tried to warn you she was hiding behind the chair, but I couldn't get the words past the duct tape."

Dan answered, "We've been looking for you for the last week. Of course we didn't have much to go on. We finally got your Social Security number at the bank your parents used. We were driving back from Madison when our people found out you were married now and living in Rockford. Sometimes the difference between success and failure is literally seconds."

"Well I'll always remember the sacrifices both of you made in trying to save my life, and Luis and I will always remember both of you."

Alice asked, "Do you feel up to telling us what happened?"

"Yes, now's as good a time as any."

Dan asked Sally to get him his notebook from the personal effects in the closet, and after placing it on a hospital tray in front of him, he waited for Kim Tuttle Monroe to tell her story.

Chapter 46

"I had just returned from the shopping mall over on Leyton Avenue. I was putting away the groceries when the doorbell rang. She had a bouquet of roses in her hand. I didn't think I was in any danger, so I opened the door. She handed me the flowers, and she said I had to sign for them. As soon as I put the flowers down, she had a gun pointed at my head."

Kim Monroe started to cry. At first it was just tears but then she lost control and started to cry. Sally grabbed a box of Kleenex from the nightstand and handed it to her. Dan and Alice just waited patiently for Kim to regain control.

She finally apologized and, after wiping away tears, continued. "She said she had a gift from Samantha Johnson and asked if I remembered the name. I had no idea who that person was. Then she forced me upstairs to my bedroom and hit me over the head with something hard.

"I woke up on my bed. At first I didn't realize I was tied down. Then I tried to scream, but she had put tape over my mouth, and nothing came out of my mouth. Then she asked me again if I knew the name, and I shook my head no. That's when she reminded me of the incident at the camp from ten years ago, and that's when I remembered the name and what we had done.

"I tried breaking free, and then I realized she had taken my clothes off. That's when I knew for sure she was going to kill me. She held a scalpel in front of my face and moved it back and forth. She told me to hold still but I couldn't. I tried again to free myself and moved my head back and forth to avoid that scalpel."

Kim Tuttle started to cry again. She put her hands up to her face and covered her eyes. Luis Monroe asked if she wanted to stop, and she pushed him away. "Luis, I've got to tell this story now."

She looked again at Alice and Dan and then continued. "She got on the bed and positioned my head between her legs. My head was trapped and I couldn't move. Then she started to slowly cut my forehead. The pain was terrible. I've never felt anything so painful in all my life."

Alice asked, "Did she say what she was cutting in your forehead?"

"No, but the surgeon who did the repair said it was the number fourteen. That was the cabin number at the camp where we all spent the summer."

"What happened next," Dan asked.

"I heard this siren in the distance. I think she knew it was the police coming to get her. She looked out the window at the front of the house and then hid behind the chair in the corner of the room. Blood was dripping down my face, into my eyes and my mouth. I saw you both look into the bedroom. I tried to warn you. My God, I tried to warn you; and then you both burst into the room, and she fired twice. The first shot hit you." She pointed to Alice, "And the second shot hit you." She pointed to Dan. "After that it was pretty confusing. She jumped out from behind the chair and slashed at you with this long knife. I've never seen a knife like that."

Dan said, "It's an autopsy knife Kim. Pathologists use it to perform autopsies."

"You fell to the floor and struggled to pick up your gun, but she kicked it away. Then she fired at me, but luckily I turned at the last second and the bullet just cut into my stomach and went into the bed."

What happened next?" Alice asked.

"She had this crazy look in her eyes. Her face was all red and she was screaming."

"What did she say?"

"I remember her exact words. *I did what you said. It's all over now. I did what you said.* Then she ran out of the room. I lost track of time then. Maybe it was five minutes, but it could have been longer or shorter, I don't remember, but the police suddenly came into the room, and then there were medics helping me onto a gurney and putting me in an ambulance. That's when I blacked out. The next thing I remember was a nurse calling my name in the recovery room."

Sally brought some water over to Kim and she gulped it down and asked for more. It took several minutes before Dan dared to ask the critical question. "Kim, I know this is going to be hard for you, but we need to know all about what happened at that camp ten years ago. Some people have told us what they know, but your explanation is the only first-hand account of what really happened. We want to hear every detail of what happened that summer to turn Samantha Johnson into a killer."

"This is going to be really hard to talk about. You see I've suppressed that awful day for all these years. Remembering Samantha Johnson's name finally shocked me into remembering everything again. For years I thought it was just a stupid prank, but now after what happened, I know it was a terrible thing to do, and it was all my idea. My God, in hindsight it was so cruel and bad."

Alice said, "It may have been, but as bad as it was, it was no reason to kill three people."

Kim paused a moment, probably to decide where to begin, and then she stared out the window as she began her story. "From the very beginning, Samantha never fit in. She was a loner; now as an adult I guess you could say she suffered from low self-esteem. Anyway, there were four of us who became friends. Everyone called us The Four Roses because we all lived in the Roses Cabin. We did everything together that summer. You could say we became of age. We all talked about sex and necked in the woods whenever we had dances with the boy's camp on the other side of the lake."

Kim looked at her husband, embarrassed by the story, but he knelt down and kissed her on the cheek and told her to tell everything exactly the way it happened, and whatever she said, he would always love her. Kim began to cry again and finally blew her nose and continued on with the story.

"A week before the end of camp, we saw Samantha disappear into the woods after dinner. She was walking toward a place we called Virgin Rock, and the way she was looking around to see if anyone was watching, we knew she was going to meet someone there. The four of us waited a few minutes and then followed her into the woods. It was still dusk when we reached the make out spot. That's when we saw it."

There was silence until Alice asked Kim, "What did you see?"

Kim finally blurted out, "We saw two women naked. Samantha was lying on her back on the rock and the other woman had her head between Samantha's legs. That's when I had the idea to take a picture with my smartphone. There was just enough light so I didn't have to use the flash. I took a few pictures, and then we snuck back to the campgrounds."

"What happened next?" Dan asked.

"That night we snuck into the office. They always hid the key on a nail above the door. I uploaded the picture to the office computer and added the words *Samantha does it for the first time* at the bottom. Then we made a couple dozen copies of the picture, and taped them to every cabin door.

"We thought it was so funny at the time but now I understand how cruel it was. Oh please God, forgive me for what I've done."

Dan then asked a final question. "Do you know who the other girl was in the picture?"

Samantha looked at Dan and answered, "It was the owner's daughter, Joyce Barker."

Joyce Barker's name came as a total surprise to Dan. Now he understood why she had never mentioned the incident when asked about that summer's unusual activities. He was certain Samantha Johnson wasn't Joyce's only lover, and each summer offered new opportunities for new conquests. God, what a sickening thought.

Everyone was quiet, just thinking about the implications of Kim's story. Finally her husband spoke. "Honey you know I love you. What you did was wrong, but you were only sixteen years old. When I think back to when I was sixteen, I did some really horrible things too. There are three girls dead, but not because of what you did, but because of what Samantha Johnson did. Please never forget, she killed those people, not you."

Luis Monroe knelt down next to his wife and they both cried while they held each other in their arms.

After a few minutes, Sally talked to Kim Tuttle. "Kim, as a physician, let me offer a little medical advice. You're going to be going through some very difficult times in the next few weeks processing what happened to you. You're going to have guilt beyond anything I can imagine. I think you're going to need some help in coping with this. My advice, for what's it worth, is to talk to your family doctor and get a recommendation for a good psychiatrist. They'll be able to help you work things out."

Kim Monroe nodded her head in agreement and thanked Sally for her advice. Dan followed up. "Kim, we may need to talk to you again." He handed her his business card and asked her to call if she needed anything or had any more information to share.

Dan said, "One more thing. I hate to bring this up, but Samantha Johnson may try to kill you again. I would advise moving away for a few weeks until we capture her."

Kim Tuttle was crying again, but Luis answered, "The police already told us the same thing. My friend has a weekend cabin near Galena. We're going to move there until the police tell us it's safe to return."

Luis and Kim Monroe thanked Dan and Alice again and left to return to their house, and Dan hoped Kim Monroe would seek the help Sally recommended.

After they left, Dan said, "Joyce Barker; who would have guessed."

Dan then gave Sally the rundown on their visit to Camp Greenwoods.

Chapter 47

A little after ten o'clock a guy in a three-piece suit knocked on the door. Alice suddenly produced an ear-to ear smile. "Bob, come in."

So this was Bob Winters. He seemed a little out of place, and Dan and Alice sharing a room created a bit of uncertainty. Nonetheless, he walked over to Alice and kissed her passionately on the lips. Next, he introduced himself to Dan and Sally. Sally broke the ice. "That was quite a kiss Bob; I wish Dan could kiss like that."

Everyone laughed and then Bob sat down on the edge of Alice's bed. She slid her gown open and showed him her dressing. So much for modesty. Bob asked the obvious question. "What happened?"

Alice and Dan then provided a twenty minute summary of the case and what had happened at Kim Monroe's house. He just shook his head at the end of the story and said, "God, you're lucky to be alive."

Alice replied with her usual barroom humor. "No shit!"

Bob then turned to Dan and Sally. "I know all about both of you. I feel I've known you both for years. It's great to finally meet you; I only wish it was under more enjoyable circumstances."

Just after his speech Jimmy, Joey, Amy, and Benny entered the room. Jimmy took one look at his best friend and shook his head. Then he turned around and headed to the nurses station where he flashed his FBI credentials and demanded that four chairs be immediately brought into the patient's room. The senior nurse looked at him and saluted. "Yes sir General; are you sure you're not a doctor. You must have trained with doctors because they like to give orders just like that."

Jimmy looked at her nametag and smiled, "I like that Nurse Higgins. I like that. You're a woman after my own heart."

Nurse Higgins complied with Jimmy's request, and four chairs were pushed into the crowded room. Sally, sensing the need for a private meeting said, "Bob, while they talk about the case, why don't you and I get some coffee."

Bob felt relieved and quickly followed Sally out into the hallway and toward the elevators.

Jimmy walked out to the nurse's station and smiled at Nurse Higgins. Holding a twenty dollar bill in his hand he asked nicely. "Nurse Higgins, would it be possible to get some coffee for our meeting?"

Nurse Higgins smiled and said, "Why yes General, there's a communal urn at the end of the hall. Feel free to get it yourself."

Jimmy put away his money and with Amy and Benny in tow, he took orders and returned with coffee for everyone.

Alice and Dan reviewed the case. The newest piece of unexpected evidence was the interview with

Kim Tuttle, and the revelation that Joyce Barker was the other woman in the incident at Virgin Rock.

Joey's comment was the most descriptive. "So now we've got a female pedophile along with a female serial killer. What's this world coming to?"

Amy brought everyone up to speed on what they had found in Samantha Johnson's apartment. The short answer was not very much. The only thing of interest was a few dozen scalpels, several disposable gowns of the type she had used in the three killings, and an unopened roll of grey duct tape. There were the usual bits of cosmetics and other toiletries any woman might have in their bathrooms, and of course as much clothes as she could cram into the few suitcases in the room.

Some cops were working 24/7 in the manager's office, much to the delight of Martha Stewart, just in case Samantha decided to return to the apartment. Forensics had easily pulled enough prints and DNA evidence to be used in any future criminal trial.

"So," Dan said, "Now we're looking for a blond with short hair. We should get the art department to modify her picture to what she probably looks like now."

Benny said, "I'll take care of that when I get back to the office."

Jimmy asked, "I guess the question now is whether she's done killing?"

Dan answered, "I think she's done killing to get revenge, but she could easily kill again in order to escape capture. We're the perfect examples of that."

Joey said, "So let's call this Joyce Barker and see if Samantha Johnson has contacted her for help."

Dan interrupted, "Not so fast. I think we should first get a Search Warrant to look at Barker's phone records. If Johnson contacted her, then we'll know it. I'm betting she's smart enough to have bought a pre-paid cellphone, but even if she's done that, we'll still have a number we can trace."

Jimmy added, "If we can get a cellphone number, then I can get the NSA to track it. Every time she makes a call, we'll know where she is."

Alice asked, "Where will she run? What's her long-term plan?"

The question was one asked by the police and FBI throughout the country every day. The question was easy to ask but hard to answer. Still, there were some general rules most criminals followed as they decided how to avoid capture, and this investigative team was well-versed in all of them.

Most, not all, people who want to hide from the law know enough to move off the grid. They've all seen enough police shows on TV to know using a credit card or bank card is an absolute no no. They need to pay for everything with cash, but most people don't carry an infinite supply of money. So how do they generate income to live on? The answer was simple they needed to find employers who would pay in cash and not ask questions or file IRS or Social Security paperwork.

Chapter 48

Samantha Johnson had been staying at a cheap motel near the University of Wisconsin campus. She had found the place several years ago when she had been trying to locate Kim Tuttle. For $69.95 per night pre-paid in cash, she had a small room and more importantly free access to a computer and the internet in the main lobby.

The call to Joyce Barker had been a total waste of time. She was not interested in helping, let alone providing temporary shelter. Her inner voice had warned her Joyce Barker would never help. What Samantha did learn, however, was the FBI and Chicago Police had been snooping at the camp asking questions. Somehow the FBI had figured out she had been involved in the killings. The take home message was very simple; she would need to be extra cautious if she was going to successfully evade capture.

More disturbing than the call to Joyce Barker was the newspaper accounts of what had happened in Rockford. The Chicago papers had reported on the incident. Somehow the Chicago cop and the FBI agent had survived. Pictures of Samantha Johnson with short blond hair had been on the front page of the Chicago Tribune. There was no mention of Kim Monroe's death, and that was very puzzling. Samantha had checked online for the obituaries in the

Rockford papers, and there was no information on Kim Monroe's death.

What had happened to Kim Monroe? Had she survived? As improbable as it seemed, Sam couldn't discount the possibility; somehow Kim had lived.

Her head began to throb again with the pain always preceding her inner voice. The voice spoke in a slow steady tone. "She's still alive and you need to find her and kill her. Your job's not done until she's dead. You'll never be free until she's gone. Do it; find her and kill her."

Samantha listened and for the first time disagreed with her personal mentor. "She's dead. I think they're just pretending she's not so they can tempt me into trying to kill her again. They've got a trap planned. Even if she's still alive, she's probably under fulltime protection. If she's alive, then she's got the number fourteen cut into her head as a constant reminder of what happened that day."

"You're kidding yourself," the voice said. "All she needs is a good plastic surgeon and the number will only be a fading memory. At least find out if she's alive. You can at least do that."

Samantha thought about the voice's advice. She just might be able to find out if Kim was still alive. She knew where Luis Monroe worked. He was a purchasing agent at the Ford plant just outside of Rockford. She found the telephone number on the internet and called the plant.

A minute later she was talking to someone in the Purchasing Department. "Could I speak to Luis Monroe please?"

The woman on the other end answered, "I'm sorry, but he's on extended leave and can't be reached."

Samantha asked, "Would this have something to do with his wife being attacked?"

"Why do you want to know?"

"I'm a friend of Kim, and I've been trying to reach her, but there's no answer at her house. I heard someone tried to kill her. Do you know if she's okay?"

The woman on the other end finally answered, "She's okay, but she's sort of in protective custody."

"Is there any way I can reach her?"

"I'm sorry but I don't know. I can certainly take a message for Luis if he calls in. Just give me your name and number and I'll pass on the message."

"Thanks, but I'll try reaching her another way. I think I know someone who would know where she's staying. Thanks for the offer though."

Samantha hung up and pounded the desk in her motel room. "She's alive. The bitch still lives, and the cops are protecting her," she screamed at herself.

She cried out in despair and continued to pound on the table until her hands were red and swollen. She finally cleaned herself up in the bathroom and sat back down at the desk in her room.

The mentor in her brain scolded, "I told you she was alive. Now what are you going to do?"

Samantha Johnson pondered the question. Her work wasn't complete, at least not until Kim Monroe was dead; but there was the reality of the police providing protection. How could she ever hope to kill her enemy with the police guarding her?

The solution she suddenly realized was time. Time was on her side. She had been planning for almost a decade; what was another two or three years? The police wouldn't keep her safe forever. Sooner or later they would all forget about Samantha Johnson and go onto other things, and then she could finish the job without interference from the police or FBI.

Samantha smiled to herself. The solution to her problem was obvious; just wait a couple of years. With that settled her problem now turned to avoiding capture by the police. The internet might be able to help.

The motel's lobby was empty and the computer reserved for guests wasn't being used. She sat down at the terminal and started her search by googling *hiding from the police*. Samantha was surprised to find dozens of websites dedicated to the topic. It took her a couple of hours to digest all of the available information, but a plan finally emerged.

First she would need to acquire a new identity. She had no idea of who to talk to, but the websites had offered good advice. She needed to find a way to get to Nogales, Mexico. The websites all identified an area in that city as the best place to buy a new identity. For the most part, people were trying to use false identities to get into the United States, but evidently other types of IDs were easily acquired.

The question of course was how to get to Nogales. She couldn't just drive across the border. The websites indicated people leaving the U.S. for Mexico were rarely checked, but why take a chance. She was certain the FBI was looking for her. Could she sneak across the border? She started another internet search. She went to Google Maps and located Nogales. There were actually two sections to Nogales, the U.S. section and the Mexican section. Getting to the American side of the border wouldn't be a problem.

Samantha studied satellite pictures of the area. A website indicated the routes normally used by illegal immigrants trying to cross the border near Nogales. All of the illegal crossings seemed to concentrate along the border just east of the city. The reason was obvious; the area to the west of the city was mountainous. The Pajarito Mountains ran from north to south.

After studying the maps of the area, Samantha had a plan. She would drive her car to an area about twenty miles west of Nogales, near Peña Blanca Lake. She would hide her car in the heavily wooded area and hike the five miles to the border. The high-tech border fence had not yet reached this area and the border was probably protected by a twenty-foot sheet metal fence. Samantha knew it would be easy to scale with the right equipment.

Samantha Johnson now had a plan. She stopped at a vending machine for a cheap lunch and walked back to her room with a new-found purpose. She found some paper and a pencil in her desk and began writing down everything she would need to reach Nogales.

Chapter 49

Dan rode shotgun as Sally drove them back to Chicago. The doctors had filled his body with enough antibiotics to kill every pathogen known to mankind. They had left Alice with Bob, and Dan promised Alice he would find Samantha Johnson; an easy promise to make but perhaps a difficult one to keep. Joey and Jimmy had been keeping him up to speed on their efforts to find her, but it seemed she had literally fallen off the face of the earth. They were still awaiting the Search Warrant allowing them access to Joyce Barker's phone, and he was hoping Johnson had at least talked to her.

The trip back to their house was made in silence, but when Dan saw his daughter run up to him he broke down in tears. He sat down in a chair in the living room and Susana lifted his little girl onto his lap. She squirmed with delight as he hugged her and kissed her over and over again. Sometimes it takes a near-death experience to realize how good life can be.

Susana had two to take care of after Sally left for the hospital, but she seemed to enjoy her new responsibility. She had become a regular part of the family after only a few months on the job.

With Sally gone, Dan moved to his office and called Jimmy. "I'm back home dude, and life is good. Any news on the Search Warrant?"

"The judge signed it a few hours ago. The BennyMeister is on it now. Knowing Benny, we should have an answer in a few hours. How are you doing?"

"Well, I've had almost as much blood taken for testing as I lost from the wound, but I'm filled up with antibiotics, and Sally says I'll be okay. Listen, when Benny gets his results, give me a call."

"Will do, and make sure you listen to Sally."

Joey was next on the list. After reviewing his and Alice's medical status, Joey called Amy into his office and activated the speakerphone. Amy asked, "How you doing partner?"

After another quick summary of his condition, he asked, "What's new?"

Amy answered, "We've sent out an APB. I've alerted Customs and Border Security in case she tries to leave the country. Yesterday I met with her father and mother separately, and I'm convinced she won't turn to them for help. She burned too many bridges with both of them. Today I'm going to talk to the cleaning crew she worked with at the morgue. One of them may know something. Any suggestions on what else to do?"

It was a good question. Amy was checking the obvious places. Dan thought for a second before he answered. "Benny will have Joyce Barker's phone records in a couple of hours. We'll need to talk to her, not just about Johnson, but then we need to alert the local cops about her possible predatory activities.

"But here's the thing, it sounds like we're dealing with a loner, someone who really hasn't developed any lasting friendships, maybe just acquaintances at work or wherever. She may not have anyone to turn to. We do know she's a meticulous planner. Maybe she figured she'd kill the four women and then just go on with her life, but now she knows we're after her, and we know her name.

"I know I'm just thinking out loud, but my gut tells me she's going to hide on her own. She's going to develop a plan, and then she's going to follow it. Of course she may have figured out Kim Monroe survived and she might try to find her and finish the job, but she's smart, and she must know Kim won't be easy to locate."

Joey said, "One thing about a psychopath on a mission, they don't tend to give up. If I were her, I'd have to finish the job."

Dan answered, "I agree Joey, but she planned these killings for almost ten years. If she analyzes the situation, she'll realize now isn't the right time to try again. It doesn't take a genius to figure out the police can't provide protection for the next five years. If I were her, I'd wait a couple of years and then try again. Time's on her side."

Joey thought about Dan's analysis. "We need to contact the Monroe's and talk to them about the problem. We need to develop a long-term plan for them. We need to get them into the witness protection program. They need to change their names and move to a new location. They need to create a new life, but if we can catch Johnson, all will be well at the Monroe household, so let's figure out how to catch her."

Dan's cellphone interrupted their conversation. It was Jimmy and Benny. Dan had everyone call into Jimmy's teleconference system for a team meeting. Five minutes later, they were all on the call. Benny started, "I've got good news. I got Joyce Barker's phone records and she received a call three days ago from a prepaid cellphone. The call lasted for seventeen minutes."

Jimmy said, "As soon as we're done here, I'm going to call the NSA and get them to put a trace on the phone. I'll follow up with getting the court order."

Joey said, "So we think Samantha Johnson buys a prepaid cellphone and then calls her romantic connection to ask for help. A seventeen minute call means there was an extended conversation, and an extended conversation means Barker may be offering sanctuary. Either way we need to follow up with her."

Dan said, "If we call her to say we know Johnson called her, then she may alert Johnson. Let's call her first to explain we know what happened at Virgin Rock, and ask her if Johnson has been in contact with her. If she is open about getting the call, then we can assume Johnson isn't hiding with her, but if she says she doesn't know anything, then Johnson may very well be hiding up there, and that's worth a trip to check things out. Let's see how she plays it on the call."

Amy said, "Let's call her right now. We'll listen in to the conversation, and we can also record it."

Jimmy and the others agreed, so three minutes later, Joyce Barker's phone was ringing. She answered on the fourth ring.

"Ms. Barker, this is Detective Dan Lawson with the Chicago Police Department. Did I catch you at a good time? I need to ask you a few questions."

"As good a time as any Detective Lawson. What can I do for you?"

"Well, during the course of our investigation, we determined there was an incident at your camp that summer."

"What was that detective?"

"It seems that there were four very close friends at the camp. They were known as The Four Roses. It seems they took a picture of you and Samantha Johnson at Virgin Rock. Both of you were nude and having sex."

Dan paused for effect. He wanted to gauge Joyce Barker's reaction. He wished he could see her face, but her long silence left little doubt as to her reaction.

Barker finally replied, "That was a long time ago detective almost ten years ago. What does it have to do with your case?"

"Well it seems Samantha Johnson was devastated when pictures of both of you in a compromising position were placed all around the camp. It seems she planned her revenge for all these years and finally began to act. She killed three of The Four Roses, and escaped capture while trying to kill the fourth woman. Now we're trying to locate her, and I'm calling to see if you might know her whereabouts."

"I have no idea where she might be detective."

"Ms. Barker, we're talking about a woman who killed three women whose only crime was pulling a stupid teenage prank ten years ago. I'd like to remind you at the time of the incident at Virgin Rock, Samantha Johnson was under age, and since you were of legal age, you may have been guilty of a crime. Also, aiding a person wanted in connection with a felony is also a crime, so are you sure you have no idea where Johnson might be hiding?"

There was once again prolonged silence. Dan could almost see the tears running down Joyce Barker's face. She knew her days as a sexual predator were numbered. Cooperating with the police, however, might help her future prospects with the local police. "Detective, she called me three days ago. She never told me what happened, but I knew because of what you had told me. I guess I should have suspected she was the killer of those two girls when you were up here, but I just couldn't believe someone would kill another person over what happened that day."

"What did you talk about?"

"We talked about twenty minutes. We hadn't talked for ten years. She said she needed a place to stay for a few weeks and wanted my help. I told her about your visit, and she finally admitted to killing the girls. She tried to convince me it was justified; she told me they deserved it; it was justice served.

"I listened to her hateful words, and finally told her I was sorry but I couldn't help. She became angry, and said she still loved me. I tried to explain what we had together wasn't love but only a romantic friendship. She started screaming at me, and that's when I hung up."

"Did she say where she was going to go?"

"No, she never shared her plans with me except to ask for my help. What are you going to do detective?"

"We're going to find her, that's what we're going to do."

"No detective, I meant what are you going to do about me?"

"I'm going to have a talk with your local law enforcement officials, and after we capture Samantha Johnson, we're going to ask you to testify at her trial."

After another long pause, she said, "I'll be happy to testify detective."

The call ended and Joey said, "It always amazes me how some criminals are always willing to help the police after they've been caught. Nothing like saving their own asses I guess."

"I don't think she's hiding up there," Amy said. "When confronted with the facts, I think she told us everything."

"I agree," Dan said, "But when we talk to the local police, we should ask them to keep an eye out for her just the same."

Jimmy said, "I'll take care of that, and I think I'll send one of our agents up there to check things out."

Joey could have sent a cop up there to do the same thing, but he knew a visit from the FBI would carry more weight than a call from the Chicago Police.

Chapter 50

It had taken almost two days of planning and a trip to the local sporting goods store specializing in camping and hiking supplies, but Samantha was now ready to begin her journey to freedom and a new life. She had bought a red wig with long curly hair and dark sunglasses. Both items had completely changed her look.

She left the hotel in the early morning and headed south on Interstate 90. At St. Louis she transferred onto Interstate 44 and spent the first night in an out of the way cheap motel near Tulsa. The next day she transferred onto Interstate 40 and headed west to Albuquerque. She spent the second night in another cheap motel, a place looking like the Bates Motel in Psycho.

She finally reached Tucson just in time for lunch at a McDonald's the next day. From there she took Interstate 19 south to Route 289 just north of Nogales and turned off onto Ruby Road, an asphalt poorly maintained road winding its way into the Pajarito Mountains. When her GPS showed the road had reached its southern-most point, Samantha began looking for a place to hide her car.

She found an old dirt road leading south toward the border. She turned her car onto the weed-infested dirt trail and slowed to five miles per hour.

The car's suspension system was tasked to the limit, but she only needed to get a few more miles out of her thirteen year-old car. A ten minute bouncing ride brought her into a clearing with a dilapidated old log cabin. The place looked like it hadn't been lived in or used for decades. It was the perfect place to spend the night and hide her car from the police or border patrol.

Samantha eased the car into a cropping of dense trees where it would be hidden from sight. She gathered her belongings and locked the car. Samantha looked at the car keys in her hand and toyed with the idea of just keeping the keys in case she decided to change her mind. Smiling to nobody in particular, she tossed the keys into the woods. There would be no turning back.

The inside of the cabin provided nothing more than protection from the elements, and the cloud of dust swirling in the one-room cabin testified to the lack of use over the years. The smell in the place was overpowering. Hundreds of dead animals had probably lived and died right under the floorboards, and she quickly determined she would set up her tent out in the clearing and only move into the cabin if the weather turned nasty.

Samantha struggled setting up the small one-man bright yellow tent. The directions written in broken English hinted at a foreign manufacturer. Finally it was up and anchored firmly to the ground.

The sales clerk at Gander Mountain had been quite helpful in filling her backpack with everything she would need for a one-week journey. She had been smart to buy some extra food at her last stop for lunch, and she sat on top of her rolled up sleeping bag casually munching on two cold Quarter

Pounders and fries; not very appetizing, but certainly filling. As dusk settled over the woods, Samantha decided to light a campfire. There was an ample supply of dead tree limbs lying around to keep the fire going for hours. Sitting by a campfire was the only good thing she remembered about her summer at Camp Greenwoods.

The smell and popping sounds of the burning wood were comforting, and she stared into the fire, mesmerized by the bright-yellow flames. She had come so close to total success. Three women had been killed and a fourth wounded, but the one failure weighed heavily on her mind. She had reviewed the day at the Monroe house over and over again in her mind. She should have just sliced the bitch open immediately after she had heard the message on the answering machine. In hindsight she had made a bad decision.

She rationalized her failure by convincing herself that Kim Tuttle Monroe would be suffering mental anguish, always looking over her shoulder for a second attack. Yes, Samantha Johnson was still in control, still in control of Kim Monroe's life. She, Samantha Johnson, would decide the time and place of the next and final attack, and right now that attack would have to wait for a few more years.

Chapter 51

Samantha unzipped the tent's entrance and peered out into the early morning light. An early morning fog hugged the ground in the clearing. Above the blanket of fog, long sunrise shadows cast an eerie feeling over the clearing. A young rabbit stared back at Sam from the edge of the clearing and then darted for safety in the woods.

After ensuring the fire's glowing embers were buried in dirt, she ate two high-energy protein bars and packed the tent and her other belongings into her backpack. When filled, the nylon backpack weighed more than fifty pounds. It was difficult to lift, and it took her more than ten minutes to adjust all of the straps to properly position the load resting on her back.

With a portable GPS in her hand, she was ready to go. She turned on the navigation system and after locating the navigation satellites overhead, the GPS system showed her location in full color on the small screen. She needed to move directly south from her present position, and with a compass as a guide, she set off on her journey to freedom.

There was no road, only animal paths crossing through the woods in no clear pattern. She walked through the forest on a carpet of fallen leaves built up from hundreds of changing seasons.

Small animals stared at her, never having seen a human before. Snakes slithered away as she advanced slowly through the forest. She looked at her watch. At her present pace, she wouldn't reach the border until noon, but it didn't really matter; her goal for the day was to just climb the fence and spend the night in Mexico.

After an hour of walking, she stopped by a large rock and released her backpack. She sat on the rock and turned on her GPS device. She was definitely making progress, just not as much as she would have liked. She downed a bottle of water. She had packed twenty bottles. The sales clerk had warned her to drink at least four bottles each day. The bottle label indicated 500 milliliters. Sam remembered from physics classes that half a liter was almost equal to one pound, so the good news was the backpack would now weigh one pound less than before.

A ten minute break was all she needed. She started out again. The rest had felt good. She wondered how soldiers managed to carry their fifty pound loads for a full day's hike. About a mile into her walk the woods began to thin and soon she was walking down a hill into a barren valley running north and south between two mountains.

Sam had chosen this location carefully. The mountains were not too steep and the valleys were mostly running in the right direction. She followed an animal path and made good time. She stopped for a rest after another hour of walking and just collapsed along the dirt path. Her GPS showed she had made excellent progress. She estimated she might reach the border in another hour. This time she rested for a full half-hour. No need to push it. She had plenty of time.

Her backpack was harder to lift this time, but she finally secured it to her back and continued on along the dirt path. Forty minutes later she could see a sign of civilization in the distance. She approached the area cautiously. She had read articles on the internet about sensors and other high-tech devices designed to pick up illegal immigrants who were crossing the border.

She took out a pair of binoculars and studied the border crossing. A sheet-metal fence had been built in this area. It looked just like the pictures she had seen. It was about twenty feet in height, and the top was covered in razor-sharp concertina wire. Sam smiled after studying the fence. She would definitely be able to scale the barrier. She had brought the right equipment for the job.

Looking through her binoculars, she followed the fence to the west and everything looked deserted. She brought the binoculars back to the east and followed the fence to the horizon. A sudden brief flash of light in the sky above the fence caught her attention. The sun had reflected off of something. Sam followed a grey speck in the sky as it moved in her direction above the fence. She was certain it was a pilotless drone searching the area for illegal immigrants.

She needed to hide before the slow-moving aircraft reached her. Looking around for someplace to hide, she spotted a large rock halfway up a hill on her left. She picked up her backpack and ran toward the safety of the rock. She hid behind the huge boulder, forcing her body as close to the ground as she could get. She was so focused on the drone she almost missed the unmistakable sound of a rattle-snake hiding in the shade of the rock near where she was lying. Should she move? Too late now; if she moved now, she would surely be spotted by the drone.

She stared at the snake and decided not to move. If she could appear non-threatening to the snake, it might not attack. She didn't want to die in this God forsaken spot, and if the snake bit her, she knew it would only be a matter of time before she died. The snake was coiled, ready to attack, but the rattler finally stopped shaking and the snake, although still coiled, became less aggressive.

Sam snuck a peek at the drone now almost directly overhead. She had been lucky to spot the surveillance aircraft. If she hadn't seen the flash of sunlight reflecting off the drone, she would have surely been spotted climbing over the fence.

The drone finally flew further west and Sam moved slowly away from the threat of the snake. Five minutes later the drone disappeared over the horizon. It seemed obvious the drone was following the fence as it flew westward. Sam had no idea when or if it might return to this remote section of the border, but she figured she had at least an hour to get over the fence and move out of the drone's coverage area.

She moved slowly away from the rock, dragging her back pack along the ground, and cautiously advanced the last two-hundred yards to the fence. Opening her back pack, she pulled out a nylon rope with a grappling hook tied to the end. She gathered the rope into a coil and threw the metal hook over the fence. The hook caught in the concertina wire and held firmly as Samantha pulled against the rope. She tied off her backpack to the free end of the rope and removed a metal wire cutter from the bag. After a final check of the bag, she began climbing up the rope. The rope had been designed with loops every two feet to assist a climber in their assault of a mountain, but the concept worked equally as well for scaling a border fence.

In no time at all, Sam had reached the top of the fence and began cutting away the razor-sharp concertina wire. It took another five minutes to remove a large enough section of wire to allow her to straddle the fence without being cut. She hoisted her backpack, one foot at a time until it rested on the top of the fence. After resting for a few minutes, and keeping an eye out for the drone's return, she lowered the backpack to the Mexican side of the border.

Carefully, she climbed down the rope and jumped the last three feet to safety. She had done it. She had reached Mexico without being captured. She rested on the ground, exhausted from her efforts. She untied her backpack from the rope and decided to leave the rope at the fence. Maybe a person trying to reach America could use it to scale the border fence.

Although she was tired, she knew she had to move further away from the fence and to the protection of the hills to the south before she could rest for the night. With a smile on her face she lifted the slightly lightened backpack onto her back and walked away from the fence with a renewed source of strength.

Chapter 52

Her first night in Mexico was spent on a hill about a mile away from the border. Sam set up camp with a sense of pride at having been able to come this far without being caught. She knew it was all about planning. The better the plan, the better the results.

After setting up her tent in half the time it took the first night, she sat on her sleeping bag eating one of those high-tech dehydrated delights; just add water and mix and it's ready to devour. Actually the spaghetti with meat sauce was pretty good after Sam heated it up on the miniature butane powered lightweight portable stove. Two Hostess Cup Cakes were more than enough for dessert.

Sam studied her position on the GPS. If she traveled southeast, she would reach a road in three miles. That might lead to a ride into Nogales, but the risks were too great. A young girl speaking English traveling alone might be a recipe for disaster; some horny male or worse yet some cops who might wonder what she was doing out in the countryside.

The alternative was to head due east and walk the twenty miles into Nogales. That meant much less risk, and above all, Sam wanted to minimize risks.

Sam was basically a city girl, and with no lights to interfere with her view of the sky, she could see more stars than she thought could possibly exist. She dreamed of better days ahead, and even though she couldn't plan ahead for every contingency, she was confident in the future.

Exhausted beyond any workout in the local gym, she moved her sleeping bag inside her tent and zipped up the flap. She fell asleep in solitude, believing in the prospects for a bright future and then ultimate revenge exacted upon the last of The Four Roses.

Chapter 53

By the time Sam woke up, the sun was already high in the sky. Her body ached from the physical efforts of the last day. She decided to dine on a ready to eat breakfast of sausage and eggs. After adding water and heating the slop, it looked terrible but tasted pretty good. She washed it down with a small container of orange juice and then cleaned the campsite.

She was all packed up and ready to go by nine o'clock. Her earlier review of satellite images indicated rather flat terrain ahead, but it was still twenty miles to Nogales. She knew she could easily walk a mile in twenty minutes as long as the land was flat, but getting into Nogales at dusk might be a problem. She decided on walking about eighteen miles. That would put her just outside Nogales by three o'clock. There was a small unpopulated area on a hill just to the west of the city and it would be a good place to rest for the night. Then she could arrive in Nogales early the next morning and have all day to find a cheap place to stay in the city.

By noon her feet were killing her. She stopped for lunch in a small grove of trees with a trickling stream running nearby and took off her shoes. Her feet were swollen from the walking and she couldn't resist sitting on a rock and soaking her feet in the cool water.

After lunch she again headed east, and began to see people and cars moving on a road just ahead. Her GPS indicated it was a fairly major road running into Nogales. She stopped and took out her binoculars and studied the roadway and local traffic. Should she hitch a ride into town? Definitely not, but she would have to cross the heavily trafficked road, and she wanted to do it without being seen.

A lightly wooded area off to her right offered protection on both sides of the road. It was a little out of her way, but the protection it afforded was well worth the extra distance to avoid any risk of being spotted. She changed direction and began walking parallel to the road, still out of sight of anyone riding along the highway. At a point just west of the wooded area she turned left and reached the woods about a half-mile from the highway. She moved slowly to the edge of the road and watched the highway, waiting for a break in traffic.

It took almost ten minutes of waiting before the highway was clear of cars. Sam did a final check in both directions and then scooted across the road and into the woods on the other side of the road. She quickly disappeared into the forest and then rested on a rock near the edge of a ravine.

She was studying her GPS when a voice in heavily accented English asked, "Who are you running from?"

Startled, Sam turned toward the voice and saw a young man in his late teens standing against a tree only ten feet from her. How could she not have seen him? "I'm not running from anyone," she said, "I'm just walking into town."

"You're running; I can tell from the way you crossed the road. You waited until all the cars were gone. You wouldn't have done that unless you were on the run."

Sam didn't answer his question. Instead she demanded, "What are you doing here?"

The guy laughed and said, "I got in a fight and accidently killed someone. The Federales are looking for me. My friends told me to hide out here. They bring me food every couple of days."

Samantha Johnson was suddenly faced with a difficult choice. The kid didn't seem like a threat, but he had just killed someone, so he was by no means as innocent as he looked. She could try to just leave and continue on her journey, but he might also be able to offer some assistance. She made a quick decision. She took her backpack off and placed it next to her. She reached into her bag for two power-bars and also moved her gun to within easy reach.

She offered him a place next to her on the rock and held out one of the bars to her new-found friend. He eagerly jumped at the chance for an unexpected meal and sat down next to her. They both ate their bars in silence and then Samantha asked, "I'm looking for a cheap place to stay in Nogales, someplace in the Centro section."

"So you're looking for drugs is it? I knew it had to be something like that."

"Is that a bad part of the city?"

"Si señorita; It is very bad; not a safe place for a young pretty girl like you. The Embarcadero section is much nicer."

"I'm not looking for nice; I'm looking for cheap; someplace I can pay for in cash, and I don't have a lot of money."

"I know a place on the Calle Triumfo. You can get a room there for the night for twenty dollars."

Sam thought about whether she could trust this kid. After all, she would have to trust someone, and this guy had already admitted to being on the run. She thought about the possibility and reached into her backpack for two bottles of water. She handed one bottle to her possible friend. "What's your name?" she asked.

"Jesus Gutiérrez," he answered.

"I'm Samantha Johnson, but my friends call me Sam."

They shook hands and Sam considered her next words carefully. "Maybe you can help me. You see I need to change my identity. I need a new passport and a driver's license. When I get to Nogales, I'm not going to need this backpack. I've got a tent inside and some food. If you can help me find someone who can get me a new passport, I'll give you all the stuff in here."

"Including the gun?" he asked. "I saw the gun when you took out the water."

"No, the gun's mine to keep, but you can have most of the other things."

The kid thought for a few seconds. My friends are going to come here tonight to give me food. They could take you to a person I know who could help you, but he's going to charge you a lot of money."

"How much money?"

"I don't know; several thousand dollars American for sure, but he's good, the best, and he has connections for someone trying to hide from the law. But there's one more thing."

"What's that?"

"I'll need to see the tent being set up, and then you and I need to use the tent for a little fun."

Samantha looked at the sneer on his face and knew what a little fun meant. She considered the possibilities. Trading a little sex for getting to the right person was certainly worth the risk. She looked again at Jesus. The kid probably had never been with a girl before. It might be over almost before it started. Then again, she had never been with a man. Was this the way she wanted to lose her virginity? She made her decision.

She reached over and gave Jesus a passionate kiss; one he would probably remember for the rest of his life. He had a smile on his face as he helped her remove the tent from the backpack. She showed him how to set it up, and then he watched her take off her clothes and make a place for both of them inside the tent. The young boy, realizing he was going to hit a homerun out of the ballpark, quickly took off his clothes and jumped on top of her.

Sam pushed him on his side and said, "Slowly, it will be more fun if we do it slowly."

Jesus nodded and kissed her tentatively on her left breast. Sam reached down between his legs and found him more than ready. It was all over in five minutes. Jesus lay on his back with a broad smile on his face. Samantha trying to build his already swollen ego said, "You're very good; you must have had many women?"

Of course she knew this was probably his first time but she needed his help, and she knew a little flattery might get her all the help she needed.

After Jesus recovered, they both went through Sam's backpack and created two piles; his and hers. Jesus didn't need any of her clothes and other personal items, so he let Sam keep the backpack. He tried to convince her to let him have the gun, but Samantha was insistent on keeping it.

Sitting in the tent, Jesus asked, "What did you do to make you run?"

Samantha answered, "I don't want to talk about it."

"You killed someone didn't you? You've got the gun, and I bet you know how to use it."

Samantha provided an answer without admitting anything. "Jesus, let's just say I know how to use a gun."

Her cold hard stare into Jesus's eyes ended the questioning.

Chapter 54

Samantha and Jesus moved back to the edge of the road by a clearing in the woods a little after eight o'clock. A car approached from Nogales and flashed its lights. Jesus stepped out into the road and flagged down the car. The beat up old Chevy pickup pulled off the road into the woods and turned off its lights. Jesus swaggered up to the driver's side and began talking in rapid-fire Spanish. Laughs followed his tale of the unexpected arrival of Samantha and his sexual conquest.

As Jesus's friends unloaded the pickup truck and carried the food supplies into the woods, Jesus led the group to his newly acquired tent. He spoke to Sam as his friends looked around the new campsite. Andrés is the leader of our gang. He'll bring you to the boarding house I talked about and tomorrow he'll introduce you to the guy who can help you. I'll always remember this day Sam, and I wish you good luck. If you need anything else, Andrés will tell you how to reach us."

Jesus pulled Sam into his arms and kissed her passionately on the lips as his friends whistled in the background. Sam picked up her backpack and followed Jesus's friends back to the car. Andrés had her sit in the front seat with her backpack while his two other friends climbed into the cargo area in the back.

Samantha Johnson waved goodbye to Jesus as the car pulled onto the highway and headed into town. The drive took only ten minutes and during the ride, Andrés told Samantha how Jesus had become a local hero by killing a rival gang's leader. He thought the Federales would stop looking for Jesus in another week, and once they tired of the pursuit, he could return to the city.

As they entered the city of Nogales, the narrow streets were crowded with people. Without many air-conditioned homes, most people escaped the heat by walking the neighborhood after dinner. Within minutes Sam was lost. Without her GPS turned on, she had no idea where they were. She finally noticed a street sign indicating they were on Calle Triumfo, and a few minutes later the car pulled up to a rundown building with a sign in Spanish indicating they had arrived at the Hacienda Triumfo. Samantha knew enough Spanish to know this was no Hacienda, but another sign in English indicated *Rooms to Rent, $20.00 per night.* Samantha pulled her backpack out of the Chevy and thanked Andrés for his help.

"I'll pick you up at ten o'clock tomorrow," he said.

Sam waved goodbye to the boys in the back and walked inside her new temporary home. A middle-aged man in an orange wife-beater sat on a stool at the front desk and looked at her in surprise. "Good evening Señorita; what can I do for you tonight?"

"I'd like a room?"

"For how many nights?"

"I'm not sure yet. It could be for several days. I'll know more tomorrow."

The manager looked at a board on the wall behind his desk. It was filled with keys. Samantha guessed it reflected an empty Hacienda Triumfo. He reached for a key and suddenly changed his mind and reached for another. "Since you might be staying for a while, I've given you a room with a balcony overlooking the street. It's the best room in the house. That will be $20.00 in advance."

Samantha took out a twenty dollar bill she had earlier moved to her pocket and handed it to the manager. In exchange, he handed her a key to room 201 and explained the elevator was broken, but the stairs were just past the elevator.

Samantha lifted her lightened backpack and found the stairs. A broken elevator seemed an exaggeration. It looked like it hadn't been used in years and had a layer of dust reinforcing her belief. She found her room on the second floor. It was a corner room and actually might have been one of the nicer ones, but nicer was definitely a relative term because the small hot room consisted of the bare minimum: a small bed with an old dirty ceiling fan overhead, a broken dresser for her clothes, an even smaller bathroom with a metal enclosed shower, and a table with one chair. The one saving grace was indeed a balcony overlooking the crowded noisy street.

Samantha unpacked her clothes and then took a shower. Even with the cold water faucet turned off, the water was only just warm, but the water still felt wonderful as she unwrapped a small bar of soap and cleaned three-days' worth of grime from her body. There wasn't any shampoo, so she used the soap to wash her hair. She dried off with a small white towel and dressed in clean jeans and a fresh white blouse.

She stuck her cashier's check along with most of her money in her shoes and kept one-hundred dollars in her pocket. It was after ten o'clock, but Sam was hungry and needed some food. She asked the manager for a recommendation. He directed her to a restaurant across the street and told her to tell them Alec told her to come there. Samantha wasn't sure whether he would get a kick-back or if mentioning his name might actually bring improved service or a lower price.

The café was almost empty. It was long past the dinner hour. She mentioned Alec's name to the woman who greeted her in broken English. "How's my brother tonight?" she asked.

"I think he's doing well. I'm staying at his hotel."

Sam was handed an English menu and she ordered Carne Asada. The skirt-steak with a side of black beans and rice delivered ten minutes later was delicious, and an hour later Sam was back in her room sitting on the balcony watching the still busy street. She reviewed the last few days in her head and realized how lucky she had been to evade capture crossing the border and to run into Jesus. Just after midnight, Sam collapsed onto her spongy bed and immediately fell asleep.

Chapter 55

After a quick breakfast at an outdoor café at the end of the street, Sam waited in front of the hotel for the arrival of Andrés. His Chevy pickup pulled up to the curb a few minutes after ten o'clock. The previous night it had been too dark to see the color of the car, but this morning the predominant color was rust, not the color, just rust. At one time the color could have been a dark blue, but that might have been twenty years ago. The original color had faded, and now the truck was clearly showing its age.

Andrés, who was alone, opened the passenger door to let her in. "Señorita Johnson, I hope you found your accommodations acceptable."

"I did Andrés, thank you for asking."

As Andrés drove east toward the Centro section of the city, Sam asked him, "What is the name of the person you're taking me to see?"

"I don't know his name. I only know his place of business. What I can tell you is he's the best in all of Mexico at what he does."

It wasn't so much the traffic as the human congestion along the narrow streets, but after crossing the main north/south road running through town, it took almost an hour to travel about three miles to an up-scale section of Nogales. Andrés parked alongside a fire hydrant and led Sam up to a gated courtyard. He rang a doorbell. A man spoke in rapid Spanish and Andrés spent a considerable length of time replying.

Finally a buzzer sounded and Andrés led Sam through the unlocked gate and into a spacious courtyard covered in a variety of beautiful flowers and potted plants. A fiftyish man emerged from a door on the opposite side of the courtyard and studied Sam with a cautious eye as he approached. He shook her hand and then spoke in perfect English. "Señorita, welcome to my humble abode. Andrés tells me you have need of my services."

"Yes, I'm looking to purchase a new identity: a new passport and other identification papers."

"Well you've come to the proper place. You might say I am an expert in these matters."

The man spoke to Andrés in Spanish. Andrés shook Sam's hand and handed her a card with a telephone number. "Call me Señorita if you need anything."

After Andrés left, the mysterious man escorted her through the door from which he had emerged. He asked her to sit down in a beautiful sitting area in a large room, probably his office.

"Would you like a coffee?" he asked.

Sam nodded yes.

"Good, I have this new Nespresso machine and it makes a wonderful cappuccino."

Samantha studied the man as he prepared their drinks. He wasn't handsome by any means, but he was well dressed. He looked exotic, and his features hinted at a strong Spanish heritage.

Five minutes later they were sitting down with their coffees. "Two things you need to understand Señorita, if I agree to help you, you must tell me everything about why you need a new identity. Also, you need to understand my services do not come cheap. But first you need to answer a question. Are you in anyway affiliated with the FBI, the police, or any other government agency?"

"No, why ask me that?"

"Because if you're lying and then I get arrested I can't be found guilty because it's entrapment."

"So now that I've answered your question, how much are we talking about?"

"Well that depends, but you can figure on about $10,000."

"That won't be a problem. I have a cashier's check that will cover that amount."

"A cashier's check isn't a problem. I have a friend at the local bank. He can cash it for you, and the authorities will not be able to trace it back to me. So now you must tell me your story."

"What is your name?"

"You can call me Roberto. That's all you need to know."

"Roberto, I killed some bad people in the United States and the authorities are looking for me."

"The police or the FBI?"

"Both."

"How were you able to get across the border without being stopped?"

Samantha then spent about half an hour explaining how she had escaped capture. Roberto listened with a smile on his face to her story. "Very ingenious Samantha. You were lucky to run into Jesus and Andrés. They're young men of the street. They know all of the players in anything illegal. So if I understand your plight correctly, you need two things I can provide. One is a new identity and the other is a place to go where you can live a new life without the fear of being caught."

Sam answered, "Yes, and I need a job to provide an income to live on."

"Yes, of course. You want to be able to blend in with the local population. That can be a problem for an English speaking woman in Mexico or South America. Tell me, do you speak any foreign languages?"

"I took French in high school. I'm not fluent but with some practice, I can get by."

"So that leaves only a few islands in the Caribbean like Martinique, Guadeloupe, and French Guiana, but the problem with these places is the FBI has good connections there, and they're really not good places to blend into the local population. People in those places tend to ask questions. Have you thought about going to Europe?"

Samantha thought about Europe. It had never occurred to her, but Europe might be an excellent place to live. She was impressed with Roberto's understanding of the possibilities. "Roberto, Europe sounds like a wonderful place to live. I never thought of Europe. Can you really make that happen?"

Roberto smiled at her. Señorita, I have connections in most countries, but Europe will cost you a little more than $10,000; I'll have more paperwork to do to ensure your success."

"How much more?"

"Roberto thought a moment. "Normally I would charge another $10,000, but I like your entrepreneurial spirit, and I want to help you, so I'll set everything up for a total of $15,000."

Sam considered her options. Fifteen-thousand dollars would deplete much of her resources, but what else could she do. She could seek out a cheaper person, but how would she find that person, and every new contact ran the risk of calling attention to her and possible arrest by the police. She looked Roberto in the eyes and held out her hand. "Fifteen-thousand dollars it is."

Roberto laughed and they shook hands. "So now young lady, we need to take a trip to my bank to cash your check and make other arrangements."

"Can I make use of your bathroom first?"

Roberto led her out of his office and into a hallway lined with beautiful works of art. It was obvious; Roberto was a man of considerable wealth.

Samantha removed her cashier's check from her shoe, used the facilities which were considerably better than what her hotel room had to offer, and returned to Roberto's office. She handed him the check. "Ah," he said, "I think if Europe is you destination, then if you wish, we'll set up a numbered account in a bank I use in Geneva for the extra money in the check. It will be safer than carrying cash around."

"How do I know you won't steal the money?"

Roberto laughed, "Because if I do, you'll turn me into the police. You might say we have a mutual need to trust each other."

Roberto reached in his desk for a camera and took several pictures of Samantha as she sat in front of the office's white wall.

Chapter 56

Roberto escorted Samantha down the street to a small bank on the next block. He was greeted at the door by a guard and immediately ushered into a small office in the back of the bank.

An elderly man with a prominent grey mustache stood up from his chair and embraced Roberto. Roberto said, "Samantha, this is my Uncle Manuel. He can help us."

They all sat down and Roberto explained in Spanish what needed to be done. He handed his uncle the cashier's check. Manuel studied the check and then entered his computer and printed a number of forms. He filled them out and asked Samantha to sign at the bottom of each form. He entered his computer again and after a few minutes spoke to Roberto in Spanish. "Samantha, he cashed the check and entered the amount into a house account. He then transferred $15,000 into my account and is now going to set up your account in the Geneva bank we use.

Uncle Manuel spent another ten minutes on his computer and then spoke to Roberto in Spanish. Roberto translated. "He now wants you to enter a password on his computer. We won't watch you do it, but remember, if you forget the password, the money will be lost forever."

Sam walked behind the desk while Manuel sat down next to Roberto. "Can I use letters or numbers?"

Roberto translated and after Manuel answered, Roberto translated again. "He says you can use letters or numbers and the password isn't case sensitive, but the password needs to be at least ten characters."

Samantha thought about ten characters she could easily remember. She smiled and then entered *thefourroses*. She knew she could easily remember the twelve characters. She entered the new password a second time and then hit enter.

"Remember," Roberto said, "never tell anyone the password because anyone with the password can gain access to your money."

"What bank is this?" Sam asked.

Roberto answered, "It's United Bank of Switzerland. They have offices in Basel and Zürich. I recommend the Zürich office and you should ask for Herr Fredrick Blummen. He's my contact there. You can mention my name."

With their business completed, Roberto insisted on buying Sam lunch. She thanked Uncle Manuel, and they then walked a few blocks to a small plaza where a number of restaurants were located. As Roberto approached a restaurant with a nice outdoor seating area, the maître d bowed in respect and quickly ushered them to the best table.

Roberto said, "This is one of the very special restaurants in Nogales. They specialize in fresh seafood. I think you'll enjoy it."

After ordering the special of the day, fresh Red Snapper, and a bottle of a Pinot Grigio, Roberto asked, "Have you been using any credit cards?"

"Not for the last week."

"Good never use credit cards again. If anyone asks you why, tell them you spent too much when you had one. Do you have a cellphone?"

"I threw away my cellphone and bought a prepaid phone."

"That's good. When you get to Europe you can get a new cellphone with your new identity."

Sam asked, "How long will it take to get my new identity?"

"Two days unless I run into problems."

"How does the process work? Why won't immigration people be suspicious?"

"Good questions. I won't tell you everything, but I have a collection of valid passports taken from people in long-term care facilities. My contacts at these places find people who, because of their illnesses, will probably never travel again. I take your picture to a contact of mine. He searches all the passports and picks one with a picture close to yours. Then we'll make you look like the person: maybe a wig, maybe some glasses, just enough to make you pretty close to the person.

Then we renew your passport at a place with one day service. I have a contact there who does the paperwork. He sends the passport back to me by FedEx, and that's all there is to it. The driver's license and Social Security card are simple compared to the passport. Those three IDs are all you'll need.

The only risk you have is if the real person dies and if that happens, we'll contact you and give you a new identity, but don't worry, it's only happened once in the last ten years."

"Roberto, you seem to have thought of everything."

"I have. By the way, where are you staying?"

"The Hacienda Triumfo."

"A good choice; it's a dump but they don't ask questions and you can pay with cash."

The waiter arrived with a whole Red Snapper and filleted it at their table. The fish tasted wonderful. It was in fact the best meal Sam had in several years. After lunch, Roberto left Samantha. He asked her to come back at four o'clock. He handed her a business card with his first name and the address of his office. "You can catch a cab at the corner. Don't do anything to get yourself in trouble."

Sam thanked him for all his help and the lunch, and then walked to the corner to pick up a taxi. She arrived back at the hotel, and after spending a few minutes in her room, walked downstairs and asked the manager where she could go shopping for some new clothes and other items. He handed her a walking map of the city and circled a section for shopping.

Chapter 57

The walk through the city was delightful. A cool afternoon breeze pushed the warm air to the east. Storm clouds appeared in the west, and Sam guessed the cool air was an advanced warning of an upcoming afternoon shower. She just made it to the shopping district before a light drizzle began falling from the sky. She ducked into a café and ordered a coffee. She sat at a table by the window and watched people without umbrellas running for cover. The few people who had umbrellas took their time walking down the street.

Sam thought about a new life in Europe. She would have to practice her French, but getting a small apartment in Paris or another French city seemed almost too much to ask for. Roberto clearly knew his stuff. She only hoped this wasn't some exotic scam; she was at his mercy and Roberto knew it. She'd be able to tell more when she met with him again.

Her attention now turned to preparing for her trip to Europe. She needed to buy some things to allow her to blend in with the tourists. Buying more things would have to wait till she arrived in her new home, but at least she needed some new clothes and certainly a new suitcase.

The rain stopped and Sam continued on her walk through the shopping district. She decided to save the purchase of a suitcase as the last item. She found a four-story department store, apparently one of the tallest buildings in Nogales and put on her best shopping face. It had been years since she had the money or the urge to buy new clothes, but circumstances had blessed her with this golden opportunity.

A $50,000 inheritance from her grandmother had been a Godsend. Her grandmother had been the only person who had ever loved her with no strings attached. The concept of unconditional love was something totally foreign to Sam, but the love for her grandmother had been the one bright spot in her unhappy life.

And now her late grandmother would be helping her in a most unexpected way with the purchase of a chance for a new life.

She felt no guilt as she perused the aisles and picked up dozens of new outfits, nothing very fancy, but enough to convince any immigration or customs official that she was not an impoverished runaway from America.

An hour later and almost one-thousand dollars poorer, she wheeled her new Louis Vuitton lookalike down the street. It was filled with all the things a young girl visiting Europe might need to fit in. She carried her new suitcase up the flight of stairs and collapsed onto her bed with the look of success on her face.

Chapter 58

Dan Lawson sat at his desk studying the case file for the hundredth time in the last few days. He had finally tossed his sling in the garbage much to the consternation of Sally. The removal of the sling meant his arm hurt all the time, but some pain killer prescribed by Sally allowed him to deal with it. The tingling in his arm was another matter. It just wouldn't go away. He wondered if he would have it as a daily reminder for the rest of his life. Alice was just released from the hospital, and he planned on visiting her tonight. Amy was working another homicide, but Dan had told Joey he wanted more time on the case.

It was funny; just last week it was the top case in the city, and today it justified zero resources. Joey understood it was personal for Dan, and he was cutting him some slack; but Dan knew at most he would have another week before Joey pulled the case from him and put it on the backburner, and the backburner meant it would never be solved unless Samantha Johnson killed again.

The trail was ice-cold. Johnson had not crossed the Mexican or Canadian borders, she had not taken any flights out of the country, she wasn't booked on any cruises leaving any of the ports; she had just plain disappeared. An FBI agent watching

Joyce Barker had been recalled after noting nothing suspicious.

If she hadn't left the country, then where was she hiding? That was the $64,000 question. She certainly had enough cash to last her many months, and getting odd jobs in exchange for cash might provide her with enough income to last several years. Where had she gone? FBI agents were watching Kim Monroe's place of hiding and they were reporting no suspicious people observing the couple. Samantha's photo had hit the national news services, and her picture had even been shown on America's Most Wanted. Things were getting desperate if you had to catch someone by showing their picture on a crime prevention show.

As Dan looked through the file wrapper, Amy's phone rang. She signaled Dan who picked up his phone and listened in on the call. "Detective Green as I was saying, I brought my car in for service yesterday and the mechanic told me someone had switched license plates with me. My wife told me there had been a news bulletin to be on the lookout for a murder suspect in a car. Jill, that's my wife, she's got a photographic memory for numbers. She was sure it was the number you guys are looking for."

The guy, his name was Fred Courtney, read off the number and sure enough it was the right number. Amy asked, "Mr. Courtney, were you anywhere near Rockford or Janesville in the last few days?"

"We went up to the Wisconsin Dells a few days ago last week. We passed both those cities on the way up there."

Did you stop at all on the drive up there, you know, someplace where the plates could have been switched?"

Courtney thought for a few moments. "We stopped for dinner at a rest stop just outside of Janesville on Friday."

Fred Courtney spent a few more minutes talking to Amy and Dan, and after giving them his phone number, he hung up after getting grateful thank yous from Amy and Dan.

Dan quickly briefed Joey who immediately put out a new APB to all government agencies to be on the lookout for Samantha Johnson driving a car with the new license number.

"What's it mean?" Amy asked.

"It means we're dealing with a really smart person who has a pretty good idea of how to evade the law."

Chapter 59

Roy Keller had been flying drones along the border for almost two years. Operating out of Yuma Air Station in Arizona, Border Security had been using the fleet of drones for three years and had directed agents to intercept illegal aliens all along the border. Today had been a rather dull day. Only one group of three people had been spotted, and he had followed the group until the Border patrol people had intercepted the illegals.

Flying at two-thousand feet above the security fence separating Mexico from the United states, his attention was suddenly directed to a rapid flash of light a couple of miles north of the border in a wooded area. Keller had flown this same mission once a week since he had first arrived at the facility, and he had never noticed anything unusual in this area.

More out of curiosity than anything else, he banked the plane to the north and flew directly over the area of the woods that had aroused his interest. His first reaction as the aircraft flew directly over the area was there was something in the woods, maybe a car, near a cabin he had seen many times, but the strange part was the car, if in fact it was a car, wasn't parked in the clearing near the cabin but in the woods. In his opinion a clear attempt to hide whatever it was.

He thought drug runners might be using the cabin as an entry point into the country. He maneuvered the plane to a lower altitude and took a closer look at five hundred feet. There was definitely a car hidden in the woods. He circled around and maneuvered his camera to look at the back of the car. He zoomed the high-tech instrument in on the license plate and hit the record button on his video system.

"Hey Art, come over here and take a look at this."

His supervisor came over and Keller explained what he had found. Art Belden took down the license plate number and entered the number in the database he used to identify known felons.

Up popped the APB on Samantha Johnson. "Holy shit Roy baby. I think we just hit the jackpot. A moment later he was calling into the FBI Field Office in Chicago. He was quickly transferred into Dan's phone at police headquarters. "Hello, Detective Dan Lawson here. How can I help you?"

"Detective Lawson, this is Art Belden with Border Security. A drone we have flying along the Mexican border has just picked up a car with the license plate number you have on your APB."

Dan quickly told Amy to pick up the call and asked, "Where is the car located?"

"It's parked in the woods near a cabin about five miles north of the border."

Belden read off the GPS coordinates of the cabin and said he would e-mail the picture the drone took just as soon as he hung up. Dan gave him his e-mail address, and after exchanging telephone numbers and thanking the agent, both he and Amy rushed into Joey's office with the information.

"No shit!" Joey remarked with his usual profanity. "You both get your asses down there and figure out what the hell is going on. Call Jimmy, I think there's a FBI field office in Phoenix. They might be able to help out."

After Dan brought Jimmy up to date, he confirmed there was indeed a Phoenix field office, and Jimmy would call to alert them to their arrival. Joey's administrative assistant booked Amy and Dan on a late-afternoon flight into Phoenix and made hotel reservations for them near the Phoenix airport. Dan had the name of the head of the FBI field office in Phoenix, and they were set up for a nine o'clock meeting the next morning.

Chapter 60

Sam rang the doorbell outside Roberto's office. Roberto buzzed her in and greeted her in the courtyard. After preparing cappuccinos, they both sat at his desk. He pulled a United States passport from his desk and handed it to Samantha.

The woman in the picture, a person by the name of Grace Millford, looked a little like Sam. "Is this going to be my new identity?"

"Yes, of course we'll have to change your hair color, and get you some blue contact lenses. We'll find a pair of glasses just like the ones in this picture and then you'll be able to pass any identity test."

"Tell me about her."

"I won't except to tell you she lives in Minneapolis, and was involved in an automobile accident. She'll never walk again."

"Why do I need to look like her?"

"When we send in your paperwork for the renewal of your passport, they'll check your new picture against the picture in their records. Don't worry, you'll look close enough; there won't be any problems."

"So what do we do now?"

"We're going to go to a beauty shop where they'll change your hair color, and then an optometrist friend of mine will fit you with some blue contact lenses and just the right type of glasses. Then we'll take your passport photo and start the process."

Roberto led the way to a beauty shop a couple of blocks from his office. He spoke to the woman at the front of the shop who looked at the picture of Grace Millford and then at Samantha. She nodded her head in approval and escorted Sam to an open chair near the back of the store. The lady, who never spoke a word, began the coloring process.

She pulled a new base color from a cabinet and applied it to Sam's light blond hair. After thirty minutes, the new color was rinsed out and after a blow dry and a new hair style, Samantha Johnson walked out of the shop looking a lot more like Grace Millford.

A five minute walk with Roberto brought them to a small local optometrist's shop. Roberto was given a hardy welcome by a middle-aged lady in a white lab coat. Roberto spoke to her in Spanish and handed her a picture of Grace Millford. The lady directed Sam to a chair, and after a brief ten-minute exam, confirmed in Spanish that Sam would be able to wear contacts without any problems.

The woman explained the process to Roberto, and he translated into English. Sam had never worn contacts, but she knew many people who did. The optometrist took out a pair of blue-colored lenses from a locked storage cabinet and handed Sam direction sheets written in English. Through Roberto's translations she was told to read everything carefully. The lady took a starter kit from the shelf and handed it to Sam. Then, with Roberto translating, the lady showed Sam how to insert and remove the lenses. She had Sam repeat the process.

The soft flexible lenses slipped through Sam's fingers, but she was finally able to place them in her eyes. She began blinking, trying to rid herself of the foreign substance. The lady told her the need to blink would pass in a few minutes. The optometrist placed some special drops in her eyes and the blinking immediately subsided.

The woman found a pair of glasses similar to the glasses in the picture and handed Sam a mirror. The new Grace Millford looked at herself and smiled. There was a remarkable resemblance. Roberto and the Grace Millford lookalike walked back to Roberto's office. He took passport photos up against the white wall and then asked her to sign a United States Passport Renewal form.

Roberto said, "Your new passport will be good for ten years. You can renew it again at the American Embassy or consulate where you wind up living. The renewal won't be a problem."

"What's next?" Sam asked.

"I'll have the new passport the day after tomorrow. Meanwhile, I'm going to contact a friend of mine in France. He'll meet you at the airport in Paris and set you up with a job and a new place to live."

Samantha left Roberto and decided to take a slow walk back to her hotel. She would walk through the shopping district again and stop for dinner before returning to her dingy room.

Chapter 61

Dan and Amy took a taxi to the FBI field office on North Seventh Street. The receptionist in the lobby called upstairs, and a minute later Agent Tim Foster greeted them and led them up to a third floor office in the corner of the building. Agent In Charge, Brenda Fuller, greeted them, and they all sat down around her desk. Dan said, "Jimmy Davis sends his regards. He told me he remembers you from his training days."

Fuller laughed, "Jimmy pulled the rest of us through physical training. I wouldn't have made it without his help. He said it was his football training. He's a great guy. So let's get down to business. Give us the background on the case. Tim and I know the basics but none of the details."

Between Dan and Amy, they were able to brief Tim and Brenda. It took almost two hours, but by the end of the briefing, they were fully up to speed.

Brenda said, "So it looks like either Samantha Johnson is hiding out in the cabin in the woods or she left her car there and then slipped into Mexico."

Dan answered, "That's how we see it."

Brenda continued, "Let's have Tim drive you down to the cabin. You guys can check things out. If she's there you'll arrest her, and if not, maybe you can find out if she crossed the border."

With the plan set, they all took potty breaks and ten minutes later they were on the road headed south on Route 10 toward Tucson and points further south.

Amy was sprawled out on the back seat asleep while Dan rode shotgun. Tim asked, "Dan, Brenda told me you're both a FBI Special Agent and a Chicago Police Department Detective. How could that be?"

"Well Tim, years ago, I got involved in a murder case that morphed into terrorism. I can't get into everything, but Director Jacobson felt there might be a mole in Headquarters, so he asked me to stay on the case. To make it legal he appointed me a Special Agent. Over the years, I've made use of my special dual status to work on some FBI cases."

"Wait a minute, wait a minute; you and the lady doctor were the ones who stopped the nuclear weapon attack in Washington. Right, come on level with me; you were in on it right?"

"Well I promised Director Jacobson I wouldn't talk about the case. Let's just leave it at that."

"She disarmed the weapon, right?"

"That doctor is now my wife."

Tim kept on trying to get Dan to talk about the case, but Dan kept on refusing. They stopped for lunch at a rest stop just outside of Tucson, and arrived at the dirt road leading to the cabin a little after two o'clock. With the drone pictures of the cabin in Dan's hand they agreed on their approach. Dan and Tim would circle the cabin through the woods and meet at the back. Amy would station herself on the edge of the clearing to provide cover, and then they would rush into the cabin.

They executed the plan perfectly. Unfortunately the cabin was empty when they crashed through the front door. Empty food wrappers, some covered with ants feeding on the microscopic scraps, indicated someone had been there recently. The license plate checked out as the stolen one, and the VIN tag on the car confirmed Samantha Johnson had indeed been here.

They found the remains of a recent campfire and a depressed area in the ground where a tent might have been deployed. Dan said, "She's one hell of a planner; I'll say that much. She's well prepared."

Tim pulled up Google Maps on his smartphone and confirmed a walk due south was the shortest distance to the border. If she had crossed the border it would probably have been accomplished by walking due south.

They headed south, trekking along the same path followed by the woman they were chasing. Dan picked up an empty water bottle and placed it in an evidence bag. Analysis would hopefully find Sam's fingerprints on the bottle.

They reached the border fence and spread out looking for clues. It took only a few minutes to spot the grappling hook Sam had used to climb over the fence. "Where do you think she went after crossing the border?" Amy asked.

Tim answered, "Nogales is the closest town, but maybe she walked over to Route 5 and caught a lift down to Hermosillo."

Dan thought about the problem. "The question we need to answer is why did she go to Mexico? Was it to live there, or was this just a stop on the way to South America?

There's another possibility," Tim said, "Nogales is a place where a person with some money can get false identity papers."

Amy asked, "How would she know that?"

Tim answered, "By looking on the internet. The place is full of web sites where people offer advice on how to escape from the cops or how to get a new identity. Even if she wanted to live in South America, a new identity would be helpful."

Dan considered Tim's theory. "I'll buy into that. So how do we go about finding out if she's in Nogales?"

Let's drive back to Phoenix. Brenda has some contacts down there with the Federales. We'll need to work with them, and if we're lucky, they'll be very helpful."

By the time they walked back to Tim's car, and drove back to Phoenix, it was after eleven o'clock. Tim dropped them off at their hotel and they agreed to meet at nine o'clock the next morning.

Chapter 62

Brenda Fuller and Jimmy set up a conference call with all of the interested parties. It was time to plan their next move.

Jimmy Davis had talked to Director Jacobson and he had gotten the NSA to monitor any calls from Samantha's prepaid cellphone, but so far, she had not used the phone to make any calls.

Dan summarized their findings at the remote cabin, and there seemed to be general agreement; Samantha Johnson had crossed the border and was probably headed for Nogales.

Joey asked, "So any ideas on what she's doing in Nogales?"

Tim Foster answered the question. "Nogales is known on the internet as a place where a person can buy a new identity. I'm guessing she's going to buy a new one. Dan tells me she's traveling with over $40,000, more than enough to buy a name change."

Jimmy asked, "What's the process these people use to steal a new identity?"

Brenda answered, "These people are very ingenious. They identify someone in the United States who has a passport but is never likely to travel again. These could be people at nursing homes or maybe people with serious health issues. These guys collect hundreds of these passports by paying other people to steal them without the person knowing it. When a person comes to them wanting a new identity, they find a passport picture that looks like them and is about the right age. Then they make the person look like the picture in the passport. It doesn't have to be a perfect match.

"Here's the neat part. They send in the passport to a Government center providing one-day service for renewing passports. They usually pay off a person in the center to process the renewal request without any questions. Now they have a new passport with a new picture of the person. It's as easy as that."

Joey said, "So you're telling us Samantha Johnson no longer exists and we don't know her new name or what she looks like."

The BennyMeister interrupted, "We do know what she looks like. She looks like Samantha Johnson. She didn't have time for major reconstructive surgery. The hair color may be different, she may have a new hair style, but she probably still has the same shaped nose and mouth."

Jimmy asked, "What are you thinking Benny?"

"We've got a facial recognition software package some people in Washington developed. If she leaves Mexico, she's probably going to go through a normal passport control process. After all, she'll feel safe with her new identity. If she reenters the U.S., they'll take her picture at Passport Control. If she flies out of Mexico to some other country, they'll have a picture of her passing through passport control. It's the new norm after nine-eleven."

Joey interrupted, "Benny there're probably thousands of people who leave Mexico every day. How are you going to analyze thousands of pictures?"

The BennyMeister answered, "I'm not, but my computer is. I think I can write a program in a couple of days that can automatically feed passport control data into our facial recognition program. Once I write the program, we'll be able to process every day's data in a few minutes."

Jimmy jumped at Benny's offer. "Benny, I like the idea. Make it happen, and let me know if you need any help."

Dan had been thinking about where she would go next. "So the real question is what will she do after she gets her new identity? She could reenter the United States, or flee to another country. I'm betting on her not coming back to the United States. She has no ties to people back here. Her only desire to come back might be to try to kill Kim Monroe again, and she can wait a couple of years until things cool down and then finish the job. After all, she spent ten years planning her revenge. What's another ten years?"

Brenda asked, "So where do you think she'll go?"

Dan pondered the question and then smiled. "She'll go where she doesn't stick out like a sore thumb, a place with a lot of foreigners, a place where she can earn enough money to live on for a couple of years."

Amy said, "That sounds like a resort area."

Dan said, "Except for the getting a job part. Remember she needs to be accepted by the locals. That means she would need to speak the language. I wonder if she took any foreign language in high school."

Joey said, "I'll have our people check with her parents. One of them will probably know."

Brenda Fuller changed the subject. "I know a lieutenant in the Federales in Nogales. He owes me a favor. He may have some contacts in the illegal identity trade. I'll talk to him. He may be able to help us."

Jimmy asked, "Dan, are you and Amy going to stay down there, or are you coming back to Chicago?"

Dan answered, "I think we need to stay as close to her last known location as we can. I think we'll stay here for a while."

Amy nodded her head in agreement.

After the conference call ended, Brenda Fuller looked in her personal contacts list and found the name of Lieutenant Jorge Rodriguez. A receptionist answered the phone and transferred the call to Rodriguez's office.

"Jorge, It's Brenda Fuller. It's been a long time."

"How are you Brenda? It has been a long time. Why the call?"

"Jorge, I'm in my office with Agent Tim Foster, Special Agent Dan Lawson, and Detective Amy

Green with the Chicago Police Department. We're working on a case involving a serial killer. Her name is Samantha Johnson and we believe she's now in Nogales trying to gain access to a new identity."

"Well, she's definitely come to the right place. Nogales is the new identity capital of the world."

"Do you know how we can track her down?"

"Well, the problem is there are hundreds of people who are in this business. We only know about half of them. We can have some of our people talk to them and watch their offices. What does the woman look like? Can you send us a picture?"

"I'll send you a picture, but we think she's probably changed the way she looks."

"I'll circulate the picture to our people and ask them to look for her, but it might help if you can send down some of your people to work with us."

"Tim, Dan and Amy will drive down today. Should they meet you at your office?"

"Yes, I'll reserve rooms for them at a hotel near our office."

Brenda looked at her watch. "They should be there by five o'clock."

"Good, I'll expect them about five."

With the phone call over, Dan and Amy took a taxi back to their hotel to checkout. Tim picked them up an hour later and they headed south to Nogales.

Chapter 63

Sam had spent most of the day just walking around the town. She had lunch in a small outdoor café in a picturesque square. The small park-like setting was filled with trees, and hundreds of birds were being fed by tourists sitting in small restaurants lining the edges of the park. Sounds of laughter from young children chasing the birds brought tears to Sam's eyes. She could never remember laughing like that. The place was filled with Americans, and it felt good just being with others like herself. For the first time she began to question whether she could ever be happy living in a foreign country.

The painful throbbing began again. Her inner voice spoke. "You must be strong Samantha. The final victory will be yours in a few years. What's a few years in the big picture? Your life won't be complete until you finish this. Hide oversees, and then in a few years you'll find her again, and your revenge will finally be complete."

Samantha listened to her inner mentor and understood the logic of the advice. She would just have to make the best of her new life.

A server interrupted her. Startled, she looked up and then smiled at the young woman. She ordered a Chicken Enchilada Special, and while she waited for the food, she tried to think about her future life in France. She suddenly had a thought. She'd buy an English to French dictionary and practice speaking French. She had never really liked French in high school, but now she was glad she at least knew a little of the language.

By the time her lunch arrived, Sam had begun to accept a new reality, one ensuring that with a new identity as Grace Millford, she would be able to find safety in a foreign country.

"I am Grace Millford," she whispered to herself as she left the café. I'm like a caterpillar changing into a butterfly "Samantha Johnson is forever dead, and Grace Millford lives on in her place."

She found an upscale bookstore catering to foreigners near the restaurant and bought an English to French dictionary. She also bought a French newspaper, Le Monde. Reading a newspaper would be the best way to brush up on her French.

She arrived back at her hotel a little after five o'clock. She sat on the balcony, trying to read the French newspaper with her dictionary by her side. It took her almost two hours to read and understand the lead story, but with the help of the dictionary, she began to remember her French vocabulary.

A brief afternoon deluge of rain scattered people on the street. It was over in ten minutes, and as the sun emerged from behind the clouds, a rare double-rainbow glistened across the sky. Sam thought it was definitely a good omen.

The smell produced by the evaporating rainwater was a mixture of life itself: sewage, aromas from nearby restaurants, and the perfume of spectacular flowers.

After eating at the same café across the street, she began packing her new luggage. She would check out of the Hacienda Triumfo in the morning and get her new identity papers from Roberto. Then, it would be on to a new life in a strange land.

She fell asleep thinking about her new life in France, and in her dream, she was speaking fluent French to vendors in an outdoor market near the Eifel Tower.

Chapter 64

Lieutenant Jorge Rodriguez was over six feet tall. He could have played linebacker for the NFL. In fact, he reminded Dan of Jimmy Davis who had played defensive tackle for the University of Illinois. He looked elegant in his uniform, and welcomed them with open arms as soon as he saw them.

"Welcome my friends, welcome to Nogales. How is my good friend Brenda?"

Tim answered, "Very good Lieutenant. She sends her regards."

"I have made reservations for you at the Marque's D' Cinia Hotel over on Avenida Prolongacion, but let's go across the street for dinner; I want to hear all about the case you're working on."

The small restaurant across the street from the Policia Federals Headquarters was filled with a variety of federal police. About half were dressed in SWAT gear and the rest in the uniforms of the federal police. The lieutenant was clearly known to the owners of the restaurant who had set aside the best table for their arrival.

The lieutenant spoke to the owner after they were seated, and then smiled at his guests. "I have taken the liberty to order a variety of items representing the locale cuisine, not the typical Mexican food you find in the States, but a much more, shall I say, sophisticated example of what our culture has to offer."

Over a wonderful dinner Lieutenant Rodriguez was briefed on the case. The description of the knife wounds shocked Rodriguez. "How could anyone do such a thing?"

Dan answered, "We've been asking the same question ourselves. It's beyond anything I have ever seen."

Over dessert, Tim asked, "What happened with the drug tunnel I read about last month?"

"Ah, the famous drug tunnel. It was 481 feet long. It was dug between two private homes, one on the Mexican side of the border and the other on the Unites States side. For years we've been trying to figure out how the drugs were getting across. An informant tipped us off, and we followed a SUV to the Mexican home and made the arrest while the men were still in the tunnel. It should be an interesting trial."

Dan finally brought them back to the business at hand. "What will we do tomorrow?"

"We're going to pay a visit to all the known forgers in the city. I don't think we'll get much help, but it's worth a try."

After thanking their host for a wonderful dinner, Rodriguez pointed to their hotel and they agreed to meet at nine o'clock the next morning.

The entrance to the hotel was through a tall pink stucco archway leading into the parking area. When Dan turned on the room's lights, dozens of roaches scampered across the room and disappeared into the woodwork. The room was just above the bare minimum for Dan, and he had a very low standard of acceptability. On the positive side, however, there was hot running water, and indoor plumbing. After checking out the bed, he left the lights on and drifted off to sleep on the ultra-soft mattress while never-ending images of the victim's knife wounds kept passing before his eyes.

Chapter 65

Samantha Johnson wheeled her luggage into Roberto's courtyard. She was early, but after a restless night and too many cups of coffee at the local café, she was more than ready to get on with her new life. Roberto showed her into his office area.

"Grace, you're early, but you're lucky, your new passport arrived just an hour ago."

Grace sat down at his desk and Roberto handed her a freshly issued United States passport, a Minnesota driver's license, and a Social Security card. Grace had never seen a Minnesota driver's license before, but it looked very official.

"I received a call from Andrés this morning. Jesus wants you to call him. You can reach him on Andrés's cellphone."

"Thanks, I'll call him later. What's next?"

"You're going to buy an airline ticket from Mexico City to Paris on Aeromexico, flight number 6103, for this Friday. There's a place near here where they will sell you one for cash without any questions." Roberto handed her a business card for the travel agency. "Ask for Lucy."

"How do I get to Mexico City?"

"The safest way is by bus. Lucy can sell you a ticket. This is the last time I'll see you. If you need to reach me for any reason while you're in France, my contact over there will get in touch with me. He'll be waiting for you just outside customs at Charles De Gaulle Airport. Good luck with your new life."

Roberto stood up and kissed the new Grace Millford on both cheeks. They shook hands, and Roberto escorted her out the gate onto the neighborhood street.

Grace sat down on a bench at the corner bus stop and turned on her cellphone. She took out Andrés's card and punched in his number. He answered on the third ring. He passed the phone over to his friend Jesus.

"Samantha, this is Jesus. I wanted to meet with you again. I'm back in town. It's safe for me now."

Grace Millford answered carefully. "Jesus, I'm glad you're back. I can't meet with you. I'm leaving town, but I want to thank you again for your help."

There was prolonged silence, and then Jesus answered, "Good luck my friend, I'll always remember you."

That was it. Grace knew Jesus's memory would only last as long as his next sexual experience, but she knew if it hadn't been for Jesus and his friends, she probably would still be trying to find a person like Roberto.

With her last farewell to Jesus completed, she looked for the travel agency as she rolled her suitcase down the street. It was easy to find, and after entering the storefront, she asked for Lucy Hernandez, the woman on the business card. Lucy spoke excellent English, and was able to book Grace on Flight 6103 to Paris.

When Grace asked for a bus ticket to Mexico City, Lucy asked, "Your plane leaves on Friday at 8:35 p.m. You can take a non-stop bus and get to Mexico City a day early or take a cheaper bus. It makes several stops and gets into Mexico City around noon on Friday. Which do you want?"

Grace thought about the tradeoff. The cost of a hotel room in Mexico City versus a horrid but cheaper two day ride on a crowded bus. Wanting to save some money, Grace chose the two day cheap fare. Ms. Hernandez booked the ticket online and then printed out the ticket along with all of the information on her flight to Paris.

Lucy called a taxi and explained that Grace had two hours before the bus departed. Grace forked over a little over nine-hundred dollars in cash for the bookings and found the taxi waiting for her as she left the travel agency.

The bus terminal was horrid, and the group of disheveled people who would be her fellow passengers for the next two days was beyond description. The good news was that she was free and now had a new identity, and she was on her way to a new life. Things were indeed looking good, very good indeed.

Chapter 66

A special NSA satellite in geosynchronous orbit over North America picked up her call as soon as she punched in Andrés's cellphone number. Almost instantly the satellite recognized the importance of the number, recorded the conversation, and located the GPS coordinates of the cellphone. At the end of the conversation, the information was relayed to a computer at NSA Headquarters in Fort Meade, Maryland, and a printout of the information landed on the desk of Staff Sergeant Miles, who was having lunch at the time.

While Sergeant Miles lunched at the NSA employee cafeteria, Dan and his team called into the morning teleconference call with Chicago. Benny was halfway through writing software code to allow the rapid analysis of the passport data being collected at all United States border entrance points and also from key Mexican exit points at airports and southern border crossings.

Joey had talked to Johnson's parents, and they confirmed she had studied French in high school. There was no other news for the two groups to exchange.

After the meeting, Lieutenant Rodriguez took his American friends to visit known forgers and suppliers of illegal documents in the town of Nogales.

Sergeant Miles returned from lunch, and it took another two hours for the information on his desk to make its way to Jimmy Davis.

In the late afternoon after getting no additional leads, Dan received the call from Jimmy. "Dan, she finally used her cellphone. The NSA has traced the GPS coordinates to a location in Nogales. She made a call from the corner of Aguirre and Alvaro Obregon streets. I'm texting you the actual voice transmission the satellite picked up."

Dan repeated the voice transmission to the rest of the group. It didn't reveal much, only that Samantha had somehow managed to get help and was leaving town. Rodriguez looked at the address. "Let's go there, I'm pretty sure I know why she called from there.

Lieutenant Rodriguez rang the doorbell on Roberto's front gate. Rodriguez announced his presence and Roberto strolled out to meet him without buzzing him in. After being greeted by FBI and Chicago Police badges, he spoke in English. "Well, well, well; if it isn't my good friend Lieutenant Rodriguez. What can I do for you today?"

Rodriguez answered, "Señor Vasquez, it's also good to see you again. I wonder if we could come in and talk to you about an important matter?"

Roberto Vasquez answered, "That depends on whether you have a Search Warrant."

"I don't Señor Vasquez, but if you don't let us in, I'm going to have my men surround your house for the next few months. I'm sure that will hamper your business activities, and I'm sure you wouldn't want that."

"Lieutenant, you don't have enough men to provide surveillance for 24 hours every day."

"Señor Vasquez, it will become my mission in life to gather enough evidence to put you in jail for a long time, and your contacts in the Nogales Government won't be able to protect you. Do you understand?"

Roberto Vasquez was silent while he considered the threat. He finally smiled and unlocked the gate. Rather than meet in his office, he led them to a table and chairs near an ornate fountain in the courtyard and sat down. "Now Lieutenant Rodriguez, what's on your mind?"

Rodriguez turned to Dan who spoke. "Señor Vasquez, we're looking for a woman who's killed three women and tried to kill a fourth. We know she's in Nogales and we know she was here today."

"How could you know such a thing Agent Lawson?"

"It doesn't matter how we know it, but we know it. Did she come to you seeking a new identity?"

Roberto, not knowing how much the FBI actually knew, decided to admit something. "Yes Agent Lawson, a woman was here this morning. She was seeking my help in matters concerning a new identity, but I told her I couldn't help her and she left."

Rodriguez spoke up. "That's your business Roberto; why wouldn't you help her?"

Roberto Vasquez laughed at the question. "My services don't come cheap lieutenant."

Dan asked, "What's the going rate for a new identity these days?"

"From what others have told me Señor Lawson, about ten-thousand dollars."

The questions and non-answers went on for another ten minutes, but it was clear Roberto Vasquez wasn't about to admit to having helped Samantha Johnson. As they were leaving the gated courtyard, Lieutenant Rodriguez said, "If I were you, I'd be very careful Señor Vasquez. You might never know when I'll be looking at your activities."

"I'll keep your warning in mind Lieutenant. Have a nice day."

Back in Rodriguez's car Dan said, "He's lying. Samantha Johnson has more than enough money to have bought a new identity."

Rodriguez said, "Getting a Search Warrant won't help. He keeps nothing in his house that could incriminate him. He buys outside experts who provide him with the best forgeries. He's just a middle man and never gets his hands dirty. We've been trying to catch him for years, but he has connections in the local Government and if we were to try to get a Search Warrant, he would know about it long before a judge approved it."

Amy said, "So you're telling us it's a dead end?"

"No, I'm not saying that. From the conversation between your suspect and this guy Jesus, I'd say she already has a new identity and she's leaving Nogales."

Dan thought about Jorge's comment. "You're probably right, but she may just not have wanted to meet with him. Can we check all the hotels in town to see if she's registered?"

"I've already started that. My men are circulating the picture to all the hotels and boarding houses. We'll see what we get. They'll have checked all the places by this afternoon. We should know by tonight."

Back at headquarters, Jorge had a report. His men had spent most of the day checking places where Samantha might have been staying but with no luck. Of course that meant nothing since many of the hotels, the ones with a one-star rating or less, didn't require a photo ID to confirm the accuracy of the name on the guest register.

Dan contacted Benny Cannon. "Benny, what's your estimate on the software program?"

"I need two more days Dan. Right now my people are trying to collect the pictures from all the Passport Control places where a person could leave Mexico. It turns out there're dozens of exit points in Mexico, and it's becoming a bureaucratic nightmare to get the information."

"Can Lieutenant Rodriguez help with getting the pictures?"

"It can't hurt. He should talk to Director Miguel Banderas, he's the head of the equivalent of our Homeland Security."

Benny gave Dan the guy's telephone number, and Dan asked Jorge for some help.

"Ah, I know Miguel. We went to university together in Mexico City."

Jorge dialed the number and spoke to his friend in Spanish. It sounded like Jorge was reliving their college days before he got to the matter at hand. His expression turned serious and he chose his words carefully. He listened for a few minutes and then ended the call with a gracias amigo. "Miguel will make it happen."

Tim received a call from the Phoenix office. The fingerprints on the bottle Dan had found in the woods were definitely Samantha Johnson's.

Dan thanked Jorge for his help, and Jorge assured them his men would continue to watch Roberto Vasquez to see if Samantha Johnson showed up again. With Tim driving the car back to Phoenix, Dan was able to arrange a flight back to Chicago out of Tucson. It wouldn't arrive until after midnight, but Dan wanted to organize the search from Chicago.

Tim dropped them off at the Tucson airport, and they all agreed to keep in touch.

Chapter 67

Grace Millford sat next to an elderly lady who smelled of the farm; Grace was the best-dressed traveler on the crowded decrepit forty year old passenger bus. There wasn't a restroom at the back, and there was usually a four-hour gap between stops. The process was always the same. The rest stops were always at a gas station with a convenience store attached. Luckily, Grace had converted some of her cash to pesos.

The first major stop was the city of Hermosillo where a dozen people left the bus and another six new disheveled passengers climbed on board. The bus had a two-hour layover in Chihuahua where the drivers changed. Grace found a McDonalds a block away from the bus terminal, and the hamburger and fries and diet coke brought back fond memories of her life back in Chicago. She used the clean restroom and stocked up on a couple of Quarter-Pounders and Super-Sized Fries to go. She had no idea when she might encounter another sign of civilization.

Exhausted from the stress of the last few days, she fell asleep while looking out the bus's dirty window and didn't awake until the sun had risen high into the eastern sky. The bus stopped at Torreon for breakfast and Za-catecas for lunch, but other than buying some drinks, Grace chose to feast on her cold hamburgers.

There was another major layover in San Luis Potosi where the drivers again changed, and Grace found a takeout place catering to the bus passengers. The lady who had been sitting next to her spoke no English, but she pointed to a few items on display and using sign language recommended a few of the meat-filled pastry items visible through the glass display case.

The food was heated in a microwave oven and Grace carried a brown bag back to the bus terminal. She ate her dinner sitting alone at a bench outside the terminal and after a visit to the restroom boarded the bus for what she hoped was the last stop before reaching Mexico City.

The bus reached the outskirts of Mexico City a little after sunrise. Grace had slept through much of the night, but the noise from rush-hour drivers leaning on their horns brought her out of her deep sleep. The driver was fighting traffic all the way into the heart of the city, but they finally arrived at the main bus terminal a little before noon.

Grace happily left the bus and quickly disposed of her pistol in a nearby garbage can. She then hailed a taxi waiting at the corner, and an hour later she was at the Aeropuerto Internacional just outside the city. The new airport stood in stark contrast to the buildings she had seen on her journey from Nogales. It was both modern and beautiful.

Grace had a little over six hours before her flight left. She checked in anyway. The check-in at the counter was uneventful: a quick look at her passport, a quick look at Grace, the picture checked out, all was good.

The lady behind the counter handed her a boarding pass and a baggage claim ticket and explained the plane was on time and scheduled to depart from Gate A3.

She tried to remain calm while going through Passport Control, but her heart was racing. The uniformed official spent a long time checking in his computer, but he finally stamped her passport and cleared her.

Grace found herself in the Duty Free area of the airport. She sat down in a deserted corner and started to cry. It was a combination of relief at having passed her first real test and thankfulness for the skills of Roberto and his people. She stopped when she looked up and saw a policeman staring at her. He asked in English. "Is everything okay?"

Grace quickly answered, "I had to leave my boyfriend."

The cop smiled, understanding the situation, and walked away.

With hours to kill, Grace walked around the duty free area. She saw a sign in English pointing in the direction of showers for rent. A fresh shower to remove the smell of Quarter-Pounders and fries seemed like a great idea. She followed the signs and found the small facility in a remote corner of the terminal. Thirty minutes later she was refreshed and ready for the long flight to Europe.

She found a bookstore where she bought a New York Times and a paperback book and sat down in a food court. Two hours before boarding, she walked the food court again and finally settled on Chinese. An hour before departure, she walked to the gate and waited for the airplane to board.

When her seat was called, she handed the clerk her boarding pass and walked down the jet-way to the airplane. She quickly found her seat and placed her purse in the overhead compartment. Coach turned out to be about half full, and luckily, the seat next to her was empty.

As the plane accelerated down the runway and lifted off the ground, Grace Millford smiled and breathed a sigh of relief. She had done it. She was on her way to a new life.

Chapter 68

Dan had been pestering the Benny-Meister. First it was errors in the software, and then it was not enough memory in his computer to deal with all the data. Finally everything was ready. Benny hit the start button, and he and Dan watched the screen. As they waited, Benny explained the process. "Each picture is loaded into the facial recognition software program. We've loaded in several pictures of Samantha Johnson. If there's a greater than ninety percent chance of a match, then the picture is moved to a second file and shows up on the screen."

"How long will this take?" Dan asked.

"I started loading pictures from when we traced the call she made in Nogales. We've got to get through sixteen thousand pictures. Figure one second per picture. That's about five hours to get through all the data since yesterday. We'll have today's data tomorrow morning. We'll always be one day behind because of the time it takes to transfer the pictures."

A picture suddenly popped up on the screen. Dan and Benny studied the photo. There was a slight resemblance to Samantha

Johnson, but the lips weren't just right. Dan sat down with a cup of coffee and Benny popped open a can of Mountain Dew from his private refrigerator. Pictures popped up on the screen at about the rate of six per hour. It was basically boring, but with brief moments of anticipation. Five hours later, they had processed all of the available data. Benny promised to stay on the job and load today's data as soon as it arrived.

Dan left for home. He hadn't seen Sally in three days and missed his time with his daughter. Debbie waddled up to him as he walked in the backdoor. He lifted her into the air much to her delight. He put the pain in his right arm out of his mind and enjoyed the love of his little girl. Sally, who came in from the library, gave him a kiss and immediately wanted a detailed update on the case.

They discussed the case over dinner. Even Susana was interested. Sally asked, "Does NSA know who owns the phone Samantha called?"

Once again Sally caught him in a serious omission. He immediately called Benny.

"Nothing new yet Dan; I still haven't gotten in today's data."

"That's not why I called. Can the NSA tell us the owner of the phone Samantha called?"

"They should be able to. I'll ask them and get back to you as soon as I know the answer."

Sally asked, "So where do you think she went?"

"Well she speaks French and English. I'm guessing she doesn't want to live in a Spanish speaking country. So that basically leaves out South America. I'm thinking some island in the Caribbean or maybe England or France."

Benny's call interrupted Dan. They've traced the telephone to a guy by the name of Andrés Garcia, and I've got the address of where the bill's sent."

Dan wrote down the information and immediately called Lieutenant Rodriguez. Jorge agreed to talk to Andrés and find out what he knew.

Dan felt he was losing it; not because Sally had thought of the other phone, but because he should have immediately thought about it. They could have confronted this guy Andrés yesterday.

Dan hit the sack right after dinner. He desperately needed to catch up on his sleep.

Once again, there was a call in the middle of the night. Sally passed Dan the phone and fell back on her pillow. It was Benny. "We've got problems; The Mexico City airport hasn't sent in their data. I spoke to their head security guard, and he says their picture taking system is down, some kind of technical problem. They've been letting people pass through Passport Control without their pictures being taken."

"Oh shit Benny, that's the most likely exit point for her."

There wasn't much either of them could do about it. It was water over the dam so to speak. Dan tried to fall asleep again but couldn't stop thinking about their bad luck. They needed another way to locate Samantha Johnson.

Chapter 69

It was during Dan's morning shower when he discovered the answer to the problem. It wasn't like it popped out of the shower head. It was just a new thought growing slowly in his brain. It was really quite obvious. Somehow, probably working with Roberto Vasquez, Samantha Johnson had acquired a new identity.

From what Dan already knew, Vasquez had access to a vast portfolio of stolen passports. He would have to have taken pictures of Samantha who had been made to look like the person whose identity she would assume. Then Vasquez would have sent in the stolen passport with two new pictures to a Passport Renewal Center in the States, but it would have to be one of the centers providing twenty-four hour turnaround service. He would have shipped everything by FedEx or some other overnight delivery service to the center, and therefore, traceable records of the mailings were available.

Dan immediately called the Benny-Meister at work. He was still there. The guy never slept. After hearing Dan out, Benny said, "Cleaver, very cleaver. I'll get on it right away."

True to his word, Benny had a smile on his face when Dan arrived at FBI Headquarters. "DHL had a record of only one package sent from Nogales to the Miami Passport Control Center in the last few days. I checked with the Miami passport office, and they processed 467 rush passport renewals in the last week. They sent me pictures and names of all the people."

Benny walked Dan over to his computer where a picture of a woman who looked a lot like Samantha Johnson was staring back at him. Benny continued. "I ran the picture through the facial recognition software and there's a greater than ninety seven percent chance of a match."

Dan stared at the picture of Samantha Johnson and the picture on the computer of Grace Millford. He didn't need the facial recognition package to see it was the same person.

Now he had a name, Grace Millford. He picked up the phone, but Benny stopped him. "I took the liberty of talking to the head of security at the Mexico City airport. He called back thirty minutes ago and told me Grace Millford boarded a flight to Paris at 8:35 p.m. last night. It landed a little over two hours ago. The good news is we know she's in France. The bad news is we don't know where in France."

Chapter 70

Grace Millford passed through Passport Control without any problems. She waited for her baggage, and after clearing customs, walked out into the airport's reception area. A surly looking man with a black mustache held a sign with her name on a placard. He could easily have passed for a private limousine driver.

She smiled at the man as she walked up to the sign. The man smiled back and shook her hand. He introduced himself as Marc Stuben. Grace started to talk, but he held up his hand. "Wait until we get to my car."

They entered a garage adjacent to the terminal, and soon they were on the road leading into Paris. Grace asked, "What do we do now?"

Stuben smiled. "My people have been able to find you a job. It will be a great cover. It's the International School of Brussels."

Grace was surprised. "Brussels is in Belgium. I thought I would be living in France."

"I was told you speak French. They speak French in Brussels and it's very cosmopolitan. An American in Brussels is like a drop of water in the ocean. You'll be safe there."

Grace thought about living in Brussels. She knew many foreigners lived there because it was the home of the European Union. It was just that she had been planning on living in France.

Stuben handed her an itinerary. She was booked on a train into Brussels leaving around noon local time. A reservation had been made at a rooming house near the Gare du Midi train station, and she had a job interview scheduled at the International School with the Headmaster tomorrow at 10:00 a.m.

As they entered the early morning rush hour traffic, Marc Stuben briefed her on the job. She would be helping the kindergarten teacher. The job paid 2000 Euros per month. It was barely enough to live on. Her story was she wanted to learn all about European history, and she thought living in Brussels for a couple of years would be a good way to accomplish this.

Stuben explained the pay was just a little above the poverty level, but she could make a lot of extra money by babysitting for the parents of the children at the school. The school was filled with the children of the most wealthy and influential people in Europe.

"Tell them you read about the job in The Bulletin; it's a weekly American magazine published in Brussels on the internet. I have a copy of the advertisement. In the interview, say you worked in a daycare center in Minneapolis. I have a letter of recommendation for you to show to the Headmaster. You should get the job because it doesn't pay very much.

"If they offer you the job, take it. They'll have you fill out some paperwork so you can get a Blue Card, that's a work permit for Belgium. They'll be able to get one for you because they'll claim you have knowledge of the American culture, and it's part of what they teach at the school."

"Where should I live?"

"Talk to the Headmaster. There may be other people who work at the school who want to share an apartment, but be careful. Many of these people may know all about Minneapolis and trap you into giving a wrong answer."

Grace would have to read up on Minneapolis. She would need to develop a believable story about her life in Minnesota. "What if I don't get the job?"

"Then give me a call. My cellphone number is at the bottom of the page, but I think you'll get the job as long as you don't screw up the interview. Set up a checking account at a bank. Roberto told me you have a numbered Swiss bank account. They can wire money to your new bank."

Stuben dropped Grace off at the Gare Montparnasse train station and handed her the packet of information on the backseat. He drove off after a quick good luck, and suddenly Grace Millford realized she was indeed a stranger in a strange land. But she spoke the language, at least a little bit. She looked at her watch. She had almost four hours until her train left.

She spotted a patisserie shop across from the train station with an outdoor seating area. She suddenly realized her dollars and pesos weren't going to do her much good in France. She walked into the Train terminal and found a currency exchange kiosk. She exchanged most of her remaining dollars and all her pesos for euros, and then walked across the street to the small café. She sat down, and a lady brought her a menu. She thought about how to order some food and practiced the right words in French. Then, when the server arrived, she ordered coffee and chocolate croissants. The lady smiled at her fractured French, but understood, and that was the important thing.

Her order arrived, and Grace Millford sat happily at her small table breathing in the morning air of the vibrant city of Paris. Maybe after she was settled in Brussels, she would visit Paris for a weekend of sightseeing. That would be fun.

The city of lights sounded more like Chicago than Nogales. Cars were honking their horns. Ambulance sirens were wailing their melancholy sounds of distress, and of course there were the police. She could see dozens of uniformed policemen walking the area around the train station. Were they looking for her? She knew they weren't, but she needed to remain vigilant, constantly looking over her shoulder for a visit from the police.

She spent an hour just watching the city wake up and go about its business, and then she walked back into the train station. She found her train on the large screen at the front of the station and moved to the entrance of Track 16. She was still early, and another train was about to leave for Düsseldorf. She bought an International New York Times at the newspaper kiosk and passed the time reading about the news of the day in her old homeland.

Chapter 71

The morning team meeting was called to order by Jimmy, and almost everyone had information to report. Tim called in from Phoenix. He had talked to Lieutenant Rodriguez who had met with Andrés Garcia. Garcia had been reluctant to talk at first, but opened up when confronted with a trip to the local jail. Yes, he had met Samantha Johnson; yes, he had driven her to the Hacienda Triumfo; yes, he had taken her to visit Roberto Vasquez. But other than that, he knew nothing more.

Dan and Benny reviewed their process for confirming Grace Millford was the new Samantha Johnson. She was now loose somewhere in France.

Jimmy said, "We need to work with Interpol now. They'll help us catch her. I know a senior detective at their headquarters in Lyon, France. I met him at an international conference on terrorism last year."

After the meeting, Jimmy and Dan talked to Inspector Claude Pelletier. "Jimmy, how good to talk to you again. I'm assuming this is not a social call."

"No it's not Claude. I'm sitting here with Special Agent Dan Lawson. We've been working on a serial killer case out of our Chicago office. Dan is the senior agent on the case. I'll let him summarize the critical facts, and then we need to agree on how to proceed."

Dan spent the next two hours taking Claude through the case from the beginning to the present day. Pelletier listened intently and asked only a few clarifying questions. When Dan finished, Claude said, "Dan, I want you to come to Lyon as soon as you can. I normally don't work on cases anymore, but this one requires some special attention. I'll work with you to catch this Grace Millford or whatever her name is."

Jimmy thanked Claude, and after taking down Claude's contact information, Dan promised to e-mail him his itinerary. After hanging up, Jimmy said, "You struck a raw nerve when you told him about how the women were gutted. I'm sure that's what made him decide to help out personally. He's a senior guy at Interpol. I'm sure you'll get all the help you need."

Dan asked, "Do you think Amy should go with?"

"I don't know; talk to Joey. Let him decide."

A follow-up phone call with Joey solved the problem. Amy's husband was sick, and she needed to stay home with the kids and her invalid mother.

Dan checked out the home of Interpol on Google Maps. It was located in the northwest section of Lyon along the Rhône River. Jimmy's administrative assistant booked him on an Air France flight leaving O'Hare Field at 8:15 p.m. He headed to his office to prepare for his trip. He needed to copy everything in the case folder so he could share all of the evidence with Claude Pelletier's colleagues.

He arrived home at five o'clock, packed quickly, gave hugs and kisses to Debbie and Sally, and when his taxi arrived, he left for the airport.

Chapter 72

The express TUV train arrived at the Gare du Midi train station a little after two o'clock. Grace bought a city map at the train station's bookstore, and after locating her hotel, she began wheeling her single bag down the street toward her destination.

Rue Joseph Claes was easy to find, and after turning left on the street, she found her hotel two blocks down on the left side of the street. Hotel was actually a slight exaggeration. The place was certainly several steps above the Hacienda Triumfo, but to call it a hotel was false advertising. It looked more like a boarding house, and walking through the front door confirmed her suspicions. The middle-aged guy behind the front counter was wearing a black undershirt with an unlit cigar in his mouth. He spoke no English so Grace attempted to communicate in French. It was a definite challenge, but after a minute of her bad French and sign language, she was handed a registration form to fill out.

She almost started writing Samantha before she corrected herself and filled out the form with the correct information. Grace needed to be more careful. She didn't need any interaction with the police. She paid the man in advance for one night and collected her key. The elevator took her to the third floor, and she easily found room 306. The old wooden door with a substantial crack down the middle creaked as she opened it up. The place was dingy and looked out at an apartment within touching distance just outside her window. She waved to a man who was looking at her from the next building. They were close enough to shake hands.

She closed the cheap-cotton drapes and unpacked her suitcase. She looked closely at her city map as she sat on her bed. She located the International School of Brussels on Watermael-Boitsfort, and then located the famous Grand Place.

With nothing to do until the interview tomorrow, Grace decided to take a long walk and check out the city. After walking along Avenue Louise with the high-priced boutique couture shops, she passed the Sablon with its many antique shops. It took her almost an hour to reach the Grand-Place. The old market square was absolutely spectacular. Old guildhalls covered in gold-leaf with golden statues on their roofs lined the square. Grace sat down at an outdoor café in the square and ordered a cappuccino and croissant. At a cost of twelve euros, she knew she'd have to watch her spending. Brussels was definitely more than a little bit overpriced.

She walked down the Petite rue des Bouchers and passed displays of fresh fish in front of the famous restaurants lining the narrow cobblestone street. She bought a Belgium waffle at a kiosk on the corner and sat on a cement bench and people-watched. She loved the beauty of the old city. She definitely knew she could call this place home for the next few years. She returned to the hotel a little after eight o'clock and immediately fell asleep.

Chapter 73

The plane landed at Charles de Gaulle airport on time. As usual, Dan was unable to sleep on the plane. Instead he ate some nondescript pasta dish for dinner and watched three old movies. He had a two hour layover for his flight to Lyon, so he exchanged some dollars for euros and had a breakfast in one of the many duty-free restaurants.

His flight was finally called, and he boarded the Airbus A320 Air France flight to Lyon. The flight landed early, and he rolled his carry-on suitcase out the airport exit and stood in line for a taxi. He spoke in fractured French to the driver. "Interpol s'il vous plait."

The driver smiled and answered, "Oui monsieur."

The drive into Lyon took only twenty minutes. The driver spoke no English and Dan spoke little French so it was a quiet ride. The building housing Interpol was something to behold. Mostly glass and reinforced concrete, it sat in a beautiful park setting along the Rhône River.

The taxi dropped him off at the front of the building, and he wheeled his suitcase in through the entrance and up to a receptionist who smiled politely at his day-old growth of beard and fatigued appearance. "Inspector Claude Pelletier please."

The young lady picked up the phone and speaking in French, spoke to someone. She hung up and said, "Inspector Pelletier will be down to see you in a moment Special Agent Lawson. Did you have a nice flight?"

"I hate flying, but it was acceptable, and how do you know my name?"

The woman smiled, "I was told to expect a representative from the FBI today with your name, and you definitely look American."

Dan was curious, "How do you know I'm American?"

"Several things: the stripes on your tie are angled the wrong way, and your suitcase is a Samsonite. They don't sell that particular model in Europe."

"You're, very observant, you should be a detective."

The young lady laughed. "I'm an intern here. Next year I'll get my degree in Criminology, and hopefully I'll eventually become a detective."

Their conversation was interrupted by a middle-aged man who came charging out of the elevator to greet his guest from the States. "Special Agent Lawson, welcome to Interpol. Let's go up to my office. My team's been expecting you."

"Please call me Dan, and I can't wait to get started."

Pelletier led him to the elevator and pressed the fourth floor button. The elevator door opened into an immense office area. The floor to ceiling glass windows only added to the feeling of open space. It was the kind of working environment any Chicago city cop would have loved to work in.

They headed to a corner of the floor and entered a large conference room with glass walls. It was clear the architect of this building loved glass, and somehow the place just looked like an efficient place to conduct business, and after all, police work was indeed a form of business.

Dan was greeted by a group of seven of Claude's colleagues. After accepting a cup of coffee, the group of international law officials got down to business.

Pelletier started the discussion. "Dan, welcome to Interpol. I've distributed a dossier on the case to all of our people, but I think a review of the case from the onset would be very valuable."

Dan obliged and when he explained the nature of the actual wounds inflicted on the victims, he could see the visible looks of shock among the group. He brought everyone up to speed, and at the end of his update the group was energized and ready to help out in any way possible.

Pelletier then asked his second in command, Theresa Pandinni, to explain what Interpol had been able to determine.

"Using the pictures of Samantha Johnson that Dan forwarded, we reviewed the surveillance cameras at Charles De Gaulle airport." A picture of Samantha Johnson, aka Grace Millford, appeared on a screen at the front of the room. "The suspect appears to be leaving the airport with a known felon, Marc Stuben. Unfortunately, they left the airport without our getting a picture of his car. Presently their whereabouts are unknown."

Dan asked, "What was this Stuben guy involved in?"

Pandinni answered, "You name it, and he's done it. He's served time for armed robbery, fraud, and embezzlement. He's a man of many talents."

Pelletier took over the conversation. "Here's the thing Dan. She's in the European Union now, so she can be in any one of twenty-eight countries. The good news is she's probably going to stay in a hotel, and if she does, then EC rules require the hotel inform the local police of all guests within twenty-four hours. We've sent out alerts to all the appropriate authorities, and if she registers at any hotel, we'll know about it, and if she tries to leave the European Union, we'll stop her when she passes through passport control."

Dan asked, "So what you're telling me is we'll have to hope she stays at a hotel?"

Pandinni answered, "No Dan; We've also got an alert out for Stuben, and the most important thing is eventually, she'll probably try to find a job. Any employer is required to file for a work permit on behalf of any non-European Union person seeking employment."

Dan was accustomed to waiting. It was part of the profession. There were just points in time on a case where waiting was the only alternative.

Claude said, "Dan, I know you must be tired. We've set you up in a nearby hotel. I'll have Theresa drive you over, and then I'll pick you up for dinner at eight o'clock. That'll give you a few hours to adjust to the time change."

The meeting broke up and Theresa Pandinni drove him to the Hilton hotel. It had a beautiful view of the Rhône River. His room was typical of most hotels. With the drapes closed, it could have been any upscale hotel in the world, except of course for the bidet, which clearly labelled it as European.

Dan looked at his watch. It was four o'clock local time. He put in a wakeup call for seven o'clock and immediately fell asleep.

Chapter 74

Grace arrived by taxi at the International School a few minutes before her ten o'clock interview. The cab entered the heavily wooded grounds along a winding road and dropped her off at a large white chateau serving as the administrative office. A smiling receptionist greeted her as she entered the foyer of the beautiful old mansion. "Good afternoon. I have an appointment with John Mannley."

"Ah yes. You must be Grace Millford. Pleased to meet you. I'm Mary Lang."

The middle-aged woman extended her hand and then called the Headmaster on the phone. After hanging up, she pointed to stairs at the back of the foyer. "He's waiting for you in his office. It's up the stairs on your immediate right."

With a high degree of nervousness, Grace walked slowly up the stairs and turned right. A cherubic and slightly overweight John Mannley rose from his desk and greeted her. He led the way to a sitting area in the corner of his office and offered her a cup of coffee. After pouring two cups and offering her some speculaas, the local cookie of Belgium, he began the interview. "I understand you've applied for the Teacher's Assistant position. How did you find out about the opening?"

Now it was time for Grace to provide all the lies necessary for her to get the job. "A friend of mine lives in Brussels. She told me about the opening. She saw it in The Bulletin."

"Well. I've seen your resume and although you don't have any teaching experience, you seem to have worked with children in the past. Why do you want this job?"

"I want to spend a few years in Europe. I always enjoyed European history in school, and I want to eventually study European history when I return to Minneapolis. After I get my degree in Education, I plan to teach European history."

"Well, you'll certainly be able to find the time to learn all about Europe here at the International School. The position pays 2000 euros per month. You'll be assisting our kindergarten teacher. The person who had the job had to go back to the States. Her mother died suddenly, and she'll have to take care of her father."

Grace asked, "I'm going to need a place to live. Do you have any suggestions?"

"Brussels is kind of expensive. We've got a bulletin board in the gym. A lot of our faculty share apartments. There're a lot of ads on the bulletin board. So can I assume you'll accept the job?"

Grace instantly smiled and replied. "Yes Mr. Mannley, I'm pleased to accept the position."

"That's wonderful Grace. On behalf of the staff, let me welcome you to ISB. Mary our receptionist will help you fill out all of the paperwork. We're going to need to apply for a work permit, but we know how to word things so they have to accept an American's application. This is an English speaking school after all. You can start tomorrow if you want."

Grace shook hands with the Headmaster and walked down the stairs with a smile on her face. Mannley had called ahead to Mary, and she had paperwork ready for Grace to fill out. She sat down at a desk in a small room adjacent to the foyer and filled out all the necessary forms.

Mary handed her a map of the campus and explained where the gym was located. Grace thanked the receptionist, walked out the backdoor, and followed the signs leading to the gym.

There was a gym class in session. Some kids, probably in the second grade, were learning how to hit a Wiffle ball with a plastic bat. She guessed many of the kids had never played baseball before. It would be like an American kid learning how to play cricket. The kids, all dressed in black gym clothes, seemed to really be enjoying the class. A young beautiful woman in her late twenties, dressed in a black ISB warm-up outfit, was teaching the class, and everyone was having fun.

Grace found the bulletin board Mannley was talking about and began reading the various advertisements. There were five ads for apartments to share. Grace studied them all, and after looking at the pictures of the apartments, settled on an ad for a large one bedroom unit within walking distance of the school. The rent was 450 euros a month. She had no idea if it was priced fairly but the place looked in good shape and it was certainly worth checking out.

She found a phone near the bulletin board and dialed the extension of the woman offering the apartment. A man answered on the third ring. "Silvia Canter's phone can I help you?"

"Yes, I'm interested in the apartment Silvia is offering to share. When do you expect her to return?"

"She's teaching a gym class right now. She should be back in about ten minutes."

"Is she dressed in a black ISB warm-up?"

"Yes, that's her."

"I think I see her teaching the class right now. I'll talk to her after the class ends."

Grace watched Silvia Canter as she continued teaching the class. She seemed friendly, just the kind of person Grace would like sharing an apartment with. After a few minutes a bell sounded and all of the kids ran off to the locker rooms to change clothes before their next class.

Grace approached Silvia Canter and introduced herself. "I saw your ad on the bulletin board. I've just accepted a job here assisting the kindergarten teacher and I'm going to need a place to live. I'm new to the city, so I don't have a good feel about what 2000 euros a month can buy, but the pictures of your place looked nice."

Silvia smiled at Grace and said, "My next class is at one o'clock. If you want, we can walk over to my place now, and you can check things out."

"That would be great. Is it available immediately?"

"Yep. Let me get some things from my desk."

Silvia led Grace to her office which she shared with the guy who answered the phone. Silvia introduced her to Mike Van Colltier. Silvia pulled some things out of her desk, and after grabbing her purse, the two left the ISB campus and walked the half mile to Silvia's apartment.

The place was in an old three-story building without elevators. The walk up to the top floor was demanding but acceptable. Silvia opened the front door and Grace walked into a small but clean apartment. She walked around the place and noticed the one rather small bed in the bedroom. "Where would I sleep?"

"Well, in the bed with me or on the couch until we get another bed. I didn't want to get the second bed until I got a roommate. I pay 1000 euros a month, and all the furniture is mine so I figure 450 euros is a fair price for the rent."

Grace continued to walk around the apartment. It was small and the walk up the stairs was a chore, but Silvia seemed like a nice person and the 450 euro rent was probably all she could afford.

After checking out the small but adequate bathroom, she smiled at Silvia and said, "I'll take it. When can I move in?"

Silvia smiled back and said, "Whenever you want."

"I'm in a hotel now. How about if I check out today and move in tonight. I've only got a few things."

Silvia said, "That's great. Let's have dinner out tonight to celebrate. Do you need any help with the move?"

"No, but thanks for the offer. Grace looked at her watch and did some quick calculations. "I'll be back here by six o'clock."

Silvia handed Grace a key to the apartment and welcomed her new roommate with a passionate hug and another smile.

Grace hailed a taxi out on the street and headed for her hotel. It had been a great day; a new job, a new place to live, and a new friend. Things were looking up.

Chapter 75

The call from the hotel operator woke Dan from a deep sleep. He shaved, took a quick shower, and was waiting in the hotel lobby when Claude Pelletier arrived.

They decided to walk the short distance to Restaurant La Scène located along the Rhône River. The maître d greeted Pelletier, who had obviously frequented this restaurant on a regular basis, and led them to a private table overlooking the river.

Claude recommended some local specialties, and after ordering, their server returned with a bottle of white wine which Claude sampled and approved. After the server poured the wine, they had some time to talk.

Claude said, "You know Dan, I am a detective; so I did a little detective work and learned some interesting things about you and your wife Sally."

Dan thought about what was coming next, and smiled at Claude.

Claude continued, "It seems you and your wife have been quite busy saving your country and what I don't understand is how a physician and Chicago detective wound up working for the FBI."

Dan, without revealing any FBI secrets, went through the explanations once again. He explained how he had met Sally while working on a simple mugging case which turned into a case involving a group of terrorists bent on the destruction of Washington with a nuclear weapon. The director of the FBI thought a mole might be working in the Washington office, so Director Jacobson wanted them to continue working on the case.

Claude shook his head in astonishment as Dan explained how he and Sally seemed to always be in the wrong place at the wrong time. Claude just looked at Dan in disbelief, but finally accepted his explanation.

The French Inquisition finally ended when the first course arrived, a dish called Quenelles made from boiled fish with a wonderful white sauce. During the main course, Claude received a phone call. Dan couldn't understand the discussion which was in rapid French, but after the call, Claude smiled and explained. "That was Theresa. It seems the Brussels police have informed us a woman by the name of Grace Millford checked into a hotel near the main railroad station. The police immediately went to the hotel to apprehend her, but she had already checked out.

"So it seems our serial killer has arrived in Brussels and has somehow found a more permanent place to establish residence."

Dan asked, "So what do we do now?"

Claude answered, "I've asked Theresa to make reservations for us on the first flight to Brussels tomorrow morning. I was stationed in Brussels before coming here so I know all of the key players in the Belgium Federal Police and also the local Brussels Police. I think Ms. Johnson's days of freedom are numbered."

With the arrival of the main course, Margret de Canard, a beautifully roasted duck breast with a delightful orange sauce, they both raised their glasses in a toast to the rapid demise of Samantha Johnson, aka Grace Millford.

After sharing a second bottle of a local red wine, and finishing off the meal with assorted sorbets, Claude walked Dan back to the hotel. Theresa called on the way back to the hotel with their itinerary. Dan needed to be ready in the hotel lobby at eight o'clock.

Chapter 76

When Grace arrived at her new home, Silvia was there to let her in. Grace wheeled her lone suitcase into the apartment. Silvia asked, "That's all you've got?"

"That's it. I travel light."

Grace knew she would have to do a better job of explaining the single suitcase. She had to make sure Silvia was not too suspicious. Silvia had set aside a dresser and a section of the closet for Grace's use, and given the lack of clothes, there was more than enough space for her things.

Silvia explained they were going to have dinner at a local friture; the Belgium name for a low-end restaurant specializing in mussels, French fries, and a variety of grilled meats. "It's impossible to get a bad meal at any restaurant in Belgium, and my ISB friends all meet there for dinner every Thursday night."

The walk to the friture took all of fifteen minutes. It was located on a residential street near the school. It seemed the Belgium government didn't impose zoning requirements separating commercial from residential. Restaurants could be found almost anywhere.

The small friendly looking place reminded Grace of the many local taverns in the Chicago area; just a nice local spot to go for a beer and an inexpensive meal. Silvia and Grace were evidently the last to arrive. Two empty chairs had been saved around a crowded corner table. Silvia introduced Grace to the group of seven girls.

The discussion quickly moved to girl talk: behind the scenes goings on at the school, an upcoming trip to Paris two of the women were taking, clothing sales at nearby stores, and some of the funny things happening in their lives.

After ordering beers, Silvia explained Grace was going to be helping Thelma DeBois teach the kindergarteners. A girl by the name of Louise said, "You're going to love Thelma; she's the greatest. Just watch out for Billy Van Der Clave; I hear he's a devil."

Then came the question Grace dreaded from Karen. "So what brings you to our school Grace?"

Grace took a deep breath and began her lie. "Well I always loved European history. I decided I wanted to live here for a while and then go back to Minneapolis and teach. There's nothing like getting first-hand experience. On my days off, I'll visit the places I've read about but never seen."

A tall lanky girl named Wendy said, "My cousins live in Minneapolis. What part did you live in?"

Grace, glad she had done a little research on the city answered, "I grew up in Plymouth, just west of the city."

Thankfully, Wendy didn't have much of an idea of where Plymouth was. Grace realized she would have to really brush up on the Twin Cities in case she met someone who actually lived there.

Silvia and Grace ordered their dinners and the conversation quickly got back to meaningless chatter. The group finally broke up a little after nine o'clock. A light rain began falling. Silvia opened a collapsible umbrella and the two walked side by side back to the apartment. "One thing you'll learn Grace, living in Belgium you need to always carry an umbrella."

"I guess I'll buy one tomorrow."

Silvia asked, "When do you start work?"

"The Headmaster said it would take a week to get my work permit approved, but I could start tomorrow if I want. He said Thelma really needs the help."

"Good, I'll set the alarm for six o'clock. That should give us enough time to get ready. The first class begins at eight."

Silvia's bed was barely large enough for two people. She insisted on Saturday they would go to the local furniture store and buy a second bed. As small as it was, sharing the bed was still better than sleeping on the small couch. It had been a long day, and Grace quickly fell asleep thinking about what was in store for her in her new life.

Chapter 77

The next day started out quite differently for Dan and Claude. The flight into Brussel's Zaventum Airport was uneventful. Dan and Claude took a taxi into the city. Claude said, "We've got reservations at the Amigo. It's one of the best hotels in the city. I stay there whenever I'm in Brussels because it's next door to the Brussels Police station; at least that's the excuse I give. After we check in, we'll visit with my old friends and as you Americans say *ratchet up the pressure.*"

The Amigo Hotel was located one block away from the Grand Place. The hotel was an extraordinary architectural accomplishment. The lobby was a perfect blend of old-world charm and modern functionality. The lobby and reception desk exuded wealth and social status. The male staff at the door dressed in black tails and top hats greeted them in both French and English. Dan began to feel self-conscious that everyone he encountered knew he was an American. What was there about his looks? He wasn't even wearing a striped tie.

Dan's room overlooking the entrance to the Grand Place was upscale and elegant. Looking out of his window, Dan spotted a group of Asian tourists following a tour guide holding a red umbrella walking toward the Grand Place. Dan hated tours. He preferred the adventure of personal discovery. That's what he and Sally enjoyed most when visiting a new city.

Claude met him in the lobby, and they took a taxi over to the Commissioner of the Federal Police's office. It was located near the Gare du Midi train station. They entered the building and Claude was immediately greeted by the receptionist. They embraced and Claude, in the Belgium tradition, planted a series of three alternating kisses on her cheeks. Claude introduced Dan to Madame Coutre, a woman who had worked for Interpol when Claude had headed up the Brussels office.

"Beatrice, we have an appointment with Commissioner Servan."

Madame Coutre reached for her phone and after making a call asked Claude to go directly up to the Commissioner's office. Claude led the way to the elevator. Up on the third floor, a middle-aged woman met them at the elevator and embraced Claude. You could see the mutual respect in their eyes as they engaged in conversation in French. Finally Claude switched to English and introduced Dan to Commissioner Servan.

She led the way to her office and soon they were being served coffee while sitting around a conference table in the corner of her office. Over coffee Dan summarized the case and as usual, Madame Servan cringed at his description of the mutilations of the victims.

An hour later, she was completely committed to helping find Samantha Johnson, aka Grace Milford as quickly as possible. She walked out of her office and spoke to her Administrative Assistant. Dan could even understand that she was asking for a person to come immediately to her office. A moment later a man she introduced as Inspector Boulanger joined the meeting. She spoke in English, "Julienne, I want you to provide my good friend Claude and Special Agent Lawson with all of the assistance they require in apprehending a serial killer who evidently has chosen to seek refuge in our country."

The three left the Commissioner's office and met in Inspector Boulanger's office. Once again Dan summarized the case. Boulanger listened carefully, taking notes as Dan focused on the key facts.

Afterwards, Boulanger sat back in his chair deep in thought. "She'll try to get a job, and that's when we'll get her, unless of course she finds someone to pay her without a permit and in cash, but that's usually manual labor or working as a nanny, but to work as a nanny, she'd need contacts. You don't just advertise for illegals needed to work as a nanny. We'll explore every option of course, but the best bet is to wait until someone applies for a work permit. From what you've told me, she has no reason to think we know her new identity, so why would she not try to get a normal job."

Dan said, "So it sounds like we need to wait, and I hate waiting. Is there anything else we can do?"

"Well," Boulanger said, "We can check some of the more obvious places where she might find employment. To get a work permit, the applicant would have to prove an American is needed over someone from the European Union. There're maybe a hundred companies that would qualify. I'll have my people make a list of those places, and then we can check them all out."

Boulanger looked at his watch. "Give me till tomorrow morning. I'll have the list by then."

By the time they returned to the hotel it was late in the afternoon. They agreed to meet at six o'clock for a quick tour of the historical sights and then dinner. Dan still hadn't adjusted to the time change. It was morning back in Chicago. His biological clock wanted him to be wide awake and ready for action, but somewhere in the last three days, he had missed almost a full night of sleep, and he still had not recovered. He quickly fell asleep.

Shaving and showering rejuvenated his body, and after dressing in some clean casual clothes, he left his room and headed for the bar off the hotel's lobby. Claude was waiting in a corner with a drink in his hand. Dan plopped down in the chair next to his and said, "I need a drink!"

"Try a Kir Royale. It's very popular over here. It's made with Crème de Cassis and Champagne."

Dan ordered the drink from the server and a few minutes later they were toasting to their new friendship and an early capture of Samantha Johnson. Dan sipped the drink. It had both a sweet and slightly bitter taste, and the champagne somehow created the perfect mixture.

Dan said, "You seem to have made some good friends in Brussels."

"It was necessary. Interpol doesn't have a lot of authority in any country. Our success is based upon establishing good relationships with every law enforcement agency. We have some unique skills, and our data bases are quite comprehensive. So you see they need us, and we need them. Close cooperation works to both our advantages."

"How long will it take to find her?"

"It's hard to say, but I think we'll get her within a week."

"Let's drink to that."

They clicked glasses and finished their drinks. Dan signed for the beverages, and they both left the hotel. They turned left and began walking down the cobblestone street, dodging tourists and local residents alike. It was a madhouse of confusion.

Claude said, "First things first my good friend. When in Rome, do as the Romans do, and here in Brussels it is an obligation to see the famous bronze sculpture of the Manneken Pis."

Two blocks down they joined a crowd taking pictures of the famous statue. Dan laughed at the little boy urinating in the fountain. "There must be some story behind this," Dan asked.

"Oh, there are many, but the one I like the best is that hundreds of years ago a little boy became separated from his mother. Everyone began looking for him, and when they finally found him, he was on this corner urinating in a fountain. To celebrate the event, this bronze sculpture was built."

"Well, that's a great story Claude, and if you believe it, I've got a bridge to sell you."

Claude didn't understand. Dan explained. "It's what Americans say when they don't believe something. They say if you believe that, then I'll sell you the Brooklyn Bridge."

Claude laughed and patted Dan on the back. "Come let me show you the Grand Place and then we'll have dinner. Claude led the way down a cobblestone street and into the famous square. They walked to the center of the large open area. Claude gestured at the beautiful guildhalls surrounding the square. "This my friend is the best of what Brussels has to offer. The city is more than one-thousand years old, and in the Middle Ages when the guilds were in power, the various guilds built these buildings around their central market. It was a competition to see which guild would create the most impressive building. At the time it was believed the more gold used in the building, the more impressive the structure."

Dan looked slowly around the Central Market. He was definitely awe-struck. One building was more ornate than the next, and most had gold sculptures on the top of each building symbolizing the guild that had commissioned the building.

They spent a half-hour walking around the square, and Claude finally said, "And now my friend, I have a special treat for you. Belgium is known for mussels and French fries, and the most famous restaurant for this specialty is Chez Leon."

As they walked down a side street leading from the Grand Place, Dan wasn't sure if this specialty would satisfy his need for real food, but he was willing to reserve judgment. Claude continued down a street named Petite rue de Bouchers. Restaurants lined the street and vendors stood outside hawking their wares. It was like a bazaar with each restaurateur enticing tourists with promises of free drinks and other benefits that would be given for entering their establishments. Claude said *no merci* to each person and continued to the end of the street where a colorful neon sign proclaimed their arrival at Chez Leon.

As Claude entered the restaurant, he was greeted by the maître d. "Mon ami Inspector Pelletier."

Claude embraced the man in the white dinner jacket and introduced Dan. "Dan this is my good friend Mario Lucca. He's the maître d at Chez Leon. We go back many years."

Lucca spoke in perfect English. Any friend of the inspector is a friend of mine. Please come with me."

They were ushered into a private area in the corner of the restaurant. Claude ordered House Specials for each of them and a bottle of white wine.

Mario Lucca stopped by from time to time asking about Claude's wife and family. Over their wines Claude explained the special relationship. "Our family ate here every Sunday for three years. Once we were interrupted by three robbers who held Mario hostage and demanded money. I quickly ended their extortion plans and put all three in jail. Needless to say, we've been friends ever since."

With Mario's intervention, we were afforded celebrity status. Dishes of appetizers we never ordered were ceremoniously brought to the table with statements of *with the complements of Mario*. The moules were the best mussels Dan had ever tasted, and there was something special about the French fries. "It's the type of potato," Claude said. "The Belgians use this special potato that just tastes different."

Claude insisted that Dan order a Dame Blanche for dessert. The chocolate sundae was extraordinary. Dan was certain it was the heated

chocolate sauce; just the perfect amount of sweet-
ness.

It was almost midnight by the time Dan rolled
into bed and fell into a much needed deep sleep.

Chapter 78

Grace was showered and ready to go to her first day on the job a little before seven o'clock. The bathroom in the one-bedroom apartment wasn't designed for two people, but with a little cooperation and mirror sharing, they both managed to get it done. They breakfasted on croissants and coffee, and left the apartment twenty minutes before eight o'clock.

Silvia walked Grace to the elementary school, one of the original buildings on campus and introduced her to Thelma DeBois. The matronly looking woman with grey hair tied in a bun looked like the perfect grandmother, a nurturing person, perfect for taking care of the young children. She was relieved to see her new assistant, and with some of the early arrivals running around the classroom, she definitely needed the help.

Silvia left for her own first-period class and Thelma began introducing Grace to kids. Some actually shook hands, but most just continued on with their own activities. Thelma said, "I let them have free time until they all arrive. Then we'll start with a story. I've got one picked out and you can read it. The kids love accents for all the characters."

After the last child arrived, everyone sat down in a large circle and Thelma stepped into the center of the circle and once again introduced Grace and explained she would be reading the story. Grace sat down in a chair in the center of the circle and started to read the chosen book. She thought back to how her father read stories every night before bed and tried to imitate his approach.

The story was about Goldilocks and the three bears. The kids squealed with delight as she read the baby bear's parts, and they all loved her imitation of the papa bear. Thelma smiled with approval from outside the circle.

After the story, Thelma worked with the kids on identifying colors. That was followed with a review of counting from one to ten, and then it was time for recess. A fenced-in playground was located on the side of the building. Thelma took a break while Grace played kickball with most of the kids.

For Grace the novelty of playing with the kids was therapeutic. It brought back memories of when she was in kindergarten without a care in the world. If only she could bring those happy times back again. Maybe this job was just what she needed to get on with her new life.

For lunch, all of the kids were marched single-file to the Middle School's cafeteria, where lunches had been pre-arranged onto trays at a long table. Most of the children began eating, but one little boy just sat there. Thelma talked to him and then took his tray back to the food line. She returned with vegetables and fruit. She sat next to Grace and said, "We always forget Michael is a vegan."

The afternoon went by quickly with a session on conversational French and then some singing of

French songs. Art was the final session of the day. The kids all put on aprons and began making cups with clay. There were certainly some interesting shapes, although none really looked like cups. Nonetheless, the kids seemed to be enjoying the project.

After the last class, Thelma led some of the kids to their school bus while Grace stayed with the others who were going to be picked up by their parents. Everyone was gone by four o'clock and Thelma relaxed at her desk while Grace pulled up a nearby chair and studied Thelma's tired face. Thelma smiled, "Well Grace, how did you like your first day on the firing line?"

Grace smiled back. "I loved it Thelma. It brought back so many memories of when I was in kindergarten."

"Well, you did very well," Thelma said, "and I'm happy to have you as my assistant. I'll tell the Headmaster everything worked out well, and you'll be perfect for the job. So now that we have a few minutes, tell me about yourself."

Grace continued with her lies and reminded herself this was going to be a frequently asked question, and she absolutely needed to find out more about life in Minneapolis.

After telling Thelma she would see her tomorrow, Grace walked over to a sports field where Silvia was coaching the girl's high school soccer team. Grace envied Silvia's good looks and the way she felt totally at ease in her role as coach. With a little criticism fit in between constant praising, she appeared to be developing quite a good team.

After the practice, they walked back to the apartment, dropped off their things and then walked two blocks down to the local supermarket. Grace was shocked at the prices of the meats and fish, but the vegetables seemed to be fairly priced. Silvia said, "Brussels is an expensive place to live."

"I'm going to have to set up an account at a bank," Grace said. "I'm going need to have some money transferred."

Silvia answered, "My bank's just down the street. We can stop on the way back to the apartment."

The small branch bank quickly set up an account for Grace, and the manager helped her transfer funds from her Swiss bank account, just enough to tide her over until her first paycheck arrived.

Chapter 79

Dan's and Claude's morning started out with a trip back to Julienne Boulanger's office. He presented them with a list of over one-hundred companies where the need for an American could be easily demonstrated. Boulanger said, "My people are going to be following up with the banks and other places she would need to register with in order to lead a normal life in Brussels.

Claude thanked Julienne for his team's efforts and after leaving his office, Claude suggested they get some coffee while they planned their strategy. Ten minutes later a taxi dropped them off at the Sablon, an area filled with antique shops and restaurants. They sat outside at a small café, and talked about the list while they waited for their coffees.

Dan asked, "Claude, if I was new to the city, how would I find a job?"

"Well, you might look in the papers, but you'd soon find out it's hard for an American to get a work permit. But once you understood what you were up against, you'd look in the English speaking magazines like the International New York Times or The Bulletin. That's an American magazine only available online now."

"So let's check these publications and see if there're any jobs for Americans being advertised."

"A good idea Dan. There's a bookstore down the street selling the International New York Times. I'll get a paper while you check to see if The Bulletin is offering any jobs."

Dan quickly found The Bulletin on his i-phone and downloaded the most recent issue. He perused the publication and easily located the advertisements for job offerings in Brussels. There were thirty-seven jobs being advertised, the majority for American companies with their European headquarters in Brussels. Dan looked at the list from the perspective of which company would want an American like Samantha Johnson and could demonstrate the job couldn't be filled by a person from the European Union.

He tore a piece from the paper tablecloth and began preparing a list. He thought about the problem. English speaking wasn't enough. It seemed everyone in this city was fluent in English. The key would be the person needed to understand the American culture and that meant having lived or grown up in the United States.

Claude returned to the table with a newspaper and began analyzing the ads while Dan continued to think about the jobs being offered in the magazine. After twenty minutes and second coffees, Dan and Claude had compiled a list of five appropriate job openings. The first was a job being offered by The Bulletin itself for a sports writer. The second was for a translator for a Belgian medical device company. An argument could certainly be made for the need for a person who understood the nuances of American idioms. Dan had read enough directions for use of products made in foreign countries where the directions were impossible to understand.

Third was an advertisement for a radio copy writer for SHAFE, the Strategic Headquarters Arm Forces Europe where the Unites States housed thousands of troops.

The fourth was for a teaching assistant at the International School of Brussels, and the fifth was for an advertising clerk at McDonalds European Headquarters.

Claude reviewed the list. He said the job at SHAFE would probably be filled by one of the soldiers spouses, and McDonald's wouldn't be able to make a case for the need for an American, but he agreed the other job offers were certainly good leads.

"Okay," he said, "let's visit each of these companies and see what turns up."

A ten minute taxi ride brought them to a small building near the airport. The Bulletin seemed to be a magazine staffed with less than fifty employees. Claude showed his Interpol credentials to the receptionist and they were soon talking to the publisher.

Claude explained who they were looking for. The publisher said they had already filled the open position with an American ex-basketball player. He also confirmed that a person with the name of Grace Millford had never applied for the job.

The second job on Dan's list was for the medical device company. The firm was located in Nivelles, about an hour's drive south of the city. "We need a car," Claude said. They took a taxi back to the hotel and walked around the corner to the Brussels Police office behind the Amigo Hotel. Claude identified himself to the receptionist, and a few minutes later they were talking to the commander of the precinct who Claude knew from when he worked in the city.

Twenty minutes later they had borrowed a police car, and Claude was driving south through a beautiful forest as they headed for the highway leading to the town of Nivelles. An hour later they found the company in an industrial park near the town. The receptionist said the president was out for a lunch meeting, but would return at two o'clock; and the head of the Human Resources department was out of town.

Claude decided to have lunch in the nearby town rather than sit in the lobby for two hours. This was Europe after all and enjoying lunch needed to be placed high on the priority list. The receptionist recommended a place close to the company and after analyzing the menu placed just outside the restaurant, Claude approved of the receptionist's choice.

Claude recommended the steak with mushroom sauce, and Dan was not disappointed. Of course the French fries were the perfect accompaniment. Claude insisted that Dan try a special raspberry flavored beer, one of the thousands of beers available in Belgium. Claude said, "Did you know more beer is consumed per capita in Belgium than in any other country in the world?"

Dan answered, "I would have thought Germany."

"That's what most people think, but it's Belgium. They really love their beer."

Dan was now certain. It was impossible to get a bad meal in Belgium. Claude insisted they blended together the best of the French, German, and Dutch cuisines. Their food was a national treasure, and the Belgians knew it.

It was three o'clock before the president of the medical device company could see them. They were ushered into his office by his assistant, and after introductions, Claude quickly got down to business. "Monsieur Claubert, we're trying to locate an American woman by the name of Grace Millford. You advertised for the position of a translator in The Bulletin, and we're wondering whether she applied for the position?"

Claubert talked to a person on his phone and quickly determined Grace Millford had not applied for the position, and it had been recently filled with an internal promotion. Claude gave the president his business card and asked him to call if Grace Millford tried to apply for the job. If she did, his people should not say the position was filled and instead set up an interview. They would then arrest her when she arrived at the company.

"What did she do?" Claubert asked.

Dan answered, "She's killed three women in the States, and she's very dangerous."

They drove back to Brussels. The rush-hour traffic seemed no different than in Chicago or any other large American city. It was bumper to bumper all the way into the city. Dan looked at his watch. "We should try to check out this International School before the end of the day. Do you think there'll be anyone there at five o'clock?"

"Let's give it a try. Maybe we'll get lucky."

They arrived at the International School of Brussels a little after five o'clock. They parked in front of a large white building that was once someone's mansion. A sign said *the Chateau* and identified it as the Administrative Office.

The front door was locked, but they knocked until someone came to the door. Claude held up his Interpol ID, and the person unlocked the door. Claude asked, "Is the Headmaster in?"

The young man who answered the door said, "I think so. Let's check his office."

They were led up a flight of stairs and found a man sitting at a desk. He stood up and the young man introduced him and explained that Dan and Claude were from Interpol. The introduction had the same effect as a visit from the FBI would provoke in the United States. Mannley immediately stood up and dismissed their guide. After the usual introductions Claude began with the same line of inquiry, but this time with different results. Yes indeed, Grace Millford had applied for a job, and in fact today was her first day on the job.

Dan asked, "Is she still at the school?"

John Mannley called someone on the phone but there was no answer. "Classes are over. She probably left for the day."

Dan asked, "Do you know where she's staying? We need to find her it's very important."

"What did she do?" Mannley asked.

"She killed three women back in the States. She's a serial killer and very dangerous."

Mannley's face turned white as a sheet. A serial killer on campus was not in keeping with his school's image. He was thinking of the bad publicity more than the safety of the children or staff. "She said she was looking to find a place to live. I suggested she check out our bulletin board. There're always a lot of people who want to share apartments."

Claude asked, "Can we see the board?"

Mannley led them out the back door of the Chateau and along a path leading to the gym. Inside the front door they found a bulletin board with several ads for apartments to share. The names of the people placing the ads were listed along with their telephone extensions at the school.

While Claude took pictures of the ads with his smartphone, Dan said, "We're going to need the addresses and phone numbers of the people advertising these apartments to share."

Back in Mannley's office he wrote down the names and phone numbers of each of the people advertising their apartments. Claude asked, "What time will she arrive at school tomorrow?"

"First class is at eight o'clock."

Claude said, "If we don't arrest her tonight, we'll be here at seven o'clock with a number of Federal Police. We'll be sensitive to the need for discretion. We'll attempt to apprehend her before she actually arrives at the classroom. We don't want a shootout at the school."

Mannley looked relieved. "Good, a gunfight at the school is definitely to be avoided at all costs."

Claude smiled, "Don't worry Monsieur; we don't want one either."

Claude gave Mannley his business card and insisted he call if he heard anything about Millford's whereabouts. As they left for the car, Dan said, "We'll find her tonight. I can feel it."

Claude laughed, "All good detectives can feel the end. I have a tingle in my bones right now too. You're right; we'll end it all tonight."

They both agreed not to risk a telephone call. That might only tip off Samantha Johnson. The better approach would be to knock on the door and quickly make an arrest.

There were five advertisements. Five places to visit, and all the ads were for apartments to share. The prices ranged from a high of 700 Euros per month to a low of 450. Dan could argue any of the five might be the one Samantha had chosen. She certainly had plenty of money to pay for any of them.

Claude looked at his watch. "There's a fifty-fifty chance she'll be eating dinner out, so we may not find anyone at these places until later tonight, but you can never tell. Let's just go down the list and check out each place.

The first apartment was located in Waterloo, a town made famous by Napoléon and Wellington. It took another forty minutes to reach the apartment complex just west of the town. They parked their car on the next block and walked toward the three-story recently constructed building. Claude said, "Let me handle this in French. It will arouse less suspicion."

Dan agreed. In the apartment's lobby, Claude rang the manager's apartment. He explained he was with Interpol and they needed to enter Fiona McNeely's apartment. Within a minute, the manager was leading them into the elevator and pointing out unit 2E. Claude asked him to knock on the door and identify himself and explain he needed her to sign something.

The manager knocked on the door and spoke in French. Then Claude eased him aside and with guns drawn, Dan and Claude waited for Ms. McNeeley to open the door. As the door opened, Claude and Dan quickly entered the apartment and searched every room. McNeeley, who was cringing in fear, explained she hadn't rented the apartment yet. Claude and Dan offered their sincere apologies and left the apartment with the manager consoling the young lady.

The second apartment was in a section called Uccle, just southwest of Brussels along the Chausee de Waterloo. The apartment was actually a cottage in front of a large house located in the back of the property. No need for a manager here. With pistols drawn, Claude and Dan rang the doorbell and waited. There was no answer. They left in their car and circled the block. Claude said, "She may have seen us coming and decided not to answer the door. If she did, she knows we're here to get her, and she'll leave in a few minutes. Let's wait here until we're sure she's not going to flee."

They waited for ten minutes, more than enough time for Samantha Johnson to try to escape, but nobody left the house. Claude looked at his watch, and they were on to the next apartment.

Chapter 80

Grace helped Silvia prepare their dinner, nothing exotic, just a roasted chicken, boiled potatoes, and fresh asparagus. After dinner they watched television and prepared for bed around ten o'clock.

They settled onto opposite sides of the small bed. Tonight Silvia was facing Grace and asked, "Do you think you'll be happy sharing the apartment with me?"

Grace looked at her and smiled. "I think it's going to work out perfectly. What do you think?"

Silvia answered Grace by kissing her gently on the lips. The kiss was more than a good night kiss or a thank you kiss; it was a tender probing kiss seeking willingness. Grace was surprised, not shocked, just surprised. Silvia was such a beautiful woman, and it felt nice to be wanted. She had not felt this way since the encounter a decade earlier at Camp Greenwoods.

Silvia's kiss finally ended. Grace looked longingly into Silvia's eyes and kissed her back. It was the type of response that couldn't be misinterpreted. Silvia held Grace in her arms and wrapped her legs around her new roommate. Grace surrendered herself to the warmth and comfort Silvia provided.

Their passion increased and soon they were both shedding their clothes. Grace had never experienced anything like what she was feeling. There was a sexual urgency she had never felt before, an almost impossible to explain sense of desire and the possibility of finally achieving sexual fulfillment.

This was not the first time Silvia Canter had found a female partner, but she thought it might be the first time for Grace. She was gentle and assuring but in total control of the situation. She led Grace down a path toward sexual ecstasy, and Grace responded with complete abandonment.

After it was over, Grace sobbed softly as Silvia held her in her arms. Silvia knew Grace was feeling embarrassed and guilty. Right now she needed to provide comfort until Grace accepted the reality of their newly defined relationship.

Grace finally kissed Silvia and told her she needed to go to the bathroom. Silvia kissed her on the cheek and Grace walked naked out of the bedroom and into the bathroom. She turned on the light, closed the door, and began to cry. She stared at herself in the mirror and then the painful throbbing started and it was worse than ever. The voice dormant for so many days spoke to her in a demanding tone. "It's happening again Sam, and in the end Silvia will be no different than Joyce Barker. She won't help you when you need it most. Silvia is no different."

"But she seems to really care about me," Grace said.

"No she doesn't," the voice said. "She doesn't care about you at all. She only wants to use you for her own pleasure. You need to end this relationship now before you can't. You need to do it now Sam, you need to do it right now."

Samantha pleaded with the voice. "I don't want to. I can't kill anymore."

"You must. You must do it now, and then when you go home in a year, you need to kill the final Rose, the Rose who started all of your troubles. Do it now Sam! Do it now!"

Samantha Johnson was locked in a trance. Her inner soul had spoken and demanded action, and deep in her heart, she knew the voice was right. She had no idea of what she would do next, but she knew she needed to listen to her inner voice because the voice was always right.

Still in a daze, her body shook as she wandered from the bathroom to the kitchen. She found a sharp long knife in the kitchen drawer. She stared at it. It felt good in her hands. It was the kind of knife that could dispense justice, the kind of knife she could use to be the instrument of action for her inner mentor.

Chapter 81

Claude had insisted on stopping for dinner. His argument made sense. People would be at home later in the evening. Dan knew he was right. The best time to charge into a house was in the middle of the night. People were slow to respond when they were shocked out of their sleep. So Claude had stopped at a restaurant specializing in Thai food near Uccle, and now they were approaching their fourth apartment. This one was located within walking distance of the school, and in hindsight, they probably should have checked on this one first, but that was water over the dam so to speak. Luckily this apartment had absolutely no security. They cautiously walked into the front entrance and looked at the mailboxes. Silvia Canter's apartment was located on the third floor.

With guns drawn they quietly walked up the stairs. Halfway between the second and third floors, they heard a horrifying scream. It was the kind of scream leaving little doubt about what was happening. Dan rushed up the stairs taking them two at a time. He pulled his gun and fought back against a sharp pain in his right arm. The screams were coming from Canter's apartment. Without thinking he slammed his good shoulder into the apartment's door and as the lock shattered, he advanced into the unknown apartment.

The screaming was coming from a room in the back. Ready for the worst and going on pure instinct, Dan burst into the bedroom. There were two nude women entwined on the bed. One was Samantha Johnson and other was probably Silvia Canter. Silvia Canter was screaming and Samantha Johnson had a deep knife wound in her belly. Dan knew immediately that she was mortally wounded. Her guts had burst from her body and the bed sheets were covered in blood.

Claude was screaming Interpol and holding out his badge. Dan pulled the mortally wounded serial killer off of the other woman. He found a bathrobe in the closet and wrapped it around the screaming woman's shoulders.

Neighbors were gathering at the front door to the apartment and Claude was assuring them the police were taking care of things. Claude made some calls, and an ambulance arrived in ten minutes followed by the Federal Police.

The woman confirmed she was Silvia Canter, but that's all she could get out of her mouth. She was in shock, and it was understandable. The medics pronounced Samantha Johnson dead at the scene, and she was taken away in a black body bag. A second ambulance arrived and Silvia Canter was brought to the local hospital with the Federal Police providing an escort. They would have to ascertain what had happened, but whatever it was, Dan's case was closed out, and most importantly, Kim Monroe and her husband could come out of hiding with no fears of a future murder.

Claude and Dan followed the Federal Police to the hospital, where Claude's presence was certainly required.

Chapter 82

It was mid-afternoon before Silvia Canter was able to talk about what had happened. She was from England and so the conversation took place in English. She admitted to having a sexual encounter with Samantha, and then Samantha had left their bedroom and five minutes later returned with a knife and attacked her.

What Samantha Johnson failed to understand was Silvia Canter was an expert in the martial arts. She had blocked the knife attack and countered with a move forcing the knife into Samantha Johnson's belly. "It all happened so fast," she said. "I didn't try to kill her; it was a reflex brought on by years of training."

It took several hours of explaining before the Federal Police realized Silvia Canter had acted in self-defense. By the time Dan and Claude had finished talking to the police, Silvia Canter was ready to be discharged. They gave her a ride back to the school. She left for the gym, and Claude and Dan visited Headmaster Mannley.

Leaving the grounds of the International School, Dan put his arm around his fellow detective. "Claude, I'm going to buy you the best dinner in Brussels. Where should we go?"

"You know my friend. There are so many great restaurants in this city, but for unknown reasons I would like to spend tonight with my good friend Mario Lucca. Let's eat once again at Chez Leon."

Made in the USA
Charleston, SC
11 November 2015